BETRAYED EXPECTATIONS

CHESTER'S RUN SERIES - BOOK TWO

CHERYL ROSARIO

Title: Betrayed Expectations–Chester's Run Series–Book Two

To Mum and Dad,
Amazing parents who have always been there for their children. You always encouraged us to follow our dreams. Everything you did was for your children and grandchildren. You are wonderful role models and have taught us how wonderful family is and how important it is to live life to the full.

Illustration by Daisy Woods.

In memory of our boy, Chester. My faithful companion as I wrote early drafts in this series

Thanks, Daisy for capturing his caring soul.

SUPPORTING HER EXTENDED FAMILY

IVY

Slumping into the vacant swing on the front porch of the Homestead, Ivy waited. Her breathing became laboured, and she trembled whenever the memory of yesterday's horrid event crossed her mind. Ivy wiped away tears. The town didn't need to see her pain surface. People needed her to be strong, by hell she'd do it for Lindy. It was Ivy's turn to dig deep and show a depth of strength and support. The one whose coping depended on support, was counting on Ivy. She'd be here for him. Inside, her head told her it was a terrible idea, but her heart incinerated the notion.

Memories of Lindy's ordeal came flooding back. She'd spent the night with Jack and Lindy's children. After leaving the hospital, they'd set up camp in the front lounge amid boxes and furniture. With mattresses crammed into the cleared space, it allowed Lindy's older kids and herself to help settle the younger ones.

The lounge room grew stuffy after the combination of the day's heat and the humidity from the downpour. Ivy recalled how it hampered the search efforts. The nine bodies occupying the room only added to the discomfort. Sophie tried to open a window, but the strong wind whipped at the house and trees. When sleep eluded them, Ivy and Sophie tried to calm themselves by recalling memorable days with Lindy, in hushed voices. Eventually, she'd nodded off just after midnight. She'd slept until her four-fifteen alarm sounded. It was time to head to the bakery. Now she found herself back at the Homestead, waiting for the moving to begin.

"Morning Ivy," a small group greeted her, as they perched themselves onto a seat or railing and waited for Natasha to appoint jobs. Ivy was grateful to be able to rely on such an active helper of the Chester's Run community. Groups of people arrived over the next fifteen minutes. Natasha took up a spot at the varnished wooden front door and the group hushed.

"Thanks to everyone for coming." Natasha's hands danced in time with her words. "I just got off the phone to Jack. Lindy is on the mend, she'll be in hospital for another night. Jack's asked for our help to settle them into their new home." Natasha's ability to coax the locals into action was amazing. "The plan is to set up both the house and bungalow, move the furniture into allocated rooms. The family's due back soon and will guide us."

Ivy shifted in her seat and took another mouthful of lukewarm coffee.

"Jack's providing a barbecue lunch, so if you could spare the time, we'd appreciate your help." There were nods and replies of agreement, Natasha continued, "If it's okay with everyone I'll designate jobs."

From the front lawn George Tuttenham, the primary school principal called out, "If you give me volunteers Natasha, I'll take care of the garden." With a sweep of his arm George pointed to the overgrown lawn and weed ridden garden beds.

"Thanks, George. Who wants to help in the garden? Not all the men. We need some sturdy men to help carry the furniture."

Everyone laughed.

Car doors banged. A minute later another group arrived.

"Sorry we're late, Natasha."

"Thanks for coming. Any volunteers to direct from the truck?"

"Give me that job," Bernie waved a hand in the air.

"Once the furniture's inside, Ivy and I'll give directions," Tessa said. "The boxes have labels and the family knows where the furniture is going."

"Okay, those working with George, head over for instructions. Those working in the bungalow, everything's already there, you can get started." Ivy doodled on the corner of the clipboard Tessa passed her while Natasha gathered a team and sent them to the bungalow. "I'll be with you in a minute. The rest of you head over to the truck, thanks. Boxes marked 'personal', leave those for the family." Natasha clapped her hands, "Let's go."

"Thanks for this," Ivy said to Natasha, watching the first group of helpers heading towards the house with their arms full.

"Not a problem. Can't comprehend how this happened." Natasha said, watching the line of volunteers waiting at the back of the truck. Men, women and children of varying shapes and sizes waited amid greetings and conversations.

"I'll be over at the bungalow if anyone needs me. You both right here?"

"Yep, we've got this." Ivy said as Natasha walked away.

"H-Hi," a voice called. Ivy turned to see Cameron standing in the driveway.

"Cameron, how's Lindy?" Ivy asked, moving closer. The drop of his shoulders and head hung low, gave her a fair indication of how he was coping. Without thinking, she approached him and rested a hand on his arm. Large eyes stared back at her. She knew the thought of losing his mother must have been devastating and unfathomable for Lindy's middle child.

"Where are the others?"

"On their way. I just needed a walk," Cameron pivoted from left to right, turning at every noise. Ivy saw the tension dripping from him as he tried to deal with people swarming the family's new home. His shoulders slumped and his hands hid deep in his pockets. His face paled. To him these people were strangers, to her they were like family. She'd known most of them all her life.

"There's people in the bungalow. Do you want to head over and sort your things out?" Ivy was hoping to get a response, but nothing was forthcoming.

"Ivy, take him over. I've got this." Tessa leaned in to take the clipboard. "Send people back if you need to." Ivy understood the hidden message. She too questioned if Cameron would cope with people he'd never met before being in his house. Stepping off the veranda, she led Cameron towards the bungalow, allowing the silence to fill the chasm between them.

Cameron hesitated in the doorway when he noticed the locals at work.

Natasha looked up, "Oh good Ivy, can you tell us which room is which?"

"That's my room," Cameron mumbled as his finger pointed to the left of the entrance.

"Cameron's room," Ivy repeated, her voice carrying above the buzz of helpers.

"Thanks," a man said to Cameron. "Okay, grab those things, follow me." He told those with him.

Natasha watched Ivy and Cameron, "Oh Ivy, whose room's that?"

"Liam's," Cameron's didn't make eye contact as he spoke. "That's his," he pointed to a bed frame leaning against the bench.

"Which bed's yours?" Ivy asked, keeping him busy as folks swarmed the bungalow in the name of community spirit.

Cameron relaxed slightly as he guided and helped move things around their new home. Ivy nodded and gave Natasha a small smile as he joined in.

IVY

The following morning started bright and early. Ivy could hear Cameron packing the last of his things upstairs in her apartment.

"I'll be over late morning," Ivy told him as he walked past the kitchen with his arms full.

"Okay." He really was a man of only a few words.

After another couple of trips, he walked into the kitchen, "I've left my key on the table upstairs."

"Oh, keep that. It's for Sophie. Could you pass it on to her?"

His legs pounded the boards as he ran back upstairs. A lot of his awkwardness disappeared. Was this something Cameron became comfortable with over time, or would he be back to square one again next time she met him?

"Well, I'll get out of your hair," Cameron told Ivy when he descended again.

"How about some breakfast before you go? I've made croissants for you to take with you, if that's okay?"

"I'd love a coffee but I might wait and eat with the others if you don't mind," this man reached down and tugged tenderly at her heart-strings and he was oblivious to it.

"Sure." Leaving her baking, Ivy headed out to the front of the shop and began making his coffee. Watching on as Cameron took it upon himself to put the chairs down and distribute wooden caddies with condiments onto each table as Ivy or Susie did every morning.

"Thanks," Ivy couldn't help but stare when Cameron smiled at her. Remembering what it was she was doing, she turned her attention back to the machine and finished his coffee. Finding a lid, she pushed it into place on the black and cream *Chester's Run Bakery* cup. Once it was secured, she handed it over the counter.

"Well, I'll see you later," Cameron said.

"Absolutely. I'll come over with morning tea." Cameron reached for the cup, but Ivy didn't let go. Her brain stalled. She was unaware of what she should be doing. Those beautiful blue eyes, the spitting image of his mother's, stared back.

The sound of the backdoor opening and Susie's singsong greeting was enough to break the spell.

"Morning," Ivy replied as Cameron gave her a shy smile and took the coffee.

"Here you go," he held out a ten-dollar note.

"It's on the house," Ivy choked out. Or was it a squeak?

"You're in business, it's not on the house," his hand still hovered over the counter when Susie walked in and took the money.

"One coffee, three-fifty." She told Cameron as she hip-bumped Ivy clear of the cash register.

Ivy understood Susie had a good grasp on the situation. Nothing got past her.

"There's your change."

"Thanks. Bye, Ivy." Cameron picked up the bag of croissants and left via the backdoor.

Ivy stood staring down the empty hallway.

"Morning," Susie repeated, drawing Ivy from her meditative state.

"Ah, morning." Ivy finally answered.

"Hey girl," Ivy sensed Susie watching closely.

"Sorry, did you say something?" Ivy tried for innocence, but she could see Susie wasn't buying it.

Sidling up beside her, Susie nudged her shoulder and began, "Look, I haven't seen you this way over any man. Not even the silly ones you've dated around here, but this one will be hard work."

Ivy looked at Susie, not sure what to say. She could deny her feelings. But Susie wouldn't be fooled. It was time to face facts; her heart ruled her head. Was it his quiet ways she loved or the conversations they shared and how he took the time to understand what was important to her?

Letting out a lengthy sigh, Ivy nodded. "But you have to admit, he's lovely. Don't you like him?"

"Not sure Cameron would approve of being called lovely. Rugged? No, you couldn't use that word for him either," Susie laughed. "Yes, I like him, I'm just saying he won't be easy to win over. That's all. There's hard work ahead if you really set your heart on this one."

If someone asked Ivy to describe her perfect man, it would have been a rugged horseman as the men in her family were, but not now. Now she'd seen the tall, shy Cameron who tugged at her heartstrings unlike any male before him. "Well, I'm going with a gentle giant for now."

They set to work opening the shop. From six-thirty they'd be flat out for the next couple of hours. Perfect. Exactly the distraction Ivy needed until she headed over to the Homestead to visit Lindy.

"What time will Lindy be home?" Susie asked Ivy.

"Mid-morning, according to Jack." Ivy told her. "I'll head over about eleven."

"Still can't get over what she did for those children," Susie said. "The town's talking about how glad they'll be to see the back of Elsa."

"Not as glad as we are, I promise you." Ivy agreed.

IVY

Ivy hefted the bucket from one hand to the other, aware the man who occupied her dreams overnight stood front and centre in her thoughts now. Not only now, Cameron had been in her mind nonstop for days. Both he and Lindy plagued her mind, and both for obvious reasons.

The heavy bucket half full of soapy water sloshed as she rested it on the far table in the sitting area of the bakery. Taking advantage of the lull, Ivy started on the tables early. The last few days took its toll, and she was up for an early night.

She bent over the bucket, grabbed the cloth, and wrung it out before wiping down the first table. She couldn't focus on cleaning the tables as her mind continued to conjure up thoughts of Cameron. It was silly to feel he deserted her when he joined his family at the Homestead, but she couldn't help it.

He'd left yesterday morning, and Ivy wasn't looking forward to a repeat of the isolation she'd faced when she returned upstairs after work last night. She ran the cloth over the table, rinsed the blue piece of fabric and then did the chairs before moving onto the next one. Walking towards the fourth table she registered a lone figure sitting there lost in his own world.

"Hey Liam," she said, drawing him from some dark place. "Everything okay?"

"Hi Ivs." He replied, stirring his coffee in an anti-clockwise direction before getting lost again. His shoulders hunched as he sat forward over the table. But he wasn't paying attention to what he was doing.

Watching him for a moment, Ivy considered what the problem could be, but she only came up with Lindy. The entire town spoke about how she endangered her own life to save Jack's children. She'd become a local hero in the space of a few hours.

Pulling out a chair, Ivy slid into it and rested her hand on Liam's arm. "Is everything all right? You look lost."

Liam sat up straighter and then flopped back down again, his hunched shoulders looking different when he leaned back. "Do you know what it's like to have the rug pulled out from under you, and you can't tell a soul?"

Ivy considered this was just a rhetorical question, but then he looked up at her and opened his mouth to continue.

"How about we take this upstairs," Ivy didn't wait for his reply. She picked up his cup and called out to Susie as she went. "I'm upstairs if you need me."

"Right you are boss," Susie said, but her eyes were on Liam and Ivy could only guess what she was thinking.

Ivy watched on as Liam flopped onto the familiar couch. His coffee now sat on the coffee table between them. She allowed silence to fill the room as she waited to see if he would talk. For five long minutes Liam huffed, groaned and even slapped himself up the side of the head, but he didn't speak. Ivy turned to glance at the clock. Why? She wasn't going anywhere.

"How could I have been such an idiot? I took his call today, believing he rang to see how Mum was doing. He asked and sounded like he cared, but that wasn't the reason for his call. No! The man was on a mission this morning." Liam reached for his coffee, which must have been cold. He sculled it and then placed the cup back on the table. For the first time since arriving upstairs, he looked at Ivy. "'*Well son,*" Liam mimicked in a deep voice. "*I've sold the business, we both need a fresh start. You'll have a job until February. So, when your mother's better, if you could head back to Melbourne and finish up on your projects, I'd appreciate it.'* The man just blurted out my fate. I didn't get a choice whether I wanted to stay with the new owners or not."

Ivy watched as Liam undid the laces on his tan boots, kicked them off, placed them under the coffee table and laid back on her couch. The week he and his siblings spent here before Jack and Lindy took ownership of the Homestead was loads of fun. Today, she saw an unfamiliar man. This man was hurting, Ivy didn't know what to do.

"Then when I questioned him about it, he said, *'Sorry son, no one from the company will have a job after the takeover. They don't need anybody. That was one condition of the sale.'* He muttered something else, but I couldn't hear what he said. So, there it is, I'm out of a job. How do you think I'll go as a sales assistant for Jack?"

Ivy let out a laugh. "You could do anything you set your mind on, Liam. But would that interest you?"

Liam's head swivelled as if on a stick, pivoting from one side to another. "But you know what, that's not the worst of it. Dad then precedes to tell me all these years he was only a third owner in the company. Mum owned the controlling interest. He told me my grandfather controlled her ownership of the business without her knowing."

"What? Lindy has two businesses?"

"Yep, but she was never privy to the arrangement until the day before her and Dad talked at my grandparents' place." Liam held up a finger as he swung back to a sitting position. "But wait, it gets better, Mum has rejected her ownership of the business, so Pa has distributed the money from the sale to us." His finger still waggling, "But I'm not allowed to say anything, oh no. *'I'm only telling you this, son, so you can consider starting up your own place. You know the business inside and out, I suggest you look at somewhere up near your mum and get away from Melbourne for a while.'*" Liam dropped back onto the couch. "The lies the man lived are unbelievable. And now he thinks he can order me around. Do I even want his bloody money?" Liam leaned forward with elbows resting on his knees. The pinched mouth through which the next few words tumbled out, appeared to pain him. He stared at his hands, set his jaw and continued, "I do want the money, in fact I need it but I wish I didn't and I wish I could talk to Cameron and Sophie about this."

Ivy got up and walked to sit beside him. She wrapped her arm around his shoulder. "I'm so sorry your father has dropped this on you. I'd hoped for all your sakes this would be over now your parents talked things through."

"Do you realise how Cameron will take this news? Ironic how Ralph took so much of his earnings when he was scouting jobs for Cameron and now, we'll get almost the same as Ralph from the business." Liam ran his fingers through his hair, "Shit, it sucks, Cameron wants nothing to do with Ralph." Ivy could feel the muscles bunching in Liam's back as he spoke of the loathing Cameron projected towards his father.

REJECTION

CAMERON

"Hi Susie," Cameron called as he reached the counter, his stomach churning and fingers tingling. Would he ever be a normal person? Able to talk to people without feeling like he'd pass out. "Is Ivy in? I umm, I left my toiletries bag here."

Susie, as always, was multitasking. One hand held a cup beneath the jet of coffee while the other was setting out three side plates, obviously for some of Ivy's delicious cakes. "Hi Cameron, she's upstairs. Go on up."

"Thanks," Cameron headed around the back of the counter.

He heard voices coming from the partially open door as he reached the top landing. Just as he was about to call out his greetings, he saw something he'd never wanted to see, ever.

Ivy's arm was draped over Liam's shoulder, and Cameron watched on as his brother placed a hand on her knee.

"What would I say to him. How would I tell him this after everything else we've endured over the past few months? Cameron's been doing so well, we've become so close. Ralph hasn't been there to manipulate us against one another. This could send him reeling."

Cameron saw enough. He didn't need his brother telling him Ivy's attention shifted from one brother to the next. Didn't Sophie and his mother talk about the wrong brother trope in the romance novels they swapped? He wasn't hanging around.

He clambered down the stairs. No. Not through the shop. He took the back entrance and went out. The image of Ivy and Liam burned behind his eyelids.

As he reached his car, his phone rang. He looked down and saw Jack's name on his screen. He so didn't want to talk to anyone, but what if something happened to his mother?

"Hi Jack," Cameron couldn't rid his voice of the sneer.

"You okay, buddy?" Ironic how even though Jack was up to his eyeballs with the move, the children and taking care of Lindy, he still had time for Cameron.

"I'm fine," Cameron opened his car door as he asked, "What's up?"

There was a slight pause before Jack spoke again. "Sophie said you were in town. If I send through a list of things for your mum, could you grab them for me, please? I'd prefer not to leave her if I could help it."

"Sure. Send it through and I'll organise it." Cameron swallowed hard and clenched his jaw.

"Thanks. Sending it through, see you at home." Jack ended the call, and Cameron looked down at his phone. This was one of the last things he wanted to do, but if he wanted to be more family oriented, he needed to put others ahead of himself. And besides, this might keep him from thinking about his snake of a brother and the woman who'd invaded his thoughts since Christmas Day.

After locking his car, Cameron pulled up the list and headed for the chemist followed by the supermarket. He needed to keep walking and doing. Anything but thinking time would work for him right now.

IVY

Wiping the last of the tables, Ivy looked up as Susie undid the ties on her apron.

"I'm heading home," Susie said as Ivy tossed the cloth into the bucket.

She puffed a stray strand of hair from her face and leaned against the table.

"Thanks for today." Ivy said as she did most days.

"No probs, see you tomorrow."

As the back door banged shut, Ivy turned at the sound of footsteps to see Liam step out from behind the counter.

"Ummm, it's time I went home, but I don't have my car." Liam's face contorted, "Would you mind giving me a lift? You could stay for dinner. I know you wanted to catch up with Mum."

"Sure," Ivy looked around, double checking she'd finished. "Just give me ten minutes to change?"

"No worries." Liam followed her back upstairs and flicked on the television.

The hard set to his shoulders told Ivy he wasn't any closer to working out what to do about his job or his father. How disruptive their lives became over the last few months. Liam throwing this at Cameron worried her sick. Being such a gentle soul, Cameron couldn't cope with the stress after everything with Lindy.

Ten minutes later they were in the car and heading for the Homestead. Liam sat in the passenger seat staring out the windscreen, not taking much notice of anything. Ivy decided not to force any conversation, instead she drove in silence with the gentle hum of the radio playing in the background.

Pulling the car to a stop at the front of the Homestead, Ivy unlocked the boot to retrieve the leftover food from the bakery. Nothing would go astray with Jack and Lindy's kids.

"Here, let me grab those," Liam said as he stepped around to pick up the three large boxes displaying her logo. He leaned in before she'd stepped back and accidently bumped into her. "Move, woman," he teased.

It was good he was showing some of his normal characteristics.

"Why thank you, kind sir," she retorted with a mocking bow, and they laughed. He was fun to be around without the stress of his predicament. But nothing about Liam set her heart pounding as it did when an image of Cameron came to mind. She looked around to see if he'd heard the car and came out to greet them. Oh, that reminded her, she'd grabbed Cameron's toiletries bag from the bathroom before she'd left. Instead of following Liam, she opened the back door and picked up her handbag with the toiletries bag inside and headed for the house.

The homestead was magical, something about it whispered a determined *'home'*, a place for a family. It was warm, bright, and so inviting. The children were running from the kitchen to the lounge, checking on Lindy as she sat, eyes closed and a gentle smile on her lips. For a moment Ivy studied those lips. They were the same as Cameron's. Why was it on Cameron, they looked so luscious?

"You okay, Mum?"

Ivy focused again on her surroundings.

"Just a dizzy spell. It's fine." Lindy answered, her eyes still closed.

"Hi Ivy. You looked like you're a thousand miles away. Everything okay?"

Heat engulfed her. She could only hope Sophie missed her heated cheeks. Thoughts of a man she had no right thinking about as she was, often had her lost in some musing or another.

Lindy's eyes opened as her lips curved into a full smile. It was the most natural thing Ivy saw, despite the state of her face.

"How's the shop, love?" Lindy asked, always the business woman.

"Great, thanks to you…again." Ivy loved how much Lindy taught her with the bakery. Not only in business, but in life. Ivy could do a hell of a lot worse than having Lindy to look up to as a mother figure. "Oh, the sales rep phoned this afternoon, we've ordered the new oven. It'll be here next week."

Sophie gave a small yelp as a grin exploded across her face. She clapped her hands. "So, this is happening?"

"It is," Ivy giggled. "Come by in the morning and sign contracts and you can start as soon as you're ready."

"Why don't you start tomorrow?" Jack's encouraging voice suggested as he walked past the two women standing on the threshold of the lounge room. He took the three steps down into the sunken room and stopped by Lindy's side.

"Won't you need me?" Sophie asked.

"What's still to be done here isn't urgent. I'm not taking over the farm supplies yet, and Cameron is here to help. Besides, I can see you're itching to get started." Jack added with a chuckle.

Ivy looked from Jack to Sophie and didn't miss her face transform to one of pleasure.

"Would you mind?" Sophie asked.

How could she mind? This was exactly what she'd been aiming for. Another qualified person to help her out. Improve the stock and get more time to herself. "Mind? No, I'd love it."

"Well, what time do I start tomorrow?" Sophie asked, showing a bucket load of enthusiasm.

"Five."

"Perfect." Sophie wore an enormous grin.

"Well dinner's ready, come on, let's get you to the table." Jack said to Lindy as he stood in front of her to help her stand. Ivy watched on as Lindy rose with little fuss and leaned on Jack up the few stairs and down the hallway.

"Hi Ivy," Evie called, running into her arms. They remained joined all the way to the dining room, "You should see my room. It's so great," Evie gushed.

In the dining room, Ivy searched for Cameron and spotted him watching her. He was walking from the kitchen through the small walkway to the dining room. Her lips curved into a smile, but she noticed his face was like thunder. What was wrong? After dinner, she'd talk to him.

"Come on," Jack called. "Let's eat."

FACING REALITY

CAMERON

Studying his body in the full-length mirror, there was nothing much to see. He'd considered working out in the past, not for the muscles but for the benefit to his general health. Maybe now was the time.

Lucky for him, he saw Ivy's interest in another man first hand. He'd not make a fool of himself there.

Losing her attention was one thing, but the knowledge she was lusting after his brother was quite another. Ivy was too good for Liam. Cameron rocked back and forth. The rise of his insecurities was never a pleasurable experience. Funny how he finally put himself out there and all his efforts ended in naught.

Needing a distraction from the rejection, he fetched his laptop. He'd found his familiar place, one he could get lost in for hours. Sitting at the kitchen table made him more focused, so he remained perched there, researching and coding till his heart was numb to his loss.

He schooled his features when he heard footsteps approaching the front door. Ignoring Liam was more difficult than it used to be, but he didn't appreciate his brother's disregard for his feelings. What a tragedy, they'd been getting along so well lately.

After dinner Cameron made up an excuse about having to finish work for his client. The questioning look from his mother put him on notice and told him how poorly his lie had gone down with her. Best to smooth it over with her tomorrow.

The tap on the front door drew him from his racing thoughts. He hadn't planned on looking until he heard the tapping. Through the glass panel in the door, he saw Ivy reach for the handle.

"Hey," she said, stepping into the room.

Cameron wished he'd put his gaming headset on. He could pretend he was taking a call and she would have left him to his misery in peace.

"Hi." He didn't look up.

"Everything okay?" Ivy leaned onto the back of the dining chair opposite him, her hands clasped together. Over the top of his computer, Cameron could see her knuckles turning white.

"Hmmm." He saw her puzzled look. "You alright?" He countered and wanted to kick himself. He was lousy at this. The words would have sufficed, but the tone gave away his pain. He was losing face. No. This wouldn't do. He needed friends, but the truth was he didn't want Ivy to be just his friend, he wanted so much more with her.

"I'm good." She released her clasped hands and clapped them together. "Your mother's worried about you. The way you took off after dinner."

"I've got stuff to do," his automatic response didn't hold weight with Ivy either.

"So, you're good? There's nothing you want to talk about?" Ivy asked again as she reached into her handbag and pulled out his toiletries bag. "You left this at my place."

"Thanks," was his only reply, because right now Ivy wasn't welcome in his home. The sooner she left the better.

GUTTERED

IVY

Three weeks passed since Lindy arrived home, and Ivy last visited the Homestead. Sophie's employment at the bakery lightened Ivy's load, which meant there was so much more time to ponder what went wrong with Cameron. Since he'd avoided her, Ivy avoided the Homestead. She rang and checked on Lindy and spoke to Jack and occasionally the children. And a couple of days ago she even rang Liam to check in with him.

"The feeling around here is morbid," he'd told her. "Ralph doesn't come into the office. There's only twelve of us left." It wasn't clear what was more devastating, the fact his life was up ended or that Liam couldn't talk to his own siblings about the situation.

Shaking those thoughts from her head, Ivy concentrated on the task at hand. She decided with Sophie and Susie closing up the shop today, it was prime time she cleaned out the spare rooms as she'd been promising herself for the last two years. Now here she was sitting among boxes of her grandmother's treasures. Ivy created four piles. The first was for the rubbish, the second for things worth keeping, though she had no use for. The third were wonderful memories Ivy would take special care of, and the last pile was for all the tissues she'd needed when rediscovering old photos of her grandparents. Though if anyone asked, she'd claim it was the dust.

Sitting among the stacks, she hefted another heavy box towards her. What did this grey wicker box hold? There was a vague recollection she'd seen it before, but nothing too familiar making it obvious at first sight.

Ivy opened the box and gasped as a photo of her mother stared back at her. The beautiful woman who succumbed to cancer over twenty years ago. A tear ran down her cheek. Already feeling low, this added a sudden heaviness to her stomach. Ivy traced the outline of her mother's face. Here she looked happy, healthy, and full of life. Ivy closed her eyes, she'd never known her mother like this. Cancer was the reason Ivy never really met this version of her mother. The picture hanging on her photo wall of her mother and Ivy together on her fifth birthday came to mind. The version of Anita Masters which Ivy remembered.

It wasn't hard to place the memory. The photo was taken not long before her mother died. Sitting in quiet contemplation, Ivy struggled to deal with the pain of her loss as a little girl. Looking into the box again, she noticed an envelope written in an elegant hand. On the front was just one word.

'Ivy'.

Her trembling hand reached in and pulled out the envelope. The significance of the lightweight letter resembled the discovery of a gold nugget. So much shiny promise with the added burden of a heavy weight.

Amid tears and sobs, Ivy heard her name being called. She looked up to see her cousin standing in the doorway of the spare room.

"Ivy, what's wrong?" Tessa asked, moving closer.

Ivy looked down at the box.

Tessa gasped. "You've only just found this?" She asked incredulous. She pulled the photo of her older cousin out and stared. "I haven't seen photos of her in years."

"I j—j…just found this box."

The box held a variety of things, all of which sent Ivy spiralling as she continued to paw through the contents. The memories were a bittersweet reminder of all she'd lost over her lifetime. Pain ripped at her heart as she studied each item. A small silver box contained a lock of her hair as a baby and two other shades of hair wrapped in plastic. A second silver box held a surprise. She and Tessa laughed through their tears at the size of the tiny pearl teeth. Ivy noticed another letter. To her it was more beautiful and symbolic than her own. Her mother's hand addressed this letter to a name she'd never heard of before. A stranger.

Lamont Gabriel Thornton

Both Tessa and Ivy looked at one another. Ivy unsure of what to do next or how to react.

"It's not sealed," Tessa pointed out as the back of the envelope flapped when Ivy pulled it from the box. "Are you going to read it?"

Ivy turned it over and glanced back at her own letter in her lap. A letter twenty years in transit, probably sitting in the box all this time. Holding out the first letter to Tessa, Ivy waited for her to read it before carefully pulling the one addressed to Lamont from its protection. What would this letter say to him?

Tessa took the second letter as the silence seeped around them. Ivy watched on as Tessa studied each word, words Ivy was yet to grasp. This was the most beautiful letter to a man who'd deserted her mother all those years ago. After twenty-five years, Ivy finally discovered who her father was. Could she forgive him as her mother asked?

With the truth revealed, Ivy pondered again her feelings about losing her mother. Like Lindy, her mother possessed a greater strength than most people she'd known.

"I'm twenty-five years old and it's high-time I found him, don't you think?" Ivy said, her voice hoarse and a little shaky.

There were so many unanswered questions. She wanted answers once and for all. She'd suffered with displaced feelings of loss all her life, but being grateful to the family who raised her, she only ever asked once about her father and received deafening silence regarding the topic. So, she hadn't been game to address it again. Even in her adult years.

At her tiny kitchen table, Ivy said, "I wonder, could I talk to Sophie about holding the fort here. I should go to England to find my father." Ivy told Tessa as she tapped her cream envelope into her palm. The letter from her mother blindsided her. With Tessa here, she'd be a great sounding board. "You've read it for yourself, the truth of what happened to her. It wasn't cancer. She'd been raped and assaulted and eventually died." Ivy swiped at tears as her cousin's arms engulfed her. "My father didn't believe her, so I think it's time I set the record straight. If nothing else comes of the meeting, at least I'll have met my father once in my life."

"What if he doesn't believe you or your mother's letter?" Tessa's gentle voice asked.

"There's always DNA testing." Ivy took a mouthful of water from the glass Tessa set in front of her, "If he'll agree to it."

The two women sat in silence, allowing the discovery to engulf them.

HIS COMPASS

CAMERON

Cameron sat opposite his mother at the kitchen table. They'd discussed the week's activities, detailing when and where each child needed to be. The parents of the children's friends were so helpful in organising play dates to give Lindy a chance to rest and recover. Which meant Cameron spent his days ferrying the children to and from their friends, while doing laundry, vacuuming, sweeping, mopping and the shopping, if Jack didn't have time to stop off at the supermarket on the way home.

At night he worked hard to complete contracts from his father. In the afternoons, if he'd been out collecting the children, one or all would beg to go to the bakery. Cameron feigned a busy workload and headed straight home. Seeing Ivy wouldn't work for him. Not at all.

Last night when Liam rang to check on him as he did every night, Cameron couldn't hold back anymore. Sitting in front of his mother, he recalled the conversation word for word. He'd never made Liam angry before, but last night he succeeded.

Liam always yelled, ranted, and raved like their father, but it wasn't anything like the intensity of last night. Their conversation was toxic. They'd come so far over the last couple of months. However, last night must have ruined all that because Liam yelled blue murder at Cameron to which he retaliated. Laying blame at Liam's feet, then in the middle of his rebuke, Liam hung up.

The whole thing left him confused. What did Liam say?

"Okay, so you've got next week all settled?" Lindy asked after checking over the calendar one last time.

"Yep, all good. Am I doing everything you want done?" Cameron asked. Lindy's tone wasn't as loving as usual which unsettled him.

"The children are happy, the laundry's done, and they've got more food coming at them than they know what to do with, thank you." It was what she hadn't said which seemed to echo between them. "Now your business, have you done anything we spoke about?"

"Actually, I've done it all." Cameron opened his laptop and pulled up his emails. Turning the screen towards his mother, he went through step by step as she'd instructed. "I began by sending all the information to the accountant. He emailed back to say they made a start with investigating Ralph's contracts. I've begun by going online as you suggested and joined some different sites. I've advertised. My friend from uni has given me some tips as well, and I've begun with a website. He's been on and improved the look of it so hopefully I can run live with it this week."

"Really?" The astonishment in her voice annoyed him.

"Give me a break, Mum, I'm really trying here." He slammed the lid of his laptop closed.

Lindy stared at him and then looked away. With her face so scarred from the bruising, Cameron couldn't read her at all.

"Seriously Mum, I'm giving it everything!"

"Something happened to you, Cameron. I heard you yelling at Liam last night and when I rang him, he refused to talk about it but he gave me a similar line, '*Mum, I'm changing and giving it my all*'," she shook her head. "What's going on because as far as Sophie and I can tell, he hasn't stepped a foot out of line for ages."

"Nothing."

Clenching her fists and her jaw, she replied, "Don't you dare…" Lindy clutched her head. The cry of pain shattered him. This was his fault. Why couldn't he tell her? She'd overdone it with her outburst.

Cameron jumped up, standing beside her saying, "Come on, let's get you back to bed." The tears in her eyes caused him heartache. Cameron wasn't being fair, but he would not tell his mother what Liam was up to. She'd probably meddle and try to sort it out. But there was nothing to sort out. He'd accepted Ivy liked his brother. End of conversation as far as he cared.

Exiting his mother's room after settling her, Cameron needed to deal with the weight of the world on his shoulders. He didn't want his mother to discover the truth, but treating Liam as his best friend was too much to ask. Halfway down the hall he stopped, leaned against the wall and expelled a rushed breath. He hoped he and Ivy could have a future together, considering she'd wormed her way into his heart. Ivy obviously never shared those feelings.

Understanding the importance of shifting his focus, he decided his best bet was to meet new people around town.

LIFE BEGINS TO CHANGE

IVY

The summons from Aunty Darla the following day made Ivy curious as to her request. The girls were handling things in the shop, so Ivy ducked out to see her aunt. Her intuition told her there was only one reason for the invitation. Darla was her grandmother's younger sister. They would have talked. Maybe there were details Ivy never heard. Her only hope was her aunty would understand the importance of her decision to travel to England.

The doorbell chimed her arrival, and she waited till Uncle Tony opened the front door.

"What are you doing there? You know to let yourself in," he admonished before pulling her into a bear hug he was famous for. "She's in the lounge."

"Thanks," Ivy said, and led the way. "Hey Aunty Darla, I've been summonsed?" Ivy couldn't stop her brows dancing with mirth.

Darla gave her niece a gentle peck on her cheek and a firm hug. Like the ones Ivy missed from her own grandmother. She waited until

Ivy settled on the couch. "Tessa dropped by after seeing you yesterday."

"I'm a big girl. I need to see him." Ivy practically pleaded, as if she required anyone's permission.

Holding up her hand, Darla continued, "I'm not trying to stop you, my girl. But your grandmother asked Tony and I to look out for you."

"And you have. I can't tell you both how important you are in my life. But I've decided." Ivy restated.

"Well, that's what we wanted to see you about. Tony and I would like you to travel with someone. At a stretch we'll both come with you, though we'd rather stay here and help Jack and Lindy. We'd prefer it if you could find someone else to travel with." Darla was direct but reasonable. Ivy couldn't dispute that.

"Would Tessa like a trip to England?" Ivy asked.

"I'm not sure, I was thinking maybe Sophie?"

Shaking her head, Ivy said, "Nope, she's the only one to take over the shop while I'm away."

"When do you plan on leaving?" Tony asked.

"Not sure, maybe in the middle of Feb, I'd need to sort things out for the shop first. I have to teach Sophie how the kitchen runs. Everything else Susie knows already." Ivy's eyes landed on a photo on her aunt's cabinet, it was a photo of her grandparents with Darla and Tony. A smile settled on her lips. Shifting her attention, she pondered, if only she and Cameron were on speaking terms. Oh well, that ship already sailed.

"Let's all think on it, and if we think of someone, fine. Otherwise, Tony and I will come with you. Just promise you won't take off without us."

"I promise you. We'll sort something out," Ivy declared, relieved they weren't considering stopping her.

Walking home to the bakery, faces and names flew in and out of her mind. But none of them were a good fit. Friends from her course days wouldn't be the type of people to share this with, Tessa had her family. Sophie would have been perfect. Maybe she should take Sophie and hire another baker. Maybe Aunty Darla's suggestion might just work. Ivy walked towards the front entrance of the shop, only to find people lined up out the door. Turning around, she headed for the back and joined the chaos at the counter.

"Who's next?" she called. All thoughts of England temporarily forgotten.

CAMERON

Following his new ritual since Lindy came home from hospital, Cameron worked well into the night, programming. And looked after the children during the day until he and Jack put them to bed. He coped on a mere four hours sleep and found there was still enough energy to keep up with the kids.

Tonight he worked later, finishing the programming for the last of his father's referrals. He was hopeful about his quotes for new jobs. He'd sent out tenders for six contracts and four asked him for a more detailed quote. The knowledge he was asking close to what his father charged and still gaining interest made him a little more confident in his ability to survive on his own.

He hadn't told his mother as yet. He wanted to have a signed contract before he showed his hand. But by stepping out, his self-belief was building.

There was a tap on his bedroom door just before Sophie stuck her head in.

"Hey, how's it going?"

"Morning Sophie. Yeah, good. Just finished with Ralph's last client. I'm done with him. For good!" Cameron smiled as a tingle of pleasure skittered through him.

"What will you do now?" Sophie asked, tilting her head.

"Au Pair." Cameron was smiling at the joke he made.

"No seriously, Cameron. You need to work." Sophie's indignant voice rose ever so slightly.

"Hey, it was a joke. I've applied for six contracts and have heard from four of them. And don't tell Mum yet. I want to tell her when I've signed a contract or two."

"Okay, fair enough. I should say congratulations, what a tremendous effort." Sophie was still hanging onto the door as she spoke. "Well, I better head to work, I don't want to be late."

"Hey Soph,"

"Yep," she popped her head back inside his room.

"Are you pleased we moved up here?"

"Oh, you bet. Ivy's great to work for and she has grand plans for expanding the business." The smile she wore lit up her face.

"Awesome. You seem happier."

"I thought you would have been more settled here, but somehow you're angrier of late." Sophie shared.

"Nah, I'm all good. I love being close to Mum again and Jack's going to give me a job a few hours a day when Mum's back on her feet, so I get out. Oh, and the kids are awesome."

"Yeah, they are. Well, I better go. See you at dinner?"

"Of course." Cameron was still smiling as he heard Sophie's car drive around the front of the house.

The ping of his computer brought him back to the present. He opened his email app to see a reply from one of his contacts. Cameron read the email, read it again and then for a third time just to be sure.

No, the first read through was correct. The email was from Phil Anders, Managing Director of Anders and Butterworth Engineering. The following words stole his breath, *'I have attached the contract for the agreed price. We understand any changes made on this end will cause payment adjustments, as stated. We hope you accept the contract as we'd love to work with you.'*

Cameron leaped off the bed.

Subject to legal approval, he might have just landed his first client. Without giving it another thought, Cameron forwarded the email to his mother's lawyer in Melbourne. He explained what happened and asked how long it would take for them to check over the contract before he could sign it, with their approval of course. The contract seemed rather straightforward, and he'd reiterated his agreement of the financial side as well.

With all that done, he checked his watch, which read five-thirty. Okay, so he'd get about two hours sleep before any of the kids came in to wake him. Closing his eyes Cameron drifted off into a deep contented sleep.

ASKING FOR GUIDANCE

IVY

*I*vy planned and predicted, worked, and scheduled everything she could think of. She wanted to have an in-depth procedures manual for Sophie to follow while she was away. Leaving Sophie and Susie in charge of the shop would be a good business decision. Both women were more than capable and trustworthy.

She studied the inventory orders for the past month and estimated around those figures. She typed up a current list of suppliers and what she brought from each one. Feeling more in control, the next task was to determine who'd be the most sensible person to be in charge of her funds.

The obvious choice would be Jack. He had a head for business and Sophie could confer with him in the evenings over things requiring his attention. Determined to sort everything out, Ivy phoned Jack to ask him for his help.

He must have been busy because the call went through to voicemail. Instead, Ivy left a message outlining her plans. Well, at this point she'd done all she could, Jack would ring back when he got a chance.

Leaving the planning for now, she ventured back downstairs to the kitchen and decided on a stocktake ahead of going back out the front of the shop to relieve the others for their breaks.

Having an extra employee left Ivy with more time to think. It was one person and one person only who invaded her mind…Cameron. His treatment of her stung painfully. Yes, she accepted he was different, but she never believed he could be so rude. Maybe she could fortify her courage and question him as to the barriers he'd erected between them.

"Hey Ivy," Jack said, dragging her from her current thoughts.

"Oh, morning, Jack. Sorry, I didn't hear you."

"Yeah, looks like you were down a rabbit hole." He said, kissing her cheek. "I got your message, sorry I was at the doctor's with Lindy."

"How is she?"

"If you came over to visit her, you'd know," Jack said, not turning away. Ivy could see he wasn't trying to hide his feelings on the matter. "Maybe your lack of attendance has something to do with this trip you're planning." Jack stared out the window and then continued. "Between you and Cameron, Lindy and I can't keep up. He's shut himself off from the world using the kids as his excuse, and now there's you who wants to travel to England to find your father." He added with a grin, "I thought looking after Lindy would be my major issue, but the two of you top that."

Having no intention of correcting his assumptions, Ivy joined in and laughed at his humour.

"I found a box Grandma left me. There are two letters from my mother, one to an adult me and another to my father. I have his name. She says if I wish to find him, I should."

Jack frowned, putting family first and taking a keen interest in them, epitomised the man he was…even his extended family.

"And you want to find him?" Jack went to the cupboard, pulled out a cup and tea bag and helped himself to a cuppa.

"I asked once, but the pain in Grandma's eyes told me never to go there again. When I cleaned out my spare rooms, I found a box full of my mother's things." Ivy pulled out a plate and walked over to the oven and opened it. "Pie, pasty or sausage roll?"

"Pasty and sausage roll thanks." He answered as he sat at her bench.

After sliding the plate towards him and fetching the bottle of tomato sauce, she pulled out a stool opposite Jack and took a seat. "Jack, I'm determined to find him. If he pushes me away, so be it. But if he doesn't, I'll have family again."

"We're your family, Ivy," Jack's jaw clenched.

Leaning over, Ivy took his hands in hers. "I know Jack, you guys couldn't love me anymore. I'd be lost without you all in my life, but I owe it to myself to meet him even if it's just this once." She couldn't hold back the plea for him to understand her situation.

"What if he rejects you? I can't stand by and see you get hurt."

"I'm willing to take the risk. Aunty Darla and Uncle Tony have made one stipulation to the trip and I respect their point of view," Ivy stated, believing Jack would've spoken with them.

"What?" Jack asked, his head jerking up. "Do they already know about this proposed trip?"

"Yep, they do. They asked I take someone with me. If I can't find anyone, they said they'll come but they'd prefer not to. And I understand." Ivy nodded as she spoke.

"I like their thinking." Jack agreed, "I'll come with you. When do you plan to leave?"

"Middle of Feb. But Jack it's not like it's an overnight trip down the highway, you have Lindy and the kids to think of, not to mention the farm supplies."

He expelled a heavy sigh, "Yep, you're right. Leave it with me. I'll try to sort something out. So, Sophie's okay to look after the shop?" Ivy could see him thinking through all the obstacles.

"I haven't said anything yet, but that's my plan," she confirmed.

"Give me a few days to work it all out and then we'll call a family meeting. What happens if he rejects you?"

"Then I've fulfilled a goal, I just want to meet him." Ivy released a small smile, got up and opened the drawer behind her and pulled out an envelope. "You should probably read this."

Jack took the offering. He read the front of the envelope and then retrieved the contents and began reading.

Ivy busied herself with the stocktake while Jack took his time to read the letter. When he finally spoke again, the tears in his eyes matched hers.

"Oh Ivs, I'm so sorry." He walked around the bench and wrapped her up in one of his warm hugs, he obviously followed in his father's footsteps. To her, Jack acted so much like her father. In fact, she had many pseudo fathers, her Grandpa, Uncle Tony, Jack, and Tessa's husband Harry. They'd all been there for her when she required some guidance and care.

"I owe it to Mum to try. She says he was an amazing man, and I was conceived with love. Hopefully, he'll be happy to see me."

"Just promise me, if he doesn't, his rejection won't hold you back from being happy. This can't make you happy, only happier because you already have a great life and family. Not to mention friends who love you."

"I promise I'll try Jack. No matter what, I'll come back home to Chester's Run. I promise you."

Ivy checked the time. "I better relieve the ladies for their lunch break. I'm sure you're needed at the farm supplies."

"You kicking me out?" he asked, wiping the crumbs from his face. His teasing shattered the tension.

She laughed and leaned in to kiss his rough cheek.

"Never." He smiled and followed her out the front.

Ivy watched him go and for a minute she stopped still. Please God, don't let his fears eventuate, but this was a risk, and with risks the outcome wasn't always favourable.

ACCEPTING RESPONSIBILITY

CAMERON

Jack's youngest son, Bradley lay kicking and wriggling on the floor as Cameron attempted to change him as he did most mornings. Lindy was up and about more and more, but they all insisted she take it easy. As the bruising came out and got darker, Lindy's energy levels increased.

"Morning love," she said, dropping a soft kiss to Cameron's stubbled cheek.

"Hey Bradley, look who it is," Cameron cooed.

"Mumma, Mumma," Bradley's legs seemed to pump harder whenever Lindy was in sight. Well, at least Lindy never needed to guess whether the kid liked her. Even though Cameron identified with Bradley's excitement when he saw his mother, a twenty-four-year-old carrying on as a toddler wouldn't be acceptable.

Finishing the job, Cameron let Bradley loose and watched as he quickly rolled over, got up on his knees and fell forward trying to get to Lindy.

They both laughed as Cameron picked the little fellow up.

"Come here, tiger. There's Mumma." He placed him in his mother's arms while returning her earlier kiss. "How'd you sleep?"

"Great. I heard Jack up with this little man at two-thirty." Turning to Bradley she asked, "Why didn't you sleep through?"

Bradley rubbed the back of his arm across his face before burying his head into her shoulder.

Dropping a kiss onto his head, Lindy headed for the door. "Come on, time for your breakfast," she informed her little man.

Cameron cleaned up the dirty nappy and Bradley's pyjamas. Next, he walked into the children's rooms, gathered up all the dirty clothes, hung towels and headed downstairs to start the day.

Nate was more than capable of overseeing breakfast creation. Caleb was rather inventive with his food combinations. This morning his scrambled eggs included a splash of maple syrup on top, while he'd thrown a few peas and cherry tomatoes into the mix. Lindy and Jack encouraged the weird combinations saying '*arguing with him will only stop him from helping*'.

"Have the horses been fed?" Cameron asked as he walked into the kitchen after dropping the washing off in the laundry.

"Yes, Cameron," Evie answered. "It was my turn this morning, all done."

"Good, thanks."

Evie's head tilted to the side as she eyed him closely. "You're in a good mood this morning, why?"

Those words made him stop. Had his moods been so appalling? "Well, because you guys are helping so much and Mum's back on her feet again and…well, this place feels like home." He didn't mean the Homestead but Chester's Run.

He caught Lindy's questioning eye and his smile automatically widened. "What? I'm not always in a bad mood," his defence was sharp.

"Yes, you are," the kids replied, which resulted in him and Lindy laughing.

"Well, how about you guys tell him when he's in a mood," Lindy suggested, but kept her gaze averted. "Cameron will know when to sort it out."

"You bet," Caleb chimed in, erupting the room into laughter.

Cameron was slowly becoming more understanding of the kids and their directness. It was easy to laugh along with them.

"Okay." Cameron began trying to plan the day. "Jack wants us to do the horses. He was up last night with a certain little rascal and didn't have time to do them this morning. We'll clean out the stables and then if we finish, after lunch we'll head over to Bernie's so you can ride the horses with the kids."

A loud cheer erupted, Cameron didn't miss his mother's smile.

"But," Cameron said, raising his pointer finger on his right hand, "We have to do inside first. So, finish breakfast, do your rooms and muck out the stables, then we'll walk around to Bernie's." Turning to his Mum, he added, "Nola will be here to pick you up at about twelve-thirty. Bradley will sleep in his pram, won't he?"

He loved her smile. Even from behind the bruises, it was magical.

"Maybe we should prepare dinner before we go," Evie suggested, looking up on the wall to see she was rostered on.

"Sounds like a plan," Caleb said as he got up to begin his first chore for the day. Clearing the table.

Cameron swallowed the last mouthful of scrambled eggs. This time using Caleb's humour he added, "Well, you heard the man."

The feeling around the table was so much happier this morning. On reflection, Cameron owned his part in the uneasy feel of the last couple of weeks. But things were looking up. The contract was due back today and from his conversation yesterday with his lawyer, the paperwork seemed in order and pretty straightforward. He'd be able to announce to his mother he'd already picked up his first client. An international one.

IVY

"You guys okay here for the next half an hour?" Ivy asked Susie and Sophie as she headed out the front of the shop.

"Yeah, why?" Susie was always the inquisitive one.

"I have an appointment," Ivy ducked out the door and out of earshot. No doubt Susie would question her later.

Checking her watch, then her hand, ensuring she'd remembered all the paperwork she required. Ivy never needed a passport before. Her belly tumbled and her sweaty hands were probably ruining the paperwork she completed with Uncle Tony's help three days ago.

Maybe while she was in England, she might visit Paris. Her dream was always to do one of those Parisian workshops to refine her baking skills.

"Morning Ivy," she looked up to see the local vet standing in front of her.

"Morning Baz, how's Marie?"

"She's great. How have you been?"

"Good, thanks," Ivy closed one hand over the other, trying to hide the passport application.

"You going overseas?" he asked with a grin.

"Not sure, but I thought I'd organise my passport just in case things fell into place." So convincing, not.

Luckily Baz only raised a brow before changing the subject.

"I was coming to see you. Marie is turning fifty in April and I was wondering if you'd be up to catering for the party. It's all hush-hush," he added, tapping his nose, and looking around to make sure no one else overheard their conversation.

"Of course, I will. When in April are you planning for?"

"Her birthday is on the 10th. I thought we'd do it the Saturday night. The kids are coming home and we decided to go all out."

"Look, I have an appointment now but could you stop by later today or tomorrow and we'll sort something out?"

"Sure. How about I stop by after my shift? Say four-thirty?"

"Perfect. I'll see you then."

Ivy checked her watch and quickened her pace, Joan would be waiting for her.

DELIGHT AND DESPAIR

CAMERON

This feeling of total exhaustion and pure pleasure was proving to be a brilliant mix. It was only in the dark hours his mind wandered to the beautiful blonde who stole his breath. But he knew better than to go there.

Checking the time, he saw he had an hour before starting dinner. The kids were washing and brushing the horses while Bradley ran around playing with the hose near the back patio.

"You right there, Mum?" Cameron asked while Bradley squealed with delight. Lindy watched him while Cameron helped the other children.

"We're all good. I'll sleep well tonight." He knew she was grateful for the outing today. Being stuck inside was driving her crazy.

The growing appreciation of friendship between man and beast, or in this case child and beast was strengthening. The outing this afternoon with the children only highlighted the interaction taking place. He'd never liked horses, but he realised it was more a case of not actually giving things a chance. The day proved a great success.

Hearing squeals of laughter, Cameron turned to see Bradley running in and out of the sprinkler. Those were the days when his mother made the most basic things enjoyable. He couldn't hide his pleasure.

"Cameron, can we leave the horses out for a couple of hours?" Nate asked.

"Okay, but make sure you guys put them away." Cameron held the gate open as the children one by one led their horses out into the paddock. Jack was uncompromising with the care of the animals, and the children were just as responsible.

"Cameron, could you please drag over the hose," Evie called. "We need to wash out the trough."

He sorted out the hose and waited for the children to exit the paddocks. "Can you all clean these things up," he was pointing to the hoses, buckets, rags, and brushes. "Mum, are you okay with these guys —I just need half an hour to get some work done?" When she waved a hand in agreement, he turned to the kids. "I'm in the bungalow if you need me. Nate, you okay to be in charge for a bit?"

"Yep. Should I start dinner?"

"Nah, all good, it's sorted. See you soon." Cameron headed over to the bungalow. He'd changed the phone settings, so he didn't receive emails or messages while he was with the children. They were more important, and knowing his own weakness at the first chance he'd get lost down a rabbit hole, following something up.

He took the laptop off charge and walked out to the dining table to begin work. But before starting, he set the timer on his phone for twenty-five minutes, ensuring he'd be back inside to start dinner on time.

Cameron's laptop beeped and buzzed with emails and messages galore. He normally dealt with them one by one, but not today. He was waiting on a reply from his lawyer, so he scanned through until the expected email came into view. Clicking on the email, Cameron read the message attached. He grinned. He was clear to sign his first ever contract. Now, he could say he was a businessman. He laughed aloud and punched the air with a clenched fist.

When his phone chimed his reminder, Cameron walked out of the bungalow feeling a small sense of achievement and whisper of caution in the back of his head. Never in his wildest dreams would he have guessed the company who'd hired him for his professional skills would include a flight to England. They'd insisted on him touring their facilities and seeing the setup for himself. Phil Anders replied to Cameron's email, with the signed contract attached, eager to begin the project. Unfortunately, he and his partner wanted to meet Cameron, but Thomas was leaving on holidays this evening for the next ten days. They finally settled on a flight on the seventh of February.

With each footstep towards the house, his grin widened and self-esteem built. He loved that he could share all this with his mother. Checking his watch, he was a minute late. The kitchen would be abuzz with Evie and Joanna getting things ready and probably turning on the veggies and the oven.

It was five now and Jack and Sophie would be home in forty-five minutes for dinner, they'd all eat at six.

He walked in to Nate and Evie, talking and laughing. He loved how close this family was.

"Where's Joanna?"

Nate laughed. "Sound asleep. Mum said to leave her, asked if I'd help you guys instead."

"It was a huge day, wasn't it?"

"The best," Evie agreed, wrapping her arms around Cameron's waist. "Thank you, Cameron, it was great."

He smiled, returned her hug, and bent to kiss the top of her head. Doing this with these wonderful children was becoming natural for him. Other than his mother, the only person he'd ever hugged or kissed like this was Sophie. His chest expanded tenfold. He was so fortunate to be a part of his mother's new life. Images came to mind of how he spent his days living alone. In fact, living wasn't the right word for it. He had only existed from one day to the next. When his mother left them, he sunk deeper into himself. In fact, at one point he just wanted to die. The pain of not having her in his life was heart wrenching. Sophie was great, but she wasn't Mum.

He heard the clatter of cutlery and realised Evie and Nate were hard at work. He refocused and began cooking.

"You're in a good mood today," Evie said as she gathered the plates from the cupboard.

"Am I?" Cameron asked, but his smile gave away his excitement.

IVY

"No Sophie, not tonight," Ivy insisted.

"Seriously, not tonight, not last night and none of the other nights either. I swear you're avoiding us." Sophie countered.

"There's a great deal happening and I'm busy getting sorted."

"Things like why you left the bakery this morning?" Susie chimed in.

"Maybe," Ivy replied, her focus on sweeping the floor.

"Your phone's buzzing, Ivy," Sophie said, heading for the counter to fetch it for her.

"Thanks," Ivy took the phone. "Hi Jack."

"Oh Ivy, I think I've worked it all out. How about you come for dinner tonight and I'll run my idea by you?"

Ivy looked at Sophie. Oh, how she wanted to say no. But she wouldn't, she needed Jack's help and didn't want to appear ungrateful. Besides she needed to get used to seeing Cameron in public, even with a broken heart. How he'd gotten under her skin so quickly was beyond her.

"Okay, sounds great. I'll see you at six, bye."

"Oh, so Sophie's invitations aren't good enough, but Jack asked and you're going," Susie teased.

When Ivy snapped, they fell silent. "Jack's helping me with the thing I'm working on. So, I'll be going to dinner. Okay?"

No one spoke, and Ivy couldn't believe she'd spoken so harshly to her workers. No, they weren't workers, they were both friends. What was happening to her?

Ten minutes of isolation time in the kitchen helped clear her mind. She heard footsteps. Looking up, she saw Sophie and Susie were heading in her direction. One glancing around as if looking for answers and the other staring back with arms crossed over her chest and an *'I told you so'* expression.

"You let it get under your skin, didn't you?" Susie whispered. Ivy dropped her head. Tears threatened, but she sniffed them back. She was bigger than the rejection of one man. Even if he was gorgeous in every way.

"I tried not to, I really did. Do you know he won't even talk to me?" gritting her teeth, she tried to focus on something else.

This time it was Sophie who responded. "Who won't talk to you?"

Ivy's head dropped.

Sophie turned to Susie. "I feel like I should know what's going on here. What got under her skin?"

Susie looked to Ivy who was bent at the waist, resting her arms on the kitchen bench. "Your brother."

"Liam?" Sophie virtually shouted.

Both women scrambled to answer. "NO!"

Susie added, "The other one."

Sophie glared at Susie for a long moment, and Ivy could see she didn't get it.

"Cameron," Ivy said, at last filling in the gaps.

"You and Cameron? Did I miss something?" Sophie's head was pivoting between the two women, as if she was watching a tennis match.

"He won't even talk to me." Ivy ran her long fingers through her hair and groaned.

"Whoa, back up. You like Cameron?"

Ivy and Susie both nodded.

"I warned her, but she went and lost her heart, regardless."

Sophie blew out a rushed breath and plonked herself onto a stool. "Please don't take this the wrong way but… Wow!"

Susie laughed, and Ivy cracked a smile.

"I told her he'd be hard work." Susie crossed her arms and leaned into the door frame.

Ivy filled Sophie in on what happened, or more like hadn't happened between them.

"I don't know what to say," Sophie said. "You guys were getting on well, as friends." She paused for a moment. "Now you've told me it does actually make some sense."

They sat in silence for a bit longer. Maybe Sophie might have a suggestion to get things back on track?

"You're the reason his confidence was growing?" Sophie squeezed clenched hands and added, "And why he's been so down lately."

Sophie tapped her hand on the bench between them. "Come on. Let's finish out the front and we'll head over. I'll drive and come back and stay the night?"

"You're not needed there?"

"Nah. I'm in bed early and out in the morning before anyone gets up so I'll come and stay."

Ivy gave Sophie a grateful smile. "Thanks, means the world."

"And as for my brother—"

"No, Sophie don't. It's over. Anyway, while it's just the two of you, I should probably mention I'm going away for a few weeks. Jack's helping me to sort it out and wants to see me about it tonight." Ivy explained.

Both women squealed with delight, "Where are you going?" Susie asked.

"Well, I'm off to the UK. I have family over there and it's time I paid them a visit," she replied matter-of-factly.

"Good for you, bring back some hunk and make someone extremely jealous." Sophie quipped.

"I will do no such thing! But, I might head to France to do a couple of short courses while I'm there. I could bring back some fresh ideas for the shop."

"What about the bakery while you're gone?" Susie asked.

"Jack will oversee everything and you will each have your responsibilities. Sophie, I'm hoping you'll be fine with the baking and Susie the front of shop will be all yours. I haven't taken a holiday in years," with a shrug, she added, "There's no time like the present."

Somehow having Sophie's support made all the difference to Ivy. She'd have dinner at Jack's and listen to his suggestions. One thing for certain, she was going to introduce herself to her father, if he was still alive.

CAMERON

The door to the garage opened, and Cameron checked his watch. Jack was on time, as usual.

"How was your day?" he heard Jack ask the children who were in the kitchen.

"Oh Dad, it was awesome," Nate gushed.

Cameron listened from the laundry as the children relived their day. He couldn't help smiling as he reflected on the part he played in Jack's children's lives.

"Sounds like everyone's enjoyed a great day. Where's Cameron?" Jack asked.

"I'm right here." Cameron said, walking into the kitchen to join the others.

Jack turned and gave Cameron one of his smiles. The one saying, *'You did good buddy'*, the one he never received from his own father. The one coaxing him out of his own world and tempting him to connect with others. Even if they were young children, Cameron understood it was a start.

"Ah, just the man I was looking for. Ivy's coming for dinner. Is there anything I can do to help?"

Cameron's brain stalled at the mention of the lively, talented, gorgeous blonde who dominated his mind. He worked hard to control his thoughts during the daylight hours but couldn't do the same with his dreams.

Realising they were all watching him, he muttered, "All good. Everything's under control."

Cameron turned his attention back to preparing dinner, hoping to cover up his discomfort of the bombshell Jack delivered. With his back to them, he listened to Joanna's tale of their day.

"Well, sounds like a great time," Jack chuckled. "And there I was slaving away at work. Where's Lindy?"

"Mum's in the library, Cameron sent her there for some quiet time." Evie explained as she counted out the knives and forks.

Cameron glanced at Jack and smiled. Lately, here and there, the word 'Mum' slipped into the conversation by Jack's kids.

"Let me say hello to Mum and I'll wash up for dinner."

Sucking in a deep breath, Cameron tried to turn his attention to his task.

How was he meant to sit in the same room as this goddess? Unfortunately, he didn't have time to ponder his answer, Sophie walked in the back door followed by Ivy.

"Hey," Sophie said in greeting.

Cameron murmured his response and kept his head down. As if counting out the serving bowls was totally engrossing.

He breathed a sigh when he heard Sophie and Ivy in the library talking to his mum. Maybe if he was clever enough, he could sit on the same side as her at the opposite end of the table.

When he heard Sophie and Ivy head upstairs with the girls, he turned off the food, grabbed the envelope he'd placed on the bench earlier and joined his mother and Jack in the library.

"Have you both got a minute?" Cameron asked, settling into one of the large overstuffed chairs by the window.

"Of course, what's up?" Jack asked.

"I just signed my first client today," he heard his voice rising as he spoke. This was a huge achievement and it wasn't lost on him.

"You did what?" his mother's smile was priceless.

"I received an offer from a firm in the UK and sent their contract to Anthony." Cameron said talking about his mother's lawyer. "He's approved it all, and we signed today." He held out a printout of the paperwork to his mother.

She took the offering, still smiling, opened, and read the contents. "Wow Cameron, this is fantastic. Your price is reasonable, and the work isn't anything beyond you from what I can tell." She continued reading and turned pages with Jack reading over her shoulder.

"Well done," Jack offered his hand to Cameron. "When do you start?"

"Well, the thing is the partners want to meet me, so I'm flying over on the seventh of February. They've booked me into a hotel in London, so I get to see all the sights I wish. But I wanted to check if you guys will be okay without me for a few weeks."

Lindy and Jack exchanged glances.

"Of course, we will be. This is your livelihood." Cameron smiled at Jack's enthusiasm, it almost outdid his mother's pleasure. "I think you've just helped me out with another dilemma. Are you up for a travelling buddy?"

"Of course," Cameron grinned, relieved at not having to do this himself. He couldn't recall ever having this response from his own father. No, Ralph was never a father, the man was only his sperm donor.

"Thanks, I'll confirm the date with them and get back to you."

Cameron was smiling wide when he left the room and headed for the kitchen where Joanna and Evie were dishing up.

"Excellent" he said, clapping his hands together, "Let's get dinner happening." Watching the girls at work, he couldn't help laugh at himself. He was picking up social skills through these children. He was still uneasy in some situations, but it showed less and less over the last few weeks. Going forward he would have to do so with his head held high even if he didn't feel it. A thought struck him, who would his travelling buddy be?

THE SOLUTION BECOMES THE PROBLEM

IVY

"Well," announced Jack once everyone served themselves. "There are some exciting times ahead for the Saunders/Kemp/Master's family."

Ivy looked up, half bemused by Jack's statement. How did her news become a Saunders/Kemp newsflash?

"Ivy has expressed a desire to travel to England. She's hoping to meet family over there she's never met before."

The table erupted with cheers on her behalf. Luckily Jack refrained from giving away too much detail about her past, but she enjoyed the children's reaction.

"I'll definitely send postcards to all of you," she promised. As she scanned the table, Cameron didn't appear at all happy for her. In fact, his mouth dropped open. Why? What was going on there?

"Aaaannnnnddd." Jack continued, "Cameron has picked up a rather important client, his first client, and gets to travel to England," the children's clapping and cheering continued.

"Will you send us postcards too?" Caleb asked.

"Well, maybe they could sign the same card because Ivy is looking for a travelling companion, so I suggest you put your heads together and sort it out. How do you like my solution? Ivy, you have a friend who will travel with you and free accommodation for three weeks." Jack summarised.

"What?" Ivy failed to hold back the surprise at his announcement.

"Organise yourself a ticket. The flight leaves on the seventh of February. You're all set." Jack concluded with a grin, Ivy could read his self-satisfaction. Boy, he'd judged this so poorly. But what could she do?

She glanced down the table at Cameron. Her hand shook as she mulled over exactly what Jack said. This arrangement was so far from perfect, but what choice did she have? She didn't. There weren't any other options, other than dragging either Jack or his parents to England, and she didn't want to be the reason for forcing them to take the trip.

After dinner Cameron stood and pushed his chair back, "Excuse me," he looked to his mother and Jack, "I've got some work to do."

"Of course, the kids and I can take care of the kitchen." Jack smiled and took Lindy's hand in his.

Ivy looked to Sophie, who watched her brother closely as he left the room. When Jack pushed his chair back, so did the children and everyone pitched in to help with the dishes. Even Ivy.

Lindy sat chatting happily about their day.

"Sophie, I think he's achieved more in the last few of weeks with these guys than you and I could ever get him to do." Lindy's face wore a grin, but she shook her head at the same time. "He's a mystery, that boy of mine."

"Mum, don't worry, I think he's landed on his feet. What he's managed with his business has been through your patience and his own grit and determination. Be happy for him, I am." Sophie kissed her mother before gathering up the last of the serving dishes and heading into the kitchen.

"You'll watch out for him, won't you, Ivy?" Lindy asked as Ivy hefted the stack of dirty dinner plates from the table.

"Sure," Ivy agreed with a smile. But how could she manage that when he couldn't even bear to be in the same room as her? But she had to admit, Cameron was dedicated to the family and supported his mother. When he loved, he loved freely. Unfortunately, such a sentiment failed to apply to her.

With the dishes finished, Jack went up to supervise baths and showers. Sophie and Ivy popped into the library for a chat with Lindy before heading over to the bungalow, so Sophie could pack some clothes.

"How exciting," Lindy said. "You must be really happy to get away for a while. You set to take on all the cooking, Sophie?"

"Yeah, I think so. Ivy has everything so well organised, I should be fine."

"I'm only organised because a few months ago a woman was sitting in my bakery for breakfast. We met over a cold cup of cappuccino. We got talking and one thing led to another and she became my mentor. Between working with me and looking after my cousin's household, she also fell in love. So, I figured if she could successfully juggle such a variety of tasks, I could follow her lead." She ended with a chuckle, and Sophie and Lindy joined in.

Ivy loved how connected she became with these ladies. They shared her pleasure and joy.

"And it was my pleasure. I've spoken with Jack, and I agree you must do this now. But just promise me you'll be careful." Ivy understood everyone cared for her. The outcome with her father was unpredictable. "Only expect the minimum response. If you get more, it's a bonus. And no matter what else, you'll have Cameron to turn to. I know he can be a bit awkward but he'll step up, I promise." Ivy's hand encased Lindy's the whole time she spoke, and it seemed natural to squeeze them in agreement to her declaration of Cameron's abilities. Even if she didn't feel as confident as Lindy.

If her father rejected her, why would she turn to Cameron for comfort, understanding, and support? Instead, Ivy allowed her lips to settle into a gracious smile, "Thanks, Lindy. I promise to be realistic about it all."

CAMERON

It was an automatic response to slam the door behind him when he entered the bungalow. He wanted to refuse Jack's request, but he wasn't one to make a scene and especially after everything Jack did for the family. But how could he spend a few weeks in Ivy's company listening to her chat daily with Liam and somehow carry on? It was probably going to sting, but at least he only promised Jack and his mother to accompany her to visit a family relative. As for playing tourist, she was on her own.

Cameron pulled out his laptop and set to work. There was plenty of reading and analytics to review. He re-read the brief, taking notes about what he wanted to see in action and how the entire engineering process could benefit from his input. Through his father's connections, he previously worked with a few engineering. He appealed to those clients eager for them to see the benefits of overhauling their systems, but they weren't open to his input, only his programming skills. Fortunately, Phil Anders respected Cameron's expertise and was willing to discuss his improvements to their initial plans. Not just the stop-gap measures, previously limited by the local company's lack of budget and their near-sightedness.

Engrossed in taking notes, Cameron babbled to himself as he researched additional information. When Ivy followed Sophie into the bungalow, it shattered his concentration. He tried to feign disinterest, but wasn't successful. She sat at the kitchen bench, leaning forward, talking with Sophie about reordering stock and the daily requirements of the bakery.

He studied her long blonde hair covering the side profile of her face. While they were deep in conversation, Cameron allowed his eyes to take in the fit of her jeans as they hugged her lower body. Each curve seemed more enticing than before.

"My contact, Max, will call you each week to confirm the order." Ivy explained to Sophie.

As she spoke, his eyes continued to travel the length of her beautiful body. Liam saw exactly what Cameron could. The woman was stunning and a masterpiece in everything except for her choice of men. He'd wanted to rant and rave about what made his brother tick, but how would such a tantrum benefit his cause? She'd only hate him for his interference.

"Hey Cameron," Sophie called. "When you're in England, can you please bring me back a tin of Quality Streets?" Sophie begged.

"Why don't you ask Ivy to get them?" Cameron snarled.

Ivy and Sophie exchanged a puzzled glance. "Because you're my brother. And family do things for each other, don't they?"

"Maybe I'll wait in the car," Ivy said to Sophie, her voice low and tight.

"No come on," Sophie said, grabbing Ivy's hand and leading her towards her room, "Come with me while I get my stuff organised."

Cameron watched as the two walked off and cursed himself. Why did he stoop so low? This woman affected him so much, how could he travel with her and be pleasant and friendly when what he really wanted was to have a relationship with her? Man, he really sucked at this relationship stuff. Connecting with a friend was hard enough, but a potential girlfriend had him twisted in knots. Oh, how his body hummed when she used to laugh and chat with him. Then he remembered how her arm was slung around Liam's shoulders and his hand on her knee.

A strangled groan expelled itself from the depth of his soul. His actions were so out of place.

"Cameron, what's wrong?" Sophie called from the hallway leading to the bedrooms. She was always there for him, bringing him down easily, and today was no exception.

He rocked back in his chair, ran his fingers through his hair and pushed himself to his feet. He was desperate to mend the bridges his attitude was burning.

He walked over to Sophie.

"Where's Ivy? I need to apologise for my behaviour lately."

Sophie bit her lip and then frowned. Cameron picked up on it immediately. Fortunately, without a word, she turned and walked towards her room.

As he reached Sophie's doorway, Ivy was pacing. Had she heard their discussion in the dining room? Maybe she was sorry for her decision. Maybe she wished she could undo the past, or face the realisation she was wrong in choosing Liam over him?

Wishful thinking, much?

If only he had the guts to put it out there.

He ran a sweaty hand through his hair, "Sorry for my behaviour. Things are way out of my comfort zone right now, and I'm dealing with them and stressing at the same time." He stood rigid in the doorway, wishing he looked in control, but how could he with his clenched fists by his side and the tension in his jaw causing him pain. He silently urged for self-control and an impossible wish that they could start again.

"How many times have I told you, when things get too much, we'll talk about it?" Sophie's voice rose slightly. "I promised you I'm here with you and I meant it."

And Cameron was pleased she did.

He nodded his agreement. Somehow, he was drawing strength from the woman across the room, not from his sister. This was a first. He watched her closely as Sophie spoke.

"I'm sure if you need to talk in England, Ivy will help you out. What you've done since moving up here Cameron has been amazing. Mum is so proud of you." Sophie walked over and hugged him as she always did. "And so am I." When she pulled back, she added, "Someone's bothered about something, maybe we could talk about it?" He could hear the hope in her voice.

Instead, he looked over at Ivy. "I just wanted to say sorry for my behaviour. I look forward to travelling to England together."

At first Ivy just gave him a nod and then realised she should speak, "Me too, Cameron, and thanks for agreeing to Jack's plan. This is something I really need to do."

IVY

Delight rushed through her, Cameron was actually paying her some attention again. He was being civil. Now would be a good time to explain her reason for travelling.

"After you guys moved out, I decided it was time to clean out the cupboards in the spare rooms and found a box of my mother's belongings. She died when I was five years old." Ivy paused and sniffed back tears forced on by her memories. "In the box I found a couple of letters from my mother, one for me and one for my father." Ivy sucked in a shaky breath before continuing. "I've never met him, but it's my mother's wish I do." Forcing herself to look up from the dark carpet, she realised Cameron was holding out a box of tissues for her. "Thank you." She blew her nose and continued. "So, I'm heading to England to meet my father. I was always told my mother died of cancer." When she paused, both Cameron and Sophie raised a brow and seemed to lean in closer. "But in her letter, she tells me exactly what happened. So, I need to see him, find out a few answers to questions I have from what she revealed."

"Why do you require an escort?" Cameron asked.

"In the letter my mother talks about one of my father's employees assaulting and raping her," Ivy couldn't monitor her shaky tone, "I want to make sure the man she says is my dad, really is. She's adamant she was pregnant before the attack, but my father refused her story. In her letter she asks me not to judge him on what happened. She says he's a wonderful man who struggled with leaving her alone with the guy while he stayed to help his much younger sister. My one hope is with the advancement in technology, he'll agree to a DNA test. Now knowing what my mother disclosed, I have to find out the whole truth."

"So, you're worried your father attacked your mother?"

"No, not at all, it's Uncle Tony, Aunty Darla, Jack and Tessa who are worried. Until now they're all the family I've known, but if there's another side in England who will meet me, I'd like the opportunity."

Cameron rubbed his hands roughly up and down his face.

"I really am grateful you've allowed me to travel with you. I'll try not to impose on you too much."

Cameron waved a dismissing hand. "It'll all work out. We'll be fine."

Sophie kept the questions coming for the next five minutes while she packed what she'd need for tomorrow and Ivy answered as best she could. The three walked out into the lounge with the situation much improved.

"Well, I'll see you tomorrow," Sophie said to her brother before she kissed his cheek and led Ivy out the door.

"Bye, Sophie. See you, Ivy. I might bring the kids by for lunch tomorrow. They've been begging me to take them to the bakery."

"Yeah, they love it. Bring Lindy as well, you can all sit upstairs and eat after the kids have made their own milkshakes. Use the backdoor if she doesn't want to see anyone."

The rift between them appeared to be mending, Ivy looked back to Cameron with a broad smile and a nod. Hopefully, by the time they left for England they would be friends again. Grateful for such a possibility, Ivy gave Cameron a wave and closed the door behind her.

PREPARING TO TRAVEL

CAMERON

"Thanks for taking us shopping," Nate said, sitting in the front passenger seat of Lindy's car.

"All good, buddy." He replied before asking Evie, "Have you finished checking off the list?" Cameron took his eyes off the road and saw bags spread out around her.

"Nearly," she answered. "I've got most of the school supplies sorted as you told me to." Evie dropped a pair of blue handled scissors into a bag. With the new school year a couple of days away, Cameron offered to take the two eldest shopping in Wangaratta. He'd wanted to get stuff for his trip as well, so figured a trip to Wangaratta was in order.

"How long before we get to the bakery?" Evie asked.

"Not long." Cameron said, slowing down as he hit the edge of town. The only sound in the car was the hum of music from the stereo, the rustle of shopping bags and the tap of Nate's fingers on the door handle.

"Cameron, can I ask you something?" Nate looked out the passenger-side window.

"Of course," Cameron said, waving to a familiar car as they drove into town.

The driver, Troy helped in the search for his mother, and he'd also bought Jack's old place. Cameron was becoming a familiar face around town, and it made him smile.

"Are you guys here to stay?"

"Who?"

"I know Lindy is, but are you and Sophie staying as well?" Nate asked. "You both seem to love it here."

"Absolutely. It's a great place. You know I work from home, don't you?" Cameron asked.

"Yes."

"With my job, I'm able to work anytime of the day or night. When I lived in Melbourne, I made that my excuse, but here my mum and your dad have forced…no, encouraged is probably a better word. Encouraged me to be more social and I'm so much happier."

"You were really awkward when we first met you," Nate told Cameron, talking with the innocence of youth.

"I still am with some people or situations, but I'm better with others." Cameron and Nate shared a grin.

"You know if you ever want to talk, I'm always here to help you, okay?"

"Thanks buddy, means a lot," Cameron hid his grin, amid the humour there was a great deal of sincerity in the comment from Nate.

As they drove along Park Road, Cameron couldn't find a parking spot, "What do you reckon, should we park around the back?"

"Yep," Evie and Nate chimed in. Getting out of the car, he followed the children in through the backdoor of Ivy's shop. Him and Ivy were friends, so he wouldn't be the person to make this more difficult than it needed to be.

Inside, they found Lindy and the rest of the clan waiting for them.

"Did you get everything?" Lindy asked as Cameron bent down to kiss her before taking his seat on the other side of the table.

"Everything on your list and a few things for me. Turned out to be a worthwhile trip." Cameron turned to see Ivy carrying over his food. "Thanks."

"Nate said the shopping trip was successful," Ivy said as she settled a veggie pasty and black coffee in front of him.

"It was." Cameron searched through the bag next to him. With a flourish, he presented a smaller bag. "Ta dah!"

"What is that?" Ivy asked.

"I wasn't sure if you had one. It's a money belt for the trip," Cameron held out the offering. "Mine's blue to match my luggage and yours is," he shrugged his shoulders hearing his nervous chuckle, "Well you can open it and see for yourself. Evie and Nate picked it out for you." He was blabbing, so he stopped talking.

Ivy took the small, black plastic bag he held out towards her. She gave a small nod. He watched as she opened the present and didn't miss her eyebrows rise and lips settle into a grin.

"Thanks Cameron, that's really..." he could see she was toying with her word selection. "Really sweet of you. Grey suede ha!"

Cameron laughed. "I wasn't sure about the colour, but Evie insisted you have a matching bag."

"You do, Ivy. The small case you used at Christmas," Evie's voice was coaxing her to remember.

"Oh, that's right, I forgot about that one. Well, I must take it with me." Ivy gave Cameron a grin, he could see there was no intention of taking it until now. He watched as she walked back to the counter, kissing both Nate and Evie on the way.

"Did you get me a surprise too, Cameron?" Caleb asked after climbing up onto his lap.

"Only if you baked me those shortbreads you promised." Caleb laughed at Cameron's questioning eyebrow but refused to answer.

The chatter around the table became excited as the children talked about returning to school. Nate was starting high school, and the unknown had him turning to Cameron. "When you were in high school, what things were you interested in?"

"For me, computers were always my thing. Liam was always the one drawing stuff and Sophie was forever in the kitchen baking."

"I wanted to be a farmer," Nate said, his head and shoulders dropped, matching his voice. The sale of the family farm was tough for Nate, as he'd previously explained to Cameron, but he wouldn't have said anything to his father or Lindy.

"Perhaps you can get a casual job on a farm?" Cameron suggested.

"Do you reckon I could?" Nate's eyes widened.

"Hey Lindy," they all looked up to see Troy standing at the other end of the table. "You're looking much better. How you feeling?"

"Definitely on the mend. Thanks again for everything."

He waved a dismissive hand. "All good." He looked at Nate and then back to Lindy, "I couldn't help overhearing what Nate was saying about a farm job. I'm actually looking to get someone in to help me with some sheep, cows and even chooks. Not sure it can continue beyond a few months, but if Nate's interested, and has someone else in mind, I'd be happy to have them working for me."

"What would we be doing?" Nate asked.

"Building fences, clearing the yard, cleaning up after the animals. Feeding and watering them. Moving them from paddock to paddock. At this stage it's only for a little while, mind."

"Could I, Lindy? I'm sure Ben would come too."

"Thanks Troy, could I speak with Jack and Tessa and let you know? If we can work out the logistics, it should be fine."

"Great, I'd be keen for them to start next week if possible?" Troy's tone was encouraging and Cameron couldn't miss the hope in Nate's eyes.

"Thanks, I'll get Jack to ring you." They all watched as Troy walked up to the counter, collected his order, and left.

Nate's pleading began. "Please Lindy, could I? I'd work really hard, I promise."

Cameron spoke up, knowing how his mother worked in these situations. "Nate, you heard Mum's plan. Just leave it for now. Wait till she talks to Dad."

Lindy's raised brow told Cameron she'd heard his reference to Jack. The awkwardness at which they referred to both Lindy and Jack was easing as the connection of family grew. Even with the children calling Lindy mum, Cameron blushed at his reference to Jack as dad, but the children would appreciate it and maybe, in time, it would become second nature.

IVY

"Can you believe you leave for Europe in the morning?" Susie asked Ivy as they all sat around one of the tables, making sure everyone understood their area of responsibility.

"No, and yes. I'm excited and nervous at the same time." Ivy came clean and explained everything to Susie about her father and was grateful for her absolute support.

"What's the worst he can do? Close the door in your face. If he does," the woman shrugged as one does with a lack of connection to a situation. "You'll just go to Paris, bake, and come home to us."

"You're right, I really have nothing to lose, but the possibility of rejection stings and it hasn't even happened yet." Ivy clarified.

"Go in expecting the worst and if you get more, it's a bonus."

"Susie, it's not like plucking a size ten jacket off the rack at Myer. This is my father, I'd love to know him or his extended family." Ivy blew out a long breath. "My mother said he had a sister. I'd love to meet her if I could."

"Sorry, I don't mean to underestimate the opportunity, but I don't want you to get hurt." Susie said, resting her hand on Ivy's arm and lightly squeezing.

"Nah, it's fine. I've got so much happening, I'm just stressed. You guys will be fine here, won't you?"

They looked over at the eight squares of butcher paper tacked to the wall, "Are you serious? You've included a reminder to buy toilet paper, I'm certain we don't even need to think for ourselves." Sophie said through spurts of laughter. "Ivy, we've got this and you're only an email away. Jack will help us out as well. Stop stressing and calm down."

Susie checked the clock on the wall. "Well, I need to get moving. I have to pick up the kids from Marty's mum."

"Thank you," Ivy said, standing and hugging her dear friend.

"You'll be fine. Enjoy yourself and don't fret about us until we give you something to worry about," Ivy laughed at the teasing tone.

When Susie left, Ivy and Sophie packed everything up and transferred the butcher paper to a spare wall in the kitchen.

"I'm sure you've covered everything here. We'll be fine. Susie's right, just bring back splendid memories and photos and hopefully a promise from your long-lost family that they'll come and visit one day soon." Sophie jumped down off the counter and wiped it clean. "Come on, Mum and Jack are waiting for us."

The girls locked up, and Sophie drove home.

As they drove up the driveway, Ivy gasped, "What the hell, whose are all these cars?"

Sophie just laughed and pulled up beside Liam's car. "Come on, they're waiting for you."

CAMERON

The sound of cheering coming from the lounge drew his attention. What the hell was going on? Cameron walked through the dining room, down the hall, and stopped at the entrance of the lounge. With three steps down into the room, it meant Cameron could see over the top of everyone. Ivy and Sophie obviously just entered, because they were kissing and greeting everyone. Harry and Tessa sat next to Darla and Tony and the children were standing about chatting and laughing. Well, all except Nate and Ben, who were due home from work any minute now.

"Cameron," his grandfather called out. Holding up his glass, he said, "Here's the other one," and they all cheered again. Liam released Sophie and was now hugging Ivy. The sight of Ivy and Liam together made his skin crawl, but he worked to stop his nostrils flaring and saying something he'd have to apologise for. He made a promise to himself, he wouldn't spoil the night. Mum and Jack obviously planned this surprise party for both of them. He would be cordial. Cameron took the few steps into the room.

"Hey Pa, you came all the way up here?"

"Of course. We couldn't let you go without a send-off. And besides, we wanted to check on your mother." Duncan pulled his grandson into a hug and whispered. "I'm so proud of you. The things you've achieved away from Ralph's reach is a credit to you." No one referred to Ralph as his father anymore. They all disowned him as part of the family. Well, all except Liam.

"Thanks, Pa."

"Are you looking forward to it?" Duncan asked, watching Cameron closely.

"Yep, I'm a bit nervous, but Ivy and I'll be there to help each other." He didn't want to associate himself with Liam's latest interest, but he had to convince them all together they'd be fine.

"Good, really lovely lass, that one." Duncan said, nodding Ivy's way.

Looking over, Cameron saw Liam and Ivy deep in conversation. Ivy pulled out her phone and began typing on it. Paused to listen, and began typing again. He couldn't help it, but he wanted to know what they were talking about. Should he sidle over and join the conversation? Why not? It was time to greet his brother. So, Cameron walked over and stood with Liam, Sophie and Ivy.

"Cameron," Liam said, acknowledging his brother. "I was just explaining to Ivy, I have friends in London, Ross and Cassy. They know you're both heading over and are expecting you to make contact. Ivy has the details."

"Thanks, that's great," It wasn't though because Cameron would fret over having to meet so many new people. In the forefront of his mind was Ivy's situation, putting him in an awkward position and he'd have to step up if things turned sour for her.

"I've just forwarded the details to you," Ivy said a second before his phone buzzed.

"Thanks."

"So, how's it all going here?" Liam asked. Obviously determined to start a conversation with his brother.

"Well, it hasn't been as relaxing as I'd hoped," Liam laughed with a mock look of surprise on his face. "Seriously, the kids have been fine and now they're all back at school there's more time to work during the day."

"The new clients, how's that going?"

"Really positive. The English firm's great and I've also picked up three small contracts as well, so I've always got something on the go."

Talking about work with his brother was the best way to remain on a safe topic. Mind, he had no intention of asking Liam about his work or Ralph, it didn't interest him at all.

IVY

As Sophie led her brothers out of the room, Jack arrived home with the boys and the food. So, Ivy helped them.

"Oh, someone's in trouble," she teased as Jack handed her bags of food from the kebab shop.

"Well, I couldn't very well ask you and Sophie to prepare food for your going away party." Jack countered.

"Look," Ben said, holding up bags of Chinese and Indian as well.

"Traitors," Ivy accused, and the boys laughed.

"You were right, Dad," Nate called, "She just called us traitors."

The teasing continued for a while, and Ivy loved the way they could stir each other up.

"You two run upstairs and wash up for dinner," Lindy ordered Ben and Nate. "How was work?"

"Awesome. Troy sent home some fresh eggs for us," Nate told her as he headed down the hall.

"How are you feeling?" Ivy asked Lindy as she stepped around the counter to help.

"Much better. I still get a bit tired, but Jack convinced me Bradley should do a couple of days a week at the preschool program. I resisted at first, but they're right. He gets to socialise and I can have a rest."

"What about when Cameron's gone?"

"Jack's looking to employ a new guy. Apparently, he's a local who's come back from Afghanistan looking for something part time. Doc spoke to Jack about it a few days ago. He was going to interview him today, I think."

Jack wrapped his arms around Lindy from behind and kissed her cheek. "Yep, interviewed him, hired him, and I've invited him over for dinner tonight." Turning to Ivy, he added, "You'd know him. Ned, Ned?" Jack was clicking his fingers, trying to remember the man's last name.

"You mean Ned Driscoll?" the hairs on the back of her neck stood to attention. Memories of the man's past and the talk of what he'd endured in Afghanistan had Ivy considering if he'd be a suitable candidate for Jack's business.

"Why, what have you heard?" Jack asked.

"Nothing bad." Ivy quickly interjected. "Only he was badly injured."

"Yeah, Doc mentioned that and asked if I'd give a veteran a chance. I'd have hired him, anyway. His track record with the army was impressive."

"Good," Lindy said, still tuned into the conversation while opening containers and finding serving spoons. "Ivy, could you round the others up, please?"

"Sure thing."

Five minutes later everyone was entering the dining room, filling plates and cups, and finding seats. Cameron, Liam, and Sophie emerged from the library as she was about to call out to them.

"Don't worry, you'll be fine," Liam said, patting Cameron on the shoulder. There was a knock on the front door and Ivy passed them all as she went to answer it.

"Hi Ned, Jack said you were coming. Come on in. It's been a long time." She leaned in and wrapped him in a hug. He was a few years older than her at school, but he was the fun, athletic type and everyone knew him.

"Good to see you, Ivy. Sorry to hear about your grandmother, she was a wonderful woman. One of the best, actually."

"How's your mother?" Ivy asked. She knew of his home life prior to him running off to war.

"I don't know. I haven't seen them since I got back."

"And Timothy?"

"I'm not ready to go there yet," he said in a strained voice as he ran a shaking hand through his hair.

Sensing this wasn't what he needed tonight, she stopped the questioning and led him to the kitchen.

He stopped short outside the dining room. Ivy picked up on his struggles immediately. The noise and number of people were too much.

"Maybe this wasn't such a good idea, I should probably go."

"Ned, come on in," Jack called from the dining room.

Ivy took his elbow and led him to the library. "Here. Take a seat."

Jack walked in with raised brows.

"Bit noisy out there at the moment," Ivy confirmed on Ned's behalf as he visibly shook. His complexion was pale and now she could see both his hands were shaking.

Jack squatted in front of him. "Sorry mate, I didn't realise."

"I need the job so I figured I should accept your invitation," Ned said, his voice shaky.

"There's Indian, Chinese, and Kebabs. What would you like to eat?" Ivy asked.

"No, I should go,' Ned said, trying to get up.

"You're not going anywhere. The noise in there will be too much for Jack's partner and she'll be in here soon, so you can sit with her and her son Cameron. I'll be back in a minute."

Ivy walked out and left Jack to monitor his guest.

"Jack's in the library with Ned. The noise was too much for him," she whispered in Lindy's ear.

Lindy gave a nod as she took her plate and excused herself. Ivy filled a plate of food as high as she could and on her way out the door she stopped by Cameron and said, "Your mum's eating in the library." He'd be grateful for the opportunity to escape the noise and constant chatter as well.

CAMERON

A minute later Cameron entered the quiet library and took in the unfamiliar face, appearing lost and out of sorts.

"Ah, Cameron," Jack said, turning when he walked in.

"Thanks, Ivy," the stranger said as she handed him an overloaded plate. The smile they exchanged seemed too intimate.

"Ned, this is Lindy's middle son Cameron, Cameron this is Ned. He's going to work at the farm supplies."

The two men shook hands and greeted one another.

"Well, if you're all settled, I'll represent the travelling duo in the dining room." Ivy said as she walked out but then stopped, "Sorry I didn't ask if you wanted a drink?"

"Umm. Water would be awesome, thanks."

Cameron's eyes tracked Ivy as she left the room, he looked back at their new guest. "You know Ivy?"

"Yes. I was a few years ahead of her at school. Though I haven't seen her since before I left for Afghanistan." Ned said. "You guys new around here?"

"Yes, my mum Lindy is Jack's partner. She moved up here last year. Then early this year my sister and I followed her. Much better option than the city."

The door opened again and Sophie popped her head in. "A bottle of water for Ned?"

"Thanks, that'd be me." Ned took the offered drink.

"This is my sister Sophie, Sophie, this is Jack's new employee." Cameron watched as he looked at her the same way he looked at Ivy. The man relaxed a little.

When Sophie left the room, the two men chattered away, slowly finding common ground. Cameron asked about where Ned had been overseas.

Cameron smiled at his mother as she watched on quietly. When the conversation ebbed, Lindy asked, "So, are you living locally, Ned?"

"Just outside of town, actually. On the road to Bright. I've bought a place with a few acres. Pleasantly quiet and no one really drops by to visit."

"No other houses in the area?"

"Yes, there's one next door, but the owners are from Melbourne and it's their holiday home. I only see them every couple of months. The peace suits me at the moment." Ned took another mouthful of food then asked Cameron, "So you're the one off to England?"

"Yep. I've picked up a new client and they want me to walk through their premises and see first-hand how everything works. I'm building a new computer program for them from the ground up." Cameron smiled at his mother. He tried to think if he'd ever given her this much reason to be proud of him, on the work front, "They'd looked for nearly twelve months trying to find a system to accommodate their needs, but the changes to individualise any program made it too messy and expensive. They put the job out to tender and I made an offer. I'll probably have to employ more man power down the track but at the moment, I'll just assess the company's needs and go from there."

The door opened again and Nate walked in. "Ivy sent me in to see if anyone needed anything. More food or drinks?"

Cameron looked at his empty plate. "I wouldn't mind something else, but I'll come and get it. Ned, do you want to come out and top up your plate?"

"If there's enough, thanks, that would be great."

"Mum?"

"Nate will get mine, thanks love," she said, holding out her empty plate to Nate.

Cameron led the way out to the dining room and although there was chatter, the noise level was more bearable. They both filled their plates and Cameron looked to Ned and asked in a whisper, "Would you mind sitting out here for a bit? I should catch up with my family from Melbourne."

Ned smiled. "I'll give it a go."

"If it gets too much, just head back into the library."

There was a spare seat beside Liam, so Cameron motioned for Ned to take it and he took one opposite. Knowing Liam as he did, he was certain his brother would entertain the newcomer for a bit. He didn't disappoint.

Ivy slipped into the seat next to Cameron and gave him a sideways glance and a smile. The glance showed off her golden eyes, but her smile took his breath away.

"How is he?" she whispered.

"Calmer now. Would it be PTSD?"

"I think so. I don't know much about it. Thanks for going in. He seemed more settled with a male there." She smiled again.

"Were you guys good friends before he left?" Cameron was just interested, or at least he told himself that.

"Not really, I saw him at school or around town. He was in the local footy team. We had different friendship groups."

"He seems like a good guy," Cameron said, just as someone called his name from the other end of the table. "What's up Caleb?"

"Can I stay in the bungalow while you're away?" his eager tone suggested he believed it was possible.

Cameron raised a brow. "I don't think your father will agree to that!"

"He will if you say it's okay," Caleb pleaded.

"Why are you asking Cameron and not me?" Sophie broke in.

"Because Cameron's the man and he's in charge," Caleb explained.

A chorus of growls echoed out from the women around the table.

"No way!"

"Who taught you that?"

"He can't be for real!"

"Caleb!" Jack's voice rose over the other voices. "You apologise to Sophie and the ladies around the table, then go in and see Mum!" The order rang loud and clear and the table silenced.

Caleb stood up to his full height, which for a six-year-old wasn't very tall at all, and looked down the table. "Sorry Sophie, sorry ladies."

Everyone watched as he walked out of the room, shoulders slumped and chin trembling. When the echo of the library door closing rang out, the room burst into fits of laughter.

"What do you teach that child?" Liam called out to Jack.

Jack replied with a pointed finger. "Apparently, you used to do something similar when you were younger."

To which the entire group began laughing again.

Something inside Cameron rippled and burst open. In one sentence, Jack gave Liam a warning, his arrogance wouldn't be tolerated. For once in Cameron's life, he enjoyed seeing Liam reprimanded from across the table. Ralph had always favoured Liam and ignored his behaviour. Cameron hid a smile, it was comforting to know Jack lived by one rule for everyone, no matter your age. The two brothers exchanged a look expressing what words hadn't for most of their lives. When Liam gave Cameron a small nod, he believed himself somehow liberated from his father's oppressive behaviour after all these years.

"Sorry, Jack." Liam said. "You're right."

Cameron and Liam were making up ground in so many areas. Except when it came to Ivy. Perhaps he was jealous he couldn't achieve such a relaxed mood when they were together. Tonight, he'd managed a conversation with Ned that not only settled the other man, but proved to Cameron he could make a success of this trip. Maybe the truth of the matter was, Ivy wasn't the woman for him and hopefully one day he'd meet someone who would make him as happy as he was around her. Cameron forked in another mouthful of food and joined a conversation with his grandparents and Tony and Darla.

THE JOURNEY BEGINS

IVY

Ivy rubbed sleep from her eyes again and checked the time. Four-forty-five. Liam volunteered to drive her and Cameron to the airport. She checked her watch again. They should be here any minute. Her bags sat at her feet by the kitchen door, the money belt secured around her waist as she checked for the hundredth time this morning. Yes, her passport was there.

"You know we're going to miss you, don't you?" Sophie said with a sigh.

"I told you last night don't start or I won't go," Ivy threatened.

"Yes, you will and you are going to love it." Sophie finger pointed at every word. "You'll have a ball no matter what happens and as for Cameron, you've got three weeks with him to let him know what he's missing out on."

Ivy laughed at Sophie's cheeky grin, "You're his sister and we—" Ivy waved a frantic hand between them, "—are not talking about him. Besides you two are more like twins and even if twins don't talk, they have this mind link thing where they know most things about each other. So, you can stop right there."

It was Sophie's turn to laugh now. "You mark my words. Cameron will come to his senses."

Ivy recognised a glint in Sophie's eyes but ended the conversation there. The less she talked about Cameron, the better. Why did she agree to spend three weeks travelling with him?

"You okay?" Sophie asked.

She'd sighed openly and loudly. "Fine. These boys are late." She said, looking at her watch yet again.

Sophie heard the crunch of the tyres first and turned to the sink to wash her hands while announcing, "Your carriage awaits, my lady."

"Haha, you're hilarious," Ivy groaned inwardly at the unknown awaiting her.

"Get out of here and have a wonderful time." The women embraced and Ivy pulled away with a tear in her eye. "And if the other thing doesn't work out the way you wish, just remember you've got us."

Ivy could only smile, she hadn't slept well last night stressing about the outcome of the situation with her father. The man could be dead. Jack encouraged her to make contact, but Ivy wanted to be at ground zero when the war broke out, if there was going to be a war.

The back door opened and Cameron came in. "Morning. You all set?"

"Morning, big brother. Yep, she's ready. Now promise me you two will look after one another," Sophie gave Cameron a pointed look.

"Seriously, I think we've determined this already. We'll both be fine. Now get out of my way so I can carry the lady's bags to the car." Cameron leaned in and planted a chaste kiss on Sophie's cheek, then grabbed Ivy's suitcase. "See you in three weeks," he called over his shoulder to Sophie as he proceeded out the open door into the cool morning air.

"You sure you'll—"

"Go. And have a great time and don't worry about anything here. Susie and I have got this."

Sophie followed Ivy out and gave them all one last kiss goodbye. Ivy watched as her home and livelihood disappeared from view. "You all set?" Liam asked, watching through the rear-view mirror. "I think so. You ready for this adventure, Cameron?" she asked. "Yep." He sighed, "As ready as I'll ever be."

LONDON

CAMERON

Dropping his backpack onto the nearest chair, Cameron walked over to the window, and looked out over London.

"Wow, this place is magnificent!" He turned when he heard their suitcases being unloaded. "I've got this," Cameron said as he strode towards the door. He'd watched enough movies to understand the expectation of tipping. "Thank you." He said, closing the door after the bellboy retreated.

"Well, how about I give you guys a bit of time to settle in and then we'll meet downstairs at the restaurant for dinner." Phil consulted his watch.

"I'm sure you guys don't need me around," Ivy said. "You've probably got business to discuss."

"No business conversation tonight, I promise and besides you're going to need to eat." Phil reassured her. "My wife should be here any minute, I'll head down and find her."

Cameron looked at Ivy. Having a familiar face would help, but he didn't want to force her. Besides it had been a long flight. He said, "Why don't you come and meet Phil's wife?"

Ivy checked her watch. "What's the time here?"

"Just past six-thirty," Cameron confirmed. He'd already changed his watch to local time.

"Okay then. Thanks. I'll just freshen up." Ivy said.

"Thanks Phil, give us fifteen?"

"Perfect, see you both then." Phil let himself out while Cameron and Ivy sorted out their luggage and selected a room each.

"See you in ten," Ivy said as she slipped into her home away from home for the next few weeks.

Cameron watched her go and smiled. He couldn't put a measure on how important it was for him to have a familiar face around. Having Ivy travelling with him was surprisingly settling. Just her presence eased his tension. In his bedroom, he took in its grandeur, the large king-size bed and bathroom off to the left. He consulted his watch and decided there was time for a quick shower and change.

By the time he emerged from his room, Ivy was sitting on the couch, finger brushing her hair and putting the long strands into a bun on top of her head. He marvelled at how easily Sophie did that, but Ivy, four years older, seemed to style it even better.

Cameron watched as Ivy slipped slender feet into a pair of flats, brushed her hand down her jeans and checked herself over in the full-length mirror as she stood up.

"Will I need a coat?" she asked.

"I don't think so. If we do, I'll come back up and get them." Cameron picked up both jackets, their scarves, and beanies, and hung them on the hall stand. And looked up to see Ivy smile.

"Have you got your door card?" he asked as he slipped his wallet into the back pocket of his jeans.

"Yep. Just in case I get too tired."

In the lobby they found Phil laughing with a woman as he tried his darnedest to hold a squirming little girl in his arms.

"There you are." Phil swapped the child from one arm to the other. "You did well. Normally when people say fifteen minutes, they take thirty. I'm impressed. Anyway, Cameron Kemp, Ivy Masters, this is my wife Clem and our daughter Portia."

"Lovely to meet you," Ivy took the woman's offered hand.

Cameron copied her lead.

Phil signalled to the hostess and ushered them inside the hotel's restaurant. Once everyone sat down, Phil asked questions and Cameron relaxed into the evening. These people were fun to be around, and it didn't take an immense effort on Cameron's behalf. They discussed everything from what the women did for work and hobbies to where Ivy and Cameron lived in Australia.

Ivy spoke with ease and gently drew Cameron into the discussion. He kept his eyes focused on hers whenever she spoke. The woman must have been born with a knack for making idle conversation a breeze.

"How long have you known each other?" Clem asked, reaching for a warm multigrain roll.

"Actually, only a few months," Cameron responded.

"Really?"

"Yep. I met Cameron's mother early…" Ivy stopped as she calculated the dates. "It was in September, but we only met," Ivy looked to Cameron, "Briefly when Jack and Lindy went away for the weekend, and again on Christmas day. Cameron's mum is marrying my second cousin and his sister started working for me in early January. So, not long at all."

"Then, Cameron you've just moved to…" Clem looked to Ivy for confirmation of the town's name.

"Chester's Run."

"Yes, I've always been close to Mum and when she decided Chester's Run was her new home, I figured with my work I could go anywhere. My sister and I followed. It's a whole new way of life from the city and so far, I can't complain."

"How far is it from Melbourne?" Phil asked.

"About two-and-a-half hours."

"Do you miss the city?" Clem countered.

"Not at all. The country gives us a freedom we never experienced in the city. When I get back, my sister and I are going to discover the local walking tracks and maybe even take up horse riding."

"Do you ride, Ivy?"

"Apparently I rode since before I could walk, though I haven't been on a horse since I lost my grandfather nearly ten years ago now."

"Would you come to our place and ride with me before you go back home?" Clem asked. "Like you, I've ridden forever. I'd love to take you out, if you're up to it."

"Thank you. Yes, sounds great."

Conversation flowed, and dinner was enjoyable. Ivy let out a yawn, "Please excuse me." Cameron watched her for a moment. She didn't look like she had the strength to finish the last mouthful of cherry pie and ice cream. Cameron breathed in slowly concealing his own threatening yawn.

"Well, I can see how tired you both are." Phil said as Ivy tried unsuccessfully to hide yet another yawn. "We'll let you get some sleep. Cameron, I'll have a car here to pick you up at eight in the morning. Ivy, it was a pleasure and we hope to see you again soon."

"I've got your number, so I'll be in touch and we'll make a day for riding," Clem added, rocking her sleeping daughter in her arms.

"Sounds perfect. Thanks for everything tonight." Ivy said, leaning in for a kiss from them both.

Cameron escorted Ivy to the lift after they said goodnight to their hosts.

"You okay?" Ivy asked.

"Me? I'm fine. Just tired." Cameron stepped aside and waited for Ivy to walk into the empty lift ahead of him.

"They were lovely people. Just believe in yourself and take time to answer their questions. Phil wasn't pushing you or too over the top. You'll be fine tomorrow." Ivy said as Cameron stepped in beside her.

"I was comfortable with him, I think it'll be all good. Thanks for coming to dinner."

Ivy's smile rocked him. Making his body stand to attention. Hell, she really was a beauty.

They walked back to their room in silence. A silence full of comfort and ease. For what it was worth, he was having second thoughts about his initial response to Jack's announcement of them travelling together. Having her here by his side gave him a strength and an ease to move forward. A smile lifted Cameron's lips. All will be well.

Inside the room, Ivy kicked off her shoes with a groan as she flexed her toes into the plush carpet. She bent down to pick them up. When she straightened, she leaned over and dropped a kiss onto his cheek.

"Thanks for agreeing to let me travel with you, Cameron. Let's hope at the end of each day we are happy with how our day panned out. Goodnight."

"Goodnight, Ivy." Cameron watched as she walked into her room and closed the door. Her nearness and floral scent had his body on high alert. If only things between them were different.

THE SEARCH BEGINS

IVY

The movement outside her bedroom woke Ivy the following morning. She remembered getting into bed, switching off the light, and that's about it. There was no resistance to sleep at all.

She stretched, rolled out of bed, and pulled on her lavender dressing gown, which she'd placed on the chair in the corner last night. After running her fingers through her hair, she popped her head out the door to say good morning.

"Sorry, did I wake you?" Cameron asked.

"It's fine. I wanted to be up early."

"What are your plans for today?"

"I'll start looking into my father's background. Mum wrote of friends who lived close by here. So, I might head out today and do that."

"Will you be okay?"

"I promise I won't contact the man, just some inquiries from people who knew him and my mum." Ivy hoped she sounded convincing, but deep down her stomach rumbled. Her mother passed away over twenty years ago. What if these contacts were no longer around?

"Take care, I admire what you're doing, I really do." Cameron was tying up the laces of his black shoes when someone knocked on the door.

"I'll get it."

"That will be breakfast," Cameron said.

"Morning."

"Your breakfast, madam."

"Just on the table, thanks," Ivy said, opening the door wider.

When the server left, Ivy walked over and made herself a cup of tea. "What time do you hope to be back tonight?"

"Phil said they always finish up by six. So back here no later than seven."

"I thought I might email Liam's friends just to say hello."

"Yep, good idea. If they want to meet us, let's try for later in the week, if that's okay with you?"

Ivy nodded her agreement as she took a bite of toast.

Cameron joined her at the table and they ate and planned for the next few days.

There was a noticeable ease of interaction between them. Even the time he'd stayed at her place, there was a connection beyond anything else she'd experienced with another person close to her own age.

Cameron checked his watch. "My ride will be here soon. You okay?"

She couldn't help the smile crossing her lips. "Yes Cameron, I'll be fine. Thank you."

He drew in a deep breath. "Well, wish me luck, I'll need it." He stood and wiped his face with the linen napkin, then walked towards the door.

Ivy joined him, "Cameron, you'll be fine. This is your career and you know what you're doing. Believe in yourself because I do and so does your family."

He shrugged on his jacket and took the scarf she offered.

"Thank you, I think we needed each other on this trip. I'll see you later." Cameron stared at her for a moment. She watched as his mouth opened and then closed again. Instead of talking, he placed a gentle kiss on her forehead. "Good luck today. Message me if you need to."

Ivy closed the door behind him and stood frozen to the spot. This man was gorgeous to look at, as well as gentle and caring. Why did she have to fall for someone like him? Did he see himself the way she did? Cameron was amazing, with so much to offer. In fact, if she was honest with herself, he was better than she deserved. Yes, he had his flaws and challenges, but he really was so special. Her reality boiled down to the fact she'd fallen for a man beyond her expectations, and he probably only saw her as Jack's little cousin.

Pulling herself out of her reverie, she walked back to the table, glancing into Cameron's bedroom as she went. It was time to finish her breakfast and head for the shower. Her mission had begun and there were no distractions, well apart from the quick emails she sent. The first to Sophie and Susie and the next to Liam's friends before getting ready to face the day.

AN ADVENTURE

CAMERON

As the car approached the offices of Anders and Butterworth Engineering, Cameron couldn't dissuade the nerves from taking hold. The factory loomed and for his career, this opportunity meant everything.

"Good morning," the friendly woman greeted him at reception. She reminded him of his mother. And this somehow calmed him, and the thudding of his heartbeats settled slightly.

"Good morning, I'm Cameron Kemp to see Phil Anders."

"Yes Mr Kemp, they're expecting you, come on through."

Cameron followed the woman away from the noise of the office to a wing on the left of the entrance. The place was grand and he couldn't help but marvel. Clean, yet professional was an understatement.

"How was your trip?"

"Not bad at all. It's my first time to England."

"Well, we must make sure you see all the sights," the woman's gentle voice offered.

"That sounds great," he croaked out and he could hear his mother saying, '*Smile. Breathe. Everything will be fine*'.

She opened a door and gestured him inside.

"Ah Cameron, come in." Phil stood to greet him. "Thanks, Mum. Cameron, I should probably mention, this is my mother, Audrey."

They looked at each other and smiled, Cameron couldn't think of what to say so he just nodded, then turned to take in the room.

He heard the door close behind him and saw an older man standing to greet him.

"And this is my father, Thomas."

"Pleased to meet you," Thomas said in his strong English accent.

"Likewise," Cameron shook the man's hand. His grip was firm but somehow respectful, if that was at all a thing. He remembered Ralph's handshakes, they were for one purpose only, a show of power. There wasn't ever any comfort in their connection for Cameron.

Cameron took the offered seat and the three of them settled down to work.

Thomas discussed the company's structure and planned expansion of the business over the next two years. He also shared the vision he and his son had for the future. Cameron listened intently, took notes and asked questions where things required clarification on the brief.

"You've picked up on several areas where we've overlooked potential issues," Thomas reflected on the growing list before him as he nodded. "Drawing our attention to these at this point in the process only adds to Phil's initial belief that you're the man for the job. Which is vital to the success of this project and our business expansion."

"You're extremely thorough," Thomas added when Audrey came in with morning tea a couple of hours later.

"I learned from the best. My uncle has his own business, he contracts for the Australian government in the nation's security. So, noting even the smallest detail is vital. That's where I learned my trade while completing my degree."

"Good to know." Phil agreed. "You've raised some issues here I hadn't expected. So, these things might hold you up initially?"

"There's so much to do, I'll keep refining the overall restructuring while you sort that out. I won't be diving in too deep this week." Cameron assured them.

"Excellent. Well, let's eat and then Phil can give you a tour of the place and introduce you to the people you'll be working with." Thomas was walking over to get his coffee when he turned back to Cameron. "I know this isn't in your job description, but if anyone raises a red flag for you, I'd appreciate you sharing that with us. It's imperative that we train our employees if their skills are lacking. We both feel we have a powerful team around us, but if there's a need for further knowledge, we're happy to provide it."

"Certainly," Cameron said.

Over morning tea, the conversation was light. More about him and Ivy and things they'd like to see. Phil and Thomas were eager to show them things England was famous for. After putting himself out there, he felt justified in the opportunity before him. As the day continued, he kept a note of the things he wanted to tell Ivy when he returned to the suite. After settling into his office for the next couple of weeks, Cameron's mind turned to Ivy, and he wondered how she was faring.

DISCOVERING WHAT'S ON OFFER

IVY

$\mathcal{I}$vy pulled out her mother's letter once again and set to work on what she'd previously refrained from. She searched the internet, looking for pictures of the old hotel where her mother worked. The website depicted a recently renovated interior. The exterior was as grand a building as she'd seen. Ivy hoped Cameron wouldn't mind a visit. She'd enjoy seeing it, if only once in her life.

Sitting back, she looked at the photos again that her mother included in the envelope. Both her parents, grinning with their arms wrapped around one another in front of a well-stocked wooden bar which spoke of a bygone era. The faded photo was hers to treasure, a past she'd not heard about. A tear tracked down her face and she allowed herself an infrequent trip down memory lane. Images raced through her mind of times with her mother. Wonderful memories of happy times together.

A short time later, she shook herself. There was work to do. Places to go. Better get back to it. The names her mother mentioned were where she'd start. Using the contact details her mother included, she drafted letters to each of them. She deliberated over the messages, fully conscious this was probably her only opportunity to make contact. Her opening line asked if they were familiar with Anita Masters and Lamont Thornton. Weird to be writing her father's name for the first time.

Ivy wrote, changed, edited, and debated over the most important words of her life for over an hour. Eventually, when she'd rehashed the letters to death, Ivy took crisp, clean hotel paper and transcribed the words conveying her hopes. Maybe one of these six people could hopefully provide her with answers to a few questions about her father.

Next, opening her laptop, Ivy composed a message to home letting everyone know how they were going. She kept the message brief and upbeat, hoping they understood there weren't any details to share. Oh, she needed to buy the postcards Jack's and Tessa's children were expecting. With the writing desk tidy, Ivy bundled up the envelopes and grabbed her purse, coat, beanie, and scarf. Then headed downstairs, all with the intention of keeping herself occupied.

Stepping out into the morning air, Ivy pulled her beanie down over her chilled ears and huddled into her coat to hold back the seeping cold. She'd known freezing, icy days, but this was like an arctic chill penetrating every millimetre of her skin, even though she wore thick layers of clothing.

Despite the cold, the locals were still out and about rushing here and there. Ivy joined the throng, looked up and down the busy street till she found what she was searching for, she dropped her head and strode towards her destination. Stepping inside the well-heated shop, she breathed a sigh. After a few minutes of shivering, she set her mind on gathering postcards. With a quick study of what was available, she grabbed one card for each of the children to send back home as she'd promised.

"You're looking cold this morning," the lady behind the counter greeted her.

"It snows a bit back home, but I don't remember it this freezing," Ivy said, shivering again as she rubbed her hands together.

The lady had a cheek to laugh. "That's an Australian accent," the woman said, "Don't worry, you'll get used to it. We all do. Eventually. I came over from Perth in the early nineties. Took a couple of years and lots of persistence."

Ivy laughed. "Could I have stamps for these, please?" she asked as she handed over the letters. When they landed on the counter, the woman caught sight of her name and address and gasped.

"Ivy Masters? As in the daughter of Anita Masters?" The two questions had Ivy feel a surge of heat in her chest. "You're from Chester's Run, Victoria, Australia." This time it was a statement, not a question. This woman knew of her mother. She must have known her

Tears sprung to Ivy's eyes. Could this really be happening? She swallowed hard. "You knew my mother?"

"Bert, come quick," The woman called into the back of the shop. A tall man with a rotund belly and a long beard, a mix of grey and brown, appeared by the woman's side. "This is Ivy, Ivy Masters," she explained, failing to hold back the tears.

The room spun, and Ivy grabbed onto the counter with a death grip.

"You must be Deb…Deb and Norbert, or Bert, as Mum said everyone called you." Ivy's eyes flashed between the couple, though their appearance blurred through tears.

Deb was now around the other side of the counter embracing Ivy in a hug. They cried together, no more words exchanged, just shared pleasure at finding one another amid the pain of their loss.

Ivy pulled back and let out a nervous laugh. "She spoke of you with love. Apparently, you did everything together."

"Aye, we did that. She was one of the good ones. Near broke my heart when she died. Anita's mother sent me a delightful letter thanking us for everything we did…for Anita." Deb reached for a tissue from the box sitting on the counter. "I can still remember the fun we used to have." Deb leaned back and studied Ivy. "Oh love, you're shaking. Come in the back and warm up."

"It's not because of the cold. I can't believe I found you, I only arrived here yesterday and, wow."

"Deirdre, love." Deb said, addressing a teenager who looked

similar to Deb. "Could you man the shop?" Deb called as she led Ivy into the back. "Bert, pop the kettle on, that's a dear."

Ivy sunk down into the large overstuffed floral sofa and drew in a deep, centring breath.

"So, what are you doing here?" Deb asked as Bert handed Ivy a delicate floral teacup and saucer. Her questioning brow was hard to miss. "Be honest with us, love."

Ivy drew out the copy of the letter handwritten by her mother. "I found this a few weeks ago." Handing it over, she sat back and clasped the steaming teacup in both hands and waited. Deb put on the glasses hanging on a chain around her neck and read the letter.

"Such a delicate hand, I'd know this handwriting anywhere," Deb said as she turned the page and continued. When she finished, she handed the letter over to Bert with a sigh. He tugged his reading glasses out of his top pocket and took his time over the words. Smiling and nodding then shaking his head as if in disagreement. "It was all such a long time ago and so much water under that bridge. My girl, what do you hope to achieve by meeting him?"

"Please, I don't wish to cause trouble, but I have a letter from Mum for him and just once I'd love to meet him. I want to know who my father was. Just once." The last two words were in a whisper, almost a plea. Did no one understand, not knowing her father left a gaping hole in her heart? Ivy managed all her life without a father, but that didn't mean she hadn't pined and longed to see him. To know the man her mother loved so deeply. No one, not even Anita's own parents, said a nasty word against him.

Bert turned the letter over and began again.

PROGRESS

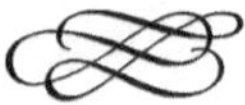

CAMERON

The hustle and bustle of the first day in the office did nothing to convince Cameron they should stay home and relax that evening. He understood the stress of what Ivy was here to do. With Audrey's help Cameron booked tickets to Phantom of the Opera, the musical. His treat to her, and honestly, he couldn't wait to watch the worldwide phenomenon as well.

Walking into their suite, he called out. "Ivy?"

"Hi Cameron," Ivy walked out of her room. "How was your day?"

"Excellent. And yours?"

"There was progress, but I can't tell if it was good or bad," Ivy dropped into a chair opposite Cameron.

"Do you mind if we have this conversation over dinner? I'm starving and I've got a treat for us." He dug into his shirt pocket and waved the two tickets in front of her.

"What have you done, Cameron Kemp?"

"You, me, dinner, and Phantom of the Opera. What do you say?"

"Ummm, let me think about that…yes please," she squealed. "You really have tickets to Phantom?"

"Like right here, right now. Come on, get organised." Cameron replied as he disappeared into his room to change. "You've got ten minutes." He called over his shoulder.

They sat opposite each other in a little booth at a cafe around the corner from the theatre. Laughing at the absurdity of their actions.

"You thought of this by yourself?" Ivy asked with a raised brow.

"No. Never and we both know that," Cameron replied, finding it easy to laugh at his own shortcomings. "Audrey, Phil's mother helped me. She spoke to me at lunch about things we should do." Cameron blushed, "I thought you'd like this."

"I do. Thank you, I'm preoccupied with making enquiries to find my father, I never would have looked into anything like this. And besides you said you didn't want to do anything this evening."

Her smile was genuine and sent the most delicious full-bodied shivers through him yet again.

"You're right, I did. But Audrey convinced me otherwise. Come on, let's relax and enjoy our night out."

They ordered a light meal and while they waited, Cameron picked up on the conversation Ivy had begun in their suite. "So, tell me about your progress on 'The Father Project'?"

"Oh, is that what we're calling it, 'The Father Project'?"

"No, I think we need a better name. What about the 'FP'?"

Ivy screwed up her nose. "The 'FP'? Not quite the ring I was going for," she mocked.

"Okay, leave it with me, but tell me what happened."

Cameron lent in closer on his elbow and listened.

"So, they know where he is?"

"Yep, and I could find him easily if I looked online. Which I will if they won't help. But I'd rather have mum's friends introduce me. They believe I'm who I say I am." Ivy gave a weak smile and Cameron didn't miss the pain in her eyes. "But they think too many people will get hurt by my sudden appearance."

"It's not sudden, Ivy, you're twenty-five years old. And from what you've told me, the man knew you existed from the time of the assault on your mother."

"Am I wrong to want this?"

"No. We're here for three weeks. You have time to convince them you don't want to disrupt lives. Only to fulfil your dying mother's wish that you meet the man she says is your father."

"You say that with confidence." Ivy's head tilted at a sharp angle and Cameron couldn't help but laugh.

"I know your family and I know you. And I know this to be the truth. You're a kind woman, Ivy Masters. Believe in yourself and know there is life after this chapter, no matter what happens here in London over the next three weeks." Cameron couldn't help the twinge of heat that skidded through his heart. He was so twisted in knots about her. Damn bloody Liam. Cameron refused to pick up the pieces for her or any other woman Liam discarded. He couldn't imagine family get-togethers in the future. No, Ivy made her choice, and it wasn't him.

"Come on, eat up." Ivy said, checking her watch. "The show starts in twenty."

Cameron hid the pain of realisation, there'd be nothing between them. Swallowing the last couple of mouthfuls of his soup, he wiped his mouth on his napkin and announced, "Ready when you are!"

Oh, if only that meant so much more than just sharing the experience of the London theatre.

IVY

"Oh. Wow!" Ivy said, attempting to match Cameron's long strides as they left the theatre three hours later. "I've seen a couple of small productions in Melbourne when I was studying, but this was… Wow!"

"Well, that was amazing, Mum tried to take me but the idea of crowds," it sounded like Cameron was berating himself. "Now, I know what I missed out on." Cameron pulled out his phone and began typing.

"Are you messaging Lindy?" Ivy asked.

"No, adding 'theatre with Mum' to my to-do list."

"You have a to-do list?" Ivy asked on a yawn.

Cameron flashed her a cheeky grin that melted her insides. "Since I agreed to move to Chester's Run, Sophie encouraged me to begin a to-do list." Cameron scrolled through his list. "Look. Learn to bake pies with Ivy, that's also on my list."

His blush was hard to miss. "You want to make pies with me?"

"Do you have anything else to add to this conversation other than questions?" Cameron teased.

Their banter was not only fun but warmed her from the inside.

"Hahaha. Well then, thank you so much for tonight," Ivy paused as she waved down a cab and they climbed in. Once the door closed, she continued, "You're so much like Sophie. Since I first met you, your confidence has soared. Do you…oh no questions, that's right."

They both chuckled.

"Sophie is so proud of what you've done for Jack and Lindy. I just wanted you to know your effort has helped so many people." There was a look Ivy hadn't seen from him before. Cameron tugged on his bottom lip and finally looked at her, and it made Ivy smile.

Watching the road ahead, he said in a low voice, "Sometimes it's hard to open up but my life without Ralph has been mind-blowing. I don't know why, but that man hated me. I wasn't Liam who fell at his feet or Sophie who dismissed his crap with a wave of her hand. Everything he did seemed to paralyse me. Shut me down."

"I believe a son needs his father, just like a daughter needs a mother. If I grew up without Anita in my life for the first five years, I have no idea what I would have been like and my grandpa had always been like a father to me. I was so fortunate."

Cameron nodded. "I had my grandpa too. He and I used to meet a few times a week without Ralph knowing. I think the man set about to undo the damage a deranged father inflicted on his son."

"You and Duncan are really close, aren't you?"

"Is that another question?" Cameron teased as a deflection. Then his face grew serious and he nodded, "We're here."

They walked into the foyer and towards the lifts together. "I remember one year we made Father's Day cards and my teacher came up and said, *'Cameron this is not for your grandpa, it's for your dad,'* " Cameron let out a harsh laugh, "So I lied and told her I didn't have a dad, well it wasn't really a lie because I didn't have a dad who cared."

"Did you get away with it?"

"No. Mum and Dad got called to the school because I got so upset about the teacher trying to make me change it. And of course, Dad was a no show, and the teacher realised what home life might've looked like for us and let the issue go. For the rest of the year, she pitied me more than anything. I don't know what Mum said, but she made me make a card for Dad at home."

"Duncan would have been so chuffed with the card, though." Ivy said, knowing how much Duncan loved his family.

Cameron's harsh features softened as he pressed the button to their floor in the lift.

"You know, that card is still on his board in the study at home. I go in and make sure it's there. Happiest moment between Grandpa and I, when we pinned it there together."

Ivy had no idea why she did it, but her arm snaked around Cameron and her head rested on his shoulder. They remained together until the door opened on their floor and they walked out into the hallway.

"Now," Cameron said, his voice raspy, "We need to make a to-do list for you for tomorrow. What's your plan of attack?"

A SICKENING BLOW

CAMERON

aking early the next morning, an onslaught of emails and messages greeted Cameron. This was what it was like being in business, and he liked it. After a quick shower, he headed out to the lounge outside his bedroom to work. He glanced at his watch and calculated the time until breakfast would arrive. Still an hour and a half, so he made himself a cup of herbal tea and settled down to work.

The next time he put his head up, Ivy was standing at the door saying good morning to the server with their breakfast.

"Sorry. I didn't hear that." Cameron apologised.

"You were working, don't worry. I was already awake." Ivy said, closing the door as the server left. "What are you working on? You were so engrossed."

"Just working through my emails and messages. And then began some programming before I head in this morning. Had a few ideas that I wanted to explain to Phil and Thomas."

Ivy took the chair next to Cameron and watched as his fingers flew over the keyboard.

"So, this is what Sophie talks about."

"What?"

"She told me you always lose yourself in your computer for hours on end."

"I suppose she also mentioned that she or Mum would bring me food and drink just to keep me functioning and hydrated?"

"Well, she might have mentioned that." Ivy nodded.

"They exaggerate."

"So, when Sophie brought over food, she didn't have to do your washing as well?" Ivy gave him a knowing look.

"She said that?" Cameron was agog with the idea that Ivy knew so much about his habits.

"Did she lie?"

"Would you believe me if I said yes?"

"Umm. No." Ivy released a laugh that had Cameron laughing out loud as well.

"Would you trust me to say that they make me look bad?"

"Still no. In fact, sitting here watching you work only reinforces their position."

"Why?"

"Because you've typed for the last ten minutes without stopping or eating your breakfast. Which, by the way, you should do because the car will be here in ten minutes."

Cameron slammed down the lid of the laptop and reached for his now cold cup that Ivy had prepared for him earlier. "What's the plan of attack today?"

"Like you said yesterday, I need to convince Deb and Bert I'm here to carry out Mum's last wish." Ivy pulled tighter on the tie of her dressing gown. "I was so young when she died. Doing this for her will keep her prominent in my memory."

"I've got to go but I believe this is the right thing for you to do." Before getting up from the table, Cameron clasped her hand in his and gave what he hoped was a gentle, reassuring squeeze.

"Time to get lost behind my screen legitimately." Cameron said, packing everything up, "Message me if you need to or feel you're out of your depth. Good luck."

He raced out the door, after looking back at the most uncertain woman he'd seen in ages, sitting there trying to decide on her next step. He felt her pain. Indecision was usually something that followed him around like a bad smell.

Cameron walked out to the waiting car. His priorities for now were his clients, but tonight hopefully he could help Ivy make headway with The Father Project.

Concentration and focus were essential today, he had issues which included the search for answers to move the project from functional to progressive in the future. Cameron was always a forward thinker and by nutting out these finer details he could gain a better understanding for the business and the industry.

"Morning Cameron," Audrey greeted him as he entered the building.

"Good morning, Audrey. Thank you for the tickets last night. Ivy and I had a great time. It will please my mum I'm involving cultural experiences into my trip." His smile made light of something that in reality would gladden Lindy a great deal.

"Excellent. What are your plans for this evening?"

"I'm not sure. Ivy's working on catching up with family, but I'm not sure how that'll pan out." Cameron said as Audrey escorted him down to his office.

"Well, if you're at a loss, let me know."

"Thanks, I will." Cameron agreed as he placed his bag on the desk.

He settled down and got to work, all thoughts of Ivy forgotten as the intensity of programming took hold.

IVY

No sooner had Cameron left when Ivy's phone buzzed. She hoped it was Bert and Deb with an answer to her request. Yesterday as she left, they'd asked her for time to deliberate over what she asked of them. To this day they were still friends with her father, and it was only out of their friendship with Anita they were considering her request. Somehow, Ivy determined there was an underlying consideration, but whatever that was, she couldn't be sure.

Reaching for her phone, Ivy saw the call was from Phil's wife. "Morning Clem."

"Ivy, morning. Hope you were up already?"

"Yes. Cameron was tapping away on his keyboard early this morning and didn't hear his breakfast arrive. So, I'm up."

"Excellent. Would you like to come over for a ride today?"

Ivy looked out her window. There was no snow, though she was certain the chill factor was practically zero, she could tell by the frost on the windows in nearby buildings. "It's not too cold to take the horses out?"

"Of course it is, but we'll be riding in the arena. I'll have enough clothes here to outfit you, what do you say?"

Ivy looked out the window again and then considered her other options. She didn't want to be idling away while waiting for Deb to get back to her. This diversion could be exactly what would calm her racing thoughts.

"Sounds great, what time?"

"I'll swing by in an hour, if that suits?"

"Okay. I'll be ready. Thanks Clem."

Ending the call, Ivy headed back into her room to shower and change. This seemed like an ideal way to entertain her over-active mind today. Hoping for a minor miracle would not advance her chances of meeting her father, so doing something practical like horse riding sounded perfect.

Ivy settled into the passenger seat of Clem's Range Rover and turned to greet Portia, but the little one was sound asleep.

"It's her nap time, so this was a perfect time to come and get you," Clem said, "I hope you don't mind?"

"Well actually, you saved me from a day of phone watching. I'm attempting to find a family member and am waiting on a call."

"Someone close?"

Ivy just shrugged. She didn't want to say yes because that would lead to more questioning, which would become uncomfortable, but she couldn't say no. She would never deny a potential father.

Fortunately, Clem changed the direction of the conversation and asked, "Who's looking after the bakery while you're away? Phil refuses to take holidays. It took Audrey six months to convince Thomas they were having a couple of weeks off."

"That's right, Cameron said Thomas was away."

"I've had to do some wheeling and dealing with Phil. He's currently considering a trip."

"What was the wheeling and dealing then?" Ivy asked.

"He wants another child and I want a holiday," the women burst out laughing and halted when Portia stirred.

Once she settled back to sleep, Clem explained, "Phil has always been a workaholic just like his father. How I got him away for a honeymoon beats me." Clem said, overtaking a little old lady travelling at least twenty under the speed limit. "What's Cameron like?"

"I don't know. I'd say similar to Phil. His sister told me once, when he works, either her or their mother would have to check on him constantly to make sure he was eating properly."

"Men," Clem said, shaking her head.

"Do you work?" Ivy asked, glancing over her shoulder again at the sweet bundle of joy.

"Yep. I work part time. I'm a fashion writer and can work around it with Portia, so am happy to keep my hand in the trade, for now. Another child might make it too hard, but we'll see."

"I hope you don't mind me saying, but you and Phil seem happy together."

"We are. Marrying each other, we made a promise that our marriage will always come first."

"How do you do that in this fast-paced world?"

"Well, the first thing is we both do things around the house together. We have a cleaner, but we are a team. And the factory is only fifteen minutes from home, so

Phil asked me to drive him to work every morning, which gives us time to talk or fight, whatever the case may be. Then he comes home with Thomas."

Ivy raised a questioning brow.

Clem laughed. "Sometimes we argue, take the holiday, for example. That turned into an argument. Phil pulled up outside the factory and we sat there arguing in a whisper for ten minutes before I gave him the ultimatum. My mother is at home with Portia and this is our time."

"Isn't it a pain to be up early to drive him?"

"Nah. I'm an early bird. Besides, few of those are fighting days, most are planning, making big decisions and just being us. I've seen it so often in my friends, kids come along and the couple forget about what they mean to one another. Phil and I don't want that for our marriage."

"I liked when we saw you together the other night, you were talking and laughing. It really struck a chord with me. And Phil was so hands on with Portia over dinner."

"Yeah, he is always home for dinner early. Family time around the table is important."

"You said you're a writer, why don't you put together a book of 'dos and don'ts' about marriage and partnerships. You'll have a New York Times bestseller on your hands then."

Even though they laughed at the suggestion, Ivy liked the smile that rested on Clem's features.

Clem turned up a long drive and before her, Ivy saw what looked like the stud farms from back home but with two vast houses, stables, sheds, and an arena on the property.

"Wow! This place is stunning!"

"I think that's why we're so passionate about keeping the spark alive in our marriage. It'd be easy to love him because of this. But when it's all said and done, that's only walls and a roof. It's what we bring to the structure that matters. For us, our children and our family."

"Definitely a book in there somewhere," Ivy teased.

CAMERON

His head was down, engrossed with the work strewn out in front of him. The notepad was full of dot points, some crossed out, while others highlighted and notations occupied small circles. To an outsider it was nothing short of carnage, to Cameron it was totally comprehensible.

"How's it going?" Phil asked from the doorway.

But Cameron didn't even flinch, engrossed wasn't a strong enough word for what was happening between him and his laptop.

Thump, thump, thump.

"How's it going in here?" Phil called out a second time, "Are you always this focused when you're lost down the proverbial rabbit hole."

Cameron looked up, momentarily confused and disorientated. "Hi."

"Are you always this intense when you work?" Phil asked again as a wry smile spread across his face.

"Apparently so. What can I do for you?" Cameron asked, sparing a quick glance at the time on his screen. "Is it really a-quarter-to-six?"

"Yep, and that's local time too. Not Australian time in case you hoped that was a possibility."

Cameron laughed at that one. "Good to know."

"I have just had it on excellent information that Ivy is at our house with Clem."

Just the mention of Ivy's name had Cameron tapping on his phone to make sure there were no messages from her. And of course, there were. Three!

"I missed her messages." Cameron screwed up his face.

"I've been told. You're coming home with us. Clem has invited you both to dinner."

"Is now a good time to reply to Ivy to tell her I received her messages?"

"Might be. So, are you always this far down a rabbit hole?"

"Sometimes worse. It's known that ripping my laptop away from me and pouring water on my head also works to get my attention."

"Brother or sister?"

"Sister. And in her defence, she was desperate." Cameron laughed at the memories of Sophie.

"So, will you be ready to leave in fifteen minutes?"

"Packing up right now." Cameron did as he declared and turned the messy pile into a spotless office within minutes. Backed up his computer to the three different cloud sources and packed away his laptop, then joined Audrey in the foyer.

"You made it with three minutes to spare," Audrey joked, making a show of looking at her watch.

"Don't worry, I'm the butt of the family's harassment for losing myself in a job." Life was teaching Cameron to laugh at himself, to let go of every little thing which upset him. There was no question, getting away from Ralph was working wonders. He discovered a strength and purpose that never blossomed before.

"Well, come on. Let's go."

Cameron loved that these people didn't judge him on his mystifying practices, they only embraced them and had some fun with him and not at his expense.

The drive to the house wound down a dark, open road. Cameron had to admit to being taken with the family that talked most of the way home and not about work. That really impressed him. They spoke of family and horses and their book collection. Cameron listened and heard not only the facts about books but the passion that Phil and his parents shared.

"Nancy said she'd follow up that lead today," Phil explained. "Mum, did she call in?"

"No, I'll call her now. Please excuse us, Cameron."

"By all means. Go ahead."

Audrey placed the call. A young woman's voice came over the car speaker. "Hi Mum, Dad and Phil, are you there too?"

"Right here, sis. We have a friend here as well."

"Let me guess. That would be Cameron, Ivy's friend."

"Did you meet her today?"

"Actually, we're sitting in Clem's kitchen waiting to eat." Nancy laughed.

"What a wonderful surprise." Thomas called out.

"What I'm calling about was the book, did you have any luck?"

"Did I have any luck?" Nancy threw back her reply with an air of self-importance, "Just get here and I'll tell you about it."

"Well then, we'll see you in five," Phil called from the back seat.

"See you soon."

"That sounds positive," Thomas nodded to his wife.

"We'll be home soon enough." Turning to Cameron, Audrey asked. "Is there something your whole family are into?"

Cameron shook his head. "My parents split up, but my mother's new partner is a wonderful man. He is amazing with mum and includes us all in everything they do."

"Oh, I'm sorry to hear about your parents." Audrey offered.

"Don't be. My father wasn't…isn't a good person."

"So, your mother, is she happy now?" the gentle inquiry had Cameron nodding. People cared, not always the ones who should, but some people did.

"Yes. If you're ever in Australia, come for a visit. I believe you'll really like her. She's an amazing woman and now has an amazing man by her side. They are both wonderful role models to their eight children."

"Eight. How do they do it? I have three and they were a handful." Audrey teased.

"Mum has my brother Liam who's twenty-six, I'm twenty-four and Sophie who turned twenty-one last year. Then Jack has Nate, he's twelve, Evie's ten, Joanna's eight, Caleb's six and gives us all a run for our money and little Bradley who's about eighteen months."

"How does your mother cope?"

Cameron let out a laugh. "I wish I knew. She hasn't been well, I stepped in to help. The younger ones ran me ragged."

"Well, you'll never get bored with that lot, would you?"

"No, but I wouldn't have it any other way."

Phil looked over at Cameron and asked, "So where does Ivy fit into all this?"

"She's Jack's second cousin."

"Jack's your mother's partner?"

"Yep, that's right. He's become the matriarch of the family. Ivy is the same as me and my siblings. We all look up to him."

"Here we are," Thomas announced, as he pulled up out the front of a large house that seemed to stretch out in both directions.

IVY

The front door opened sending Portia into a tizzy and the women laughed.

"See? I told you," Nancy said of her niece. "She's a daddy's girl."

Portia struggled until she was down and they watched as she staggered like a drunken sailor on a mission to the front door to greet her father.

Phil met his daughter halfway and scooped her up in his arms, blew raspberries on her belly and listened to her giggles with pure delight.

"Who's daddy's girl then?" Phil asked Portia. She clapped her hands and cuddled into him.

"We're blessed we get to share this a few times a week," Thomas told Cameron as he escorted him down the hallway.

"It's something special."

"Hey ladies," Thomas said, greeting his daughter and daughter-in-law with kisses. He stopped in front of Ivy, "So, you must be the other Aussie? Welcome to England."

"Thank you, and thanks for allowing me to stay with Cameron. It was very kind of you."

"Oh, nonsense," Thomas said as Audrey stepped up beside him.

"You must be Audrey?" Ivy said, holding out her hand to greet the other woman.

"Lovely to meet you," Audrey smiled.

"How was your day riding?" Thomas asked Clem and Ivy.

"Portia, did you tell daddy you had a ride on the horsey?"

Portia clapped her pudgy hands together and repeated, "Ors, ors." And looked around confused when everyone laughed.

Cameron walked over to greet Ivy. "How was your first ride after all this time?"

"So good, I forgot how much I loved it." Her face lit up and a smile caressed her lips. "Think I need to talk to Jack about an agistment at his place."

"You're going to buy a horse?" His eyebrows shot up under his long fringe.

"After today, I think so."

"Well, maybe Sophie and I should think seriously about it then, you wouldn't mind, would you?" Cameron tipped his head to one side.

"No, not at all. I'd love to have late afternoon trail rides with you guys and the kids."

"Good!"

"Excellent!"

Ivy smiled at Cameron before tuning back into the family conversation. There was a natural comfort which oozed in the home of these near strangers. Not that the Anders' treated them anything other than dear friends.

"Well come on, let's eat. Portia's going to get grumpy and over tired soon." Phil announced, still giving his daughter lots of attention while remaining in the conversation.

"Mum, I popped over to see Uncle Gabe today. Something's not right. He barely focused on our conversation. When I asked if something was wrong, he said he received some news."

"What kind of news?" Audrey asked.

"All he said was his past was catching up with him."

Ivy watched Audrey and her husband exchange glances. "Thanks Nance, we'll call him after dinner. So, Cameron and Ivy, how did you enjoy the show last night?" Thomas asked, changing the subject.

"Amazing," Ivy offered. "I must admit to having a new pastime. It was wonderful to get lost in the world of live theatre for a while."

"Did you try out the little cafe I suggested?" Audrey asked.

"We did. The food was so simple, yet masterfully done. It actually gave me a few ideas about a change in direction for my bakery back home."

"Oh, I didn't realise you owned a bakery?" Audrey's voice rose with excitement.

"You'll get to taste her wares for dessert, Mum," Clem added. "Ivy made Caramel Slice, Anzac Biscuits and a Lemon Delicious Pudding."

"How is it I can't smell them?"

"She's been here all day, Dad." Nancy admonished. "And guess what? She even cleans up after herself." Nancy cupped her hands over her mouth and widened her eyes, which had the others laughing.

"You making fun of me?" Thomas asked his daughter as he looked down the table at her under his bushy eyebrows.

Squeezing her thumb and pointer finger together, Nancy said, "Maybe just a little." Turning to Ivy and Cameron, she added, "Dad doesn't think we girls can cook and clean up. He thinks we believe it's an anomaly."

Ivy smiled as Cameron jumped to her defence. "Ivy is so much like my mother, a clean-up as you go gal. But my sister who now works at Ivy's bakery is just as Thomas believes. She can cover every surface with dirty dishes in minutes. Mum and I learned very early on to follow behind her and clean up. The results of her cooking were worth the hassle."

"Good to know, you mark my words Ivy Masters, Audrey and I will grace your table in…" Thomas looked around for support.

"Chester's Run," Ivy offered.

"Yep, that's it. Don't doubt it for a minute. I'd like to meet Jack the horseman and see this beautiful town Cameron talks so much about."

"You're both most welcome. I have a spare room and so do Lindy and Jack. In fact, you're all very welcome to come and join us." Ivy couldn't hide her pleasure at the thought of talking horses and country Australia with this English family. Oh, how she wished her father and his family would be as open and friendly like this.

"Well, delightful as ever," Thomas said as he closed his plate with his utensils and wiped his mouth with his serviette. Nancy, Cameron, and Ivy helped Clem do the dishes while Phil bathed Portia.

Thomas and Audrey excused themselves so they could make their phone call.

"Get dessert ready," Thomas warned, "We'll be back."

Just after they walked out, Ivy's phone rang.

"Ivy Masters," she answered when she didn't know the caller number.

"Hi Ivy, it's Deb here."

"Oh Deb, thank you for calling me back." Not sure what else to say, Ivy waited during the prolonged silence.

Eventually Deb spoke, "Bert and I talked about your situation last night and this morning we rang Lamont. I'm sorry, Ivy, but he refused to see you. He offered you his best but said there was too much water under the bridge now and too many people would get hurt by you showing up." Deb's voice softened, "I'm so sorry, love."

Ivy went completely still. Outright refusal was a possibility, but never an option in her mind. Just one meeting to see the man who fathered her was her hope. Anything more was a dream. But not even that would eventuate. Try as she may, the tears wouldn't stop. She slipped in to a chair at the table, as her body could no longer support her weight.

"He won't even meet me?" her strangled voice asked.

"No love. He feels it's best this way." The silence spoke of rejection of not only her but also her mother's memory.

"You told him I had a letter from Mum for him?"

"I did Ivy, but nothing I said swayed him. He honestly believes this is for the best. Sorry again, but promise to stop by and see us before you go, okay?"

"Okay," Ivy whispered down the phone through her tears.

CAMERON

The phone slipped from Ivy's slackened hands and clattered to the table. Cameron dropped the tea towel onto the bench and arrived at Ivy's side in three long strides.

"What happened?" The idea of bad news from home skittered through him. The shattered expression told Cameron this wasn't good. "Ivy, talk to me."

The silent tears continued as she shook her head. As if attempting to reject the outcome.

"It's my father," Ivy began, her whisper barely audible to him. The pain on her face was excruciating. "He's refused to meet me," she finally mumbled.

Cameron couldn't help himself, even though embracing others was not comfortable for him. He pulled Ivy into his arms and let her cry it out.

Nancy handed her a warm face cloth a few minutes later, and Cameron looked up to see the two women staring at them.

"Do you mind if we skip dessert?" Cameron asked.

"Of course," Clem said, picking up the phone. "I'll have Ronald drive you home."

A few minutes later Cameron led a devastated Ivy out to the waiting car.

"Can I call her tomorrow?" Clem asked Cameron.

"Yep, that should be fine. Could you please apologise to the others and tell them I'll see them at work tomorrow?"

"Sure," Clem rested her hand on his arm. "If you need anything, call us. Anytime."

"Thanks, I will." Cameron helped a still inconsolable Ivy into the back seat and closed the door. He looked back to see Clem and Nancy standing at the top of the front steps, confused and minus the cheerful nature of the evening they'd shared. "Thank you for tonight, sorry we have to race off like this."

"Cameron, it's fine. Go. Get her settled. I hope she's okay."

Ivy leaned against the car door in silence.

Seriously! How did Cameron get himself into a situation like this? This woman needed comforting, and he couldn't think of a thing to say or do. He knew what it was like to have an abusive, self-centred father. But God, couldn't Ivy find some peace with the small window of opportunity she had to meet her own dad. Even if it was just this once.

The drive was a long one and proved even longer in the silence surrounding them. After thanking the driver, Cameron helped Ivy out of the car and walked her up to their suite.

"Can I get you anything? Should I call Mum so you can chat to her?" he was desperate to help.

She headed off to her room, her body swaying slightly. When Cameron saw her face, her brows were tight and pulled down towards clouded and unfocused eyes. The tremble in her hands seemed to engulf her body.

He watched her go. A sense of helplessness invaded him. In his own room Cameron turned the telly on low and sat in contemplation. If this was what fathers did, then he'd never have children. He wouldn't risk being a self-absorbed man like his father and brother were. He could hear the occasional sob coming from Ivy's room and it broke his heart.

When his phone rang, he wasn't actually sure he wanted to talk to anyone. At seeing Phil's name on the screen, he thought better of it and answered.

"Hi Phil," His voice was low, almost pained.

"Is she okay? What happened?" Phil asked.

"Sorry, it's not my story to share. I think she's heartbroken at the moment." Cameron paused because he heard Ivy's voice. "Can you hang on a minute, Phil?" He didn't wait for an answer. He dropped the phone onto the bed and walked out and stopped just outside Ivy's doorway.

"He won't meet me." Ivy explained to the other person on the phone.

"I knew it was a possibility," her voice a little rough now.

Cameron ran his fingers through his hair. He shouldn't be eaves-dropping on her private conversation.

"I love you too. You've been my strength."

She was obviously listening again.

"Sorry to wake you. Okay, I'll try. Night."

The silence seemed to creep around the suite like a vulgar noise. Unbearable and deafening but unstoppable at the same time.

Who was Ivy talking to? Was that Liam? The words 'I love you too' echoed in his ears.

Remembering Phil was still on hold, Cameron walked back to his room and continued the call. Offering nothing but hoping to console his business associate, and most likely Clem as well. "She just needs time." He said in closing. "I'll see you in the morning."

"Well, just let her know we're thinking of her and are only a phone call away." Phil told him.

"Sure, thanks for calling. Bye." Cameron dropped the phone on his bed and expelled a long, harsh breath. He really needed sleep, but first he'd check on Ivy. But would she want him there? He didn't have to be a genius to know the person she spoke to was Liam, so why would she be relying on him to console her?

Cameron wrestled with his inner demons. Something his mother instilled in her children was to be aware of them, but on this occasion his inner demon won. Liam was there for her so why should he put himself out? Rubbing his hands over his face, Cameron decided it was shower time followed by bed. Ivy knew where he was if she needed him.

FEELING THE LOSS

IVY

hen breakfast arrived the following morning, Ivy stayed in bed. The rejection from her father stung. Although she kept telling herself this trip to meet her father could amount to nothing, the reality was still painful. In fact, deep down Ivy pondered whether she would accept no for an answer?

The genuine pain was after they got home, when Cameron ignored her. Was a difficult situation like this too much for him to handle? Because in her experience, life cast these painful challenges at you frequently. Luckily, when she rang Aunty Darla and Uncle Tony last night, they were there for her.

Aunty Darla talked her through the options. Maybe she should just accept it all and move on to Paris? She looked online after the call last night, and there were a couple of last-minute availabilities in the courses she wanted to take. So, heading to Paris early might actually work. Nothing else was keeping her here…unless she fought back.

She'd heard the tiptoeing of Cameron's retreating footsteps after she ended the call from Chester's Run. Some moral support would have been great, but obviously that's beyond him. Why couldn't Cameron cope in situations like this? Ivy didn't have the head space to unravel him. The pressing matters she needed to deal with were what to do about her father. Ivy rolled over onto her back and sighed. Then groaned out loud.

Where to start?

What to do?

There were decisions that demanded answers. What to do next was her greatest dilemma, and she'd decide her next step today. Time would not make this any easier.

"Talk to Deb,' Ivy whispered. And she forcefully rolled out of bed. Seeing Deb's face would hopefully give her answers to her more pressing questions. She checked the time on the bedside clock and almost laughed. Their shop opened from early to late. So now was as good a time as any.

Shower was the first thing on her list. Then a small bite of breakfast. That would give her time to summon up the courage to hear and see the truth.

Emerging from her room thirty minutes later, she saw Cameron had gone. The breakfast tray was still on the table, with a note in his scrawled writing tucked under the right-hand corner. Ivy lifted the tray slightly and pulled out the note.

Morning Ivy,

I'm so sorry about what happened last night with your father. I've headed off to work but can come back whenever you want. Phil is fine with that.

Oh, by the way Phil and Clem rang last night to check on you. I wasn't sure what to say, so I just explained you needed time. I hope that was all right?

Jack and Mum phoned this morning. I mentioned to them what had happened. Mum insists you call when you get my note.

Take Care

Cameron.

Ivy released a sardonic laugh. Seriously, this man was so confusing. Well, at least one thing in that letter made sense. She walked back into her room and grabbed her laptop and placed a call to Lindy and Jack. Nine in the morning London time made it almost dinner time in Chester's Run.

"Ivy love, how are you?" Lindy's voice echoed through the headphones. "I hope you don't mind, but we pressured Cameron into telling us what happened."

"That's fine." Ivy explained about the chance meeting with Deb and Bert and the reply she received from her father.

"What options are you considering?" Jack's voice rang out from somewhere in the background.

"Hi Jack. I thought my first option was to see Deb and Bert this morning. Maybe I could get a better understanding of the situation if I see their faces while asking the questions I couldn't think to ask last night."

"That sounds like a great place to start." Jack agreed.

"What are you hoping to find out?" Lindy asked.

"Why's a big one, but I'm not sure they can help me." Ivy said, running her fingers through her long strands, which she'd still not tied up.

"Have you got paper and pen handy?" Jack asked, now moving into the picture.

"Hang on," Ivy picked up the laptop and walked back to the dining table. Found the note pad Cameron used and patted around the table to find the pen. "Okay, I'm ready."

"Ask what he wants done with your mother's letter to him." Jack began. "Whatever they say remember to enclose a letter of your own."

Ivy puffed out an angry breath.

"Ask Deb and Bert for any photos of your mother. Hopefully, they will have some of your father as well. Don't forget to scan them so you have more memories of your mother."

"Good idea."

"If they offer you an email address, take it. Not sure they will though." Jack seemed to have put a great deal of effort into this. Ivy's heart lightened.

"The other thing you can do," Lindy began, "Is ask for their memories of Anita and record them. These things are treasures you can keep."

Ivy began tearing up. "I hadn't thought of that."

"Ivy, I don't mean to be negative about what's happened. But now salvage what you can for your own future. Your mother's memories are the most important thing for you and your children." Lindy added.

"So, you suggest I go in, ask things like where did she work, live and visit while she was here?"

"Yes, that's it. Make it about your mum now. Put your father behind you, for the moment. Together we'll pick up the pieces on that front when you get back home, love."

Ivy smiled into the camera for the first time. "Thanks, Lindy. You put it all into perspective for me."

"Good," Jack said, nodding his head in approval. He disappeared from her screen. It was only when he called out to the children she realised why. "Quick guys, Ivy's rung us, come and say hello."

Right there was the best thing to happen to her in a few days. It even topped the horse riding with Nancy and Clem yesterday.

"Hey guys,"

"Hi Ivy," the questions flew thick and fast, so Lindy took control.

"One at a time. Caleb, you go first."

"Is it cold, Ivy?"

"Freezing Caleb."

"What have you done?" Joanna asked next.

"Would you believe I went horse riding?" Ivy told them while sending some photos for them to see.

"What else?" Evie added.

"Oh yeah, that's right," Ivy said after a moment's thought. "Cameron got us tickets to Phantom of the Opera, it was amazing. Something we will have to do when I get home guys. You'll love it." Cheers erupted and Ivy laughed. Then her phone rang. "Hang on a minute. I'll just take this."

Ivy took the call from Clem. "Hi Clem, can I call you straight back. I've got my family from Chester's Run online."

"Actually, Portia and I are downstairs. Can we come up?"

"Of course. See you soon." Ivy cut the call and looked back to the screen. "Whose turn for a question?"

"Mine," Nate answered quickly, "Have you made any friends?"

"We have. The people Cameron is working for are lovely and you'll get to meet Clem and Portia in a minute, they're on the way up."

When a knock sounded, Ivy jumped up to answer it.

"Morning. You okay?" Clem asked, giving Ivy a questioning look.

"Come and meet my family," Ivy ushered both Clem and Portia to the screen. "Guys, these are our new friends, Clem and Portia." Turning to Clem, she added, "This is my adopted family."

"She's not adopted," Jack explained. "I'm her second cousin Jack, and these are my children." Jack named them all.

"Lindy's the one we adopted," Caleb added to a roar of laughter.

"That's Caleb, he's the joker of the family," Ivy explained, her lips splitting into a huge grin.

"Hello everyone. Are you missing Ivy and Cameron?"

"Yes!" the children yelled.

"Enjoy yourself and ring back whenever you can," Lindy instructed.

"Hang on before you go," Ivy called out, "How's Sophie doing?"

"The bakery is fine," Nate told her with a grin. He understood exactly what she was asking. "And Sophie is great too."

Ivy let out a laugh. These people were her safe place, and right now she loved them all for it. "Love you guys. We'll ring back soon. I promise."

"Excellent, can't wait to speak again." Lindy smiled into the camera.

"Bye," the rest of them chorused.

"Bye." Ivy whispered, fighting back tears as Lindy cut the connection.

She leaned into the embrace from Clem and gave a weak laugh. "Thanks, I needed that."

"We all do. Now, tell me what's really going on, you scared us last night."

CAMERON

It was one thing to be helpless in a situation and completely another to choose helplessness. Cameron watched the screen go black and released a pitiful groan making him feel hopeless. Lindy refrained from mincing words when she was on the warpath and this morning was no different. But he had too much work to do now, so this conversation between his head and his heart needed to wait.

Thomas and Phil would join him for a meeting in thirty minutes. He had more preparation to do. So, he pushed aside the awareness of wrongdoing, or the fact he took 'the coward's way out last night' which were his mother's words, Cameron attempted to delve into the task at hand. He'd be confronting his defect at some point soon.

He couldn't concentrate in here, his mother's harsh tone rung in his ears. Gathering everything up, he headed to the boardroom early to organise himself. He had to regain some focus. This morning when he'd entered, Audrey wasn't at the front desk. Another woman, Claire, greeted him and passed on messages from the owners. He wanted to apologise in person to Audrey for leaving early, but he'd have to do that later.

"Claire, I'm just going to set up in the boardroom."

"That's fine. The door's open." Cameron nodded and walked down the corridor.

With the information he'd gathered, he printed out the paperwork for the owners and sat back in his chair, mentally preparing himself for the meeting.

Getting into the zone for work wasn't hard for Cameron, he'd used it as his escape most of his working life. The men entered and Cameron began with a breakdown of his understanding of each department and the flow on effect of it all, which Phil and Thomas studied intensely and offered suggestions where appropriate. Cameron took notes, rejigged, and confirmed, and continued. Claire interrupted the meeting an hour and a half in.

"Thomas, could you please take the call on line two, it's Audrey."

"Thanks," Thomas called. "Sorry Cameron, I need to take this."

Phil watched his father leave the room and then focused on Cameron. "How's Ivy this morning?"

"Not sure. She wasn't up when I left. But the news shattered her last night."

"What happened?"

"Sorry, not for me to say. If she wants to share it, then that's up to her." Cameron spread his hands out and shrugged.

"Fair enough." Phil dug into his pocket and pulled out an envelope. "Are you guys into football?"

Cameron let out a laugh. "According to my brother, I wouldn't know what to do with any piece of sporting equipment if my life depended on it."

Phil chuckled. "So, you don't want these tickets. It's a Manchester United v Chelsea game on the weekend."

Cameron looked at the envelope and then back at Phil. "You won't use them?"

"Not if you want them."

"Maybe we could go together, if you're okay with explaining the game to a sports moron."

"That could work."

Thomas walked back into the room, his usually neat hair messy and his face pale. "Dad, is everything alright?"

Thomas waved off the query and turned to Cameron. "Now, where were we?"

IVY

With her hands outstretched towards little Portia, Ivy scooped her up and cuddled her close when the little girl fell into her arms. "Not much to tell, I came over on a whim to meet my father, but he's rejected the invitation. Apparently, he has no desire to rehash the past."

"Oh, no. Ivy, I'm so sorry." Clem leaned in and hugged her.

Why couldn't Cameron do something like that? His distance hit her gut like a jagged rock making its way through a narrow stream.

"So, what will you do now?" Clem asked.

"Lindy," Ivy pointed to the computer, "Suggested I go back to my mother's old friends and ask for their memories of her. Something I can take back with me." Ivy closed her eyes against another round of tears. "She passed away when I was five. My grandparents raised me."

Portia reached her hands out to her mother, and Clem instinctively opened her arms and pulled her in close. "I couldn't imagine Portia having to grow up without me."

"My childhood was great. I knew nothing different, and when my grandparents became my carers, I couldn't have been more loved."

"So why are you trying to meet your father?" Clem asked, her delicate features twisted into a grimace.

"I finally cleaned out my spare rooms and found a box my grandmother put away for me to open when I was older, the box contained letters from my mother to both me and my father." Ivy hugged herself, "Her last wish was for me to deliver it to him. That's all I wanted to do."

"And now?"

"I think I'll do as Lindy suggested. Talk to Mum's friends again today and then I'll maybe change my plans and head to Paris early." The thought of leaving brought tears to Ivy's eyes.

"What will you do in Paris?"

"I've always thought of studying in Paris. Now would be a great opportunity to do a couple of cooking workshops while I'm over here. I think that was my backup plan for when my father rejected me."

"What about Cameron?"

"I'll come back and we'll fly home together."

"Ivy." Clem began.

"What?"

"Would you welcome a tagalong?"

"You want to go to Paris?"

"If you'll have me. I'm sure Phil won't mind. How long will we be?"

"Seven or eight days. What will you do with Portia?"

"Well, there's my mother and Aunty Nance," Clem said, looking at Portia, "And even Audrey would love to help out."

"If you can arrange it."

"Leave it with me. Now, do what you have to do and I'll ring you in a couple of hours."

"Okay," A tingle of delight raced through her. Ivy hadn't smiled this widely in a long time.

They layered themselves into their winter gear, huddling against the cold, and headed out. Promising to be in touch in a couple of hours, Ivy waved them off. If only Clem could see her way free to head to Paris. The thought of travelling alone wasn't totally daunting, but having a familiar face would be great.

Clem and Portia drove off waving, as Ivy headed out to meet with Deb and Bert. This was her chance to say goodbye and hopefully do as Lindy recommended, make this a journey to discover memories of her mother.

She entered the shop to find Bert serving a customer. Ivy walked around the tiny space, drawing in deep breaths, preparing herself for the topic she would raise with this couple. When Bert finished with the customer he looked up and she gave him a sweet smile, hoping to put him at ease. Making things difficult wouldn't benefit her end goal here. The customer walked out and Ivy stepped up to the counter.

"Morning Bert."

"Hey love. How you doing?" the older man asked.

"Alright. He's made his decision and I won't fight it. That's not what my mother would have wanted, though I believe she trusted him to meet me." Dropping her eyes for a moment before continuing, she breathed in deeply, "Anyway, what I've come for is to see if you and Deb would have any photos of my mum. Some new memories for me to treasure."

"Really, that's all you want?"

"Bert, I'm not here to cause trouble or heartache. Just to fulfil my mother's final wish."

Bert checked his watch. "Deb will be back in about ten minutes and Deidre can takeover in here. Would you mind waiting?"

"Not at all. Thanks Bert."

Ivy meandered through the small space and picked up trinkets for the kids back home while she waited. She smiled at her purchases. The children would enjoy these.

Deb arrived as Bert was finalising the sale.

"Thought we'd see you again," Deb laughed as she stepped up to the counter behind Bert.

It was wonderful to feel at ease with this couple. "I'm hoping for some memories to take with me when I go," Ivy explained.

"Let's see what we can do," Deb said, looking at Bert and then back to Ivy with a relaxed smile. "Follow me." When Ivy was settled, Deb walked over to a large bookcase and opened a cupboard door. "What will you do now?"

"I'm heading to Paris in the next day or two. I'll stay there for a week then come back to meet up with my friend and we'll fly home."

"Do you know people in Paris?" Bert asked.

"No. I'm hoping to travel with a new friend I've made and do some pastry and speciality bread-making workshops. Rejection was always a possibility, but I hadn't really prepared for it. So, getting away is probably a good thing." Ivy had a sudden thought. She gently bit down on her lower lip, clasped her hand together and leaned forward, "Could I ask something of you?"

"You want us to give your father the letter?" Deb sounded confident at her guess.

"No. You read my mother's letter, she assigned the task to me, but if he changes his mind about receiving the note, would you mind passing on my details?" Ivy fumbled through her backpack and found a piece of paper and pencil. She paused and looked up for an answer.

"So, you're really just going to walk away?" Bert asked.

"I don't know the man. Yes, there is a gaping hole in my heart, but I won't beg for his attention. I have a great life and I hoped knowing him would only make it better. If that's not the case, then I will move on." Ivy shrugged, meeting the man's disbelieving eyes. She'd been open and honest, and now it was time to bow out gracefully.

"Yes," Deb offered, "Leave us your details because I would love to stay in touch with you as well, if you don't mind?"

"It would be my pleasure," Ivy swallowed back the emotion. Nothing would replace the father she'd never meet, but one thing she realised overnight amid her tears, how her life panned out didn't depend on one person, in this case her father. The people she wanted in her life were her choice. The same went for Cameron, she'd suffer both their rejections and move on.

CAMERON

Opening the door to their suite, Cameron didn't miss the sight of Ivy's overstuffed backpack leaning against the wall.

"Hello," she called from her room as he dropped his bag onto the end of his bed.

"You going somewhere?" he asked as he walked back into the lounge.

Ivy appeared in the doorway and made her way to the couch. "Paris is happening earlier," there was a smile but he also heard the flat monotone voice. "I hope you don't mind?"

"No, of course not. What about your father?"

"I spoke to Jack and Lindy this morning. Your mother made me see I was better off putting space between me and the situation. Umm," Ivy pointed to her room, "I've left my suitcase in there. We'll be away about a week."

"We?" Who was she travelling with?

"Oh, didn't Phil tell you?" Ivy said, turning another page of her travel brochure. "Clem and I leave on the seven-o'clock train in the morning."

"You and Clem. That's great." How stupid to feel jealous of her travelling with someone else.

The dressing down from his mother earlier put thoughts of Ivy and his treatment of her in his mind all day. Now was as good a time as any to address it.

"She's got babysitters for Portia, and Phil was encouraging her to go when she mentioned it. So, we're going." Ivy concluded with a grin and a shrug.

"How are you feeling about The Father Project?"

Ivy gave an overly bright smile. He suspected she was hiding the pain.

"Moving on!" she tried to joke.

"I'm sorry I didn't wake you this morning to check on you, I thought you needed sleep." Her eyes bulged as she sized him up? Yep. She was definitely sizing him up.

"Yeah. Sleep was a bit elusive during the night." Her clipped tone told him she'd noticed his neglect. "Oh, by the way I bought some gifts for the children," Ivy pointed to the table, "And I wrote the postcards too. Could you write on them and post them tomorrow, please?"

"Sure. I can do that." Cameron opened the bag of goodies, "How much do I owe you?"

"Don't worry about it. I've got this." Her tone eased, but not by much.

"So, have you booked into any workshops?" Cameron asked, relieved she was still chatting with him.

"Yep, we do one on day three of the trip and another on days five and six."

"Is Clem doing the workshops too?"

"She said she'd give anything a go once and twice if she liked it. So, I'm hoping she likes it." Ivy's chuckle sounded more relaxed.

"What do you want to do tonight? Since you're leaving me to fend for myself for a week." Cameron asked, picking up a miniature London cab Ivy brought.

"I thought we could order in as I have to be ready to leave by five-forty-five in the morning."

"How are you getting to the station?"

"Phil and Clem are picking me up on the way."

Cameron waited, hoping Ivy would invite him along for the ride. But no offer was forthcoming. He clenched his fists, not sure if he directed that at Ivy or himself for creating the tension. In order to shift his focus, he walked over to the hall table.

"Have you seen the menu for the restaurant downstairs?"

Ivy pointed to the credenza on the opposite wall. "I think it's there."

"Can we compromise on dinner? My shout, I'll take you down to the restaurant." When she agreed, Cameron trembled slightly and slowly released a breath, and noticed the small smile on her lips. He tried to ignore how good a smile from her was. He picked up the phone and made a booking before heading for the shower.

MOVING ON FROM REJECTION

IVY

*H*er alarm failed to beat Cameron's wake up call.

"Thanks, I'm awake." Ivy replied to his knocking and calling out. Rolling over, she groaned aloud. At home she was always up at this time, but it was a bitter pill to swallow on her holidays. But her lips morphed into a grin when she realised why she was waking so early.

"Paris, here I come," she murmured as she rolled out of bed. She couldn't wipe the smile of pleasure at the knowledge that Clem was accompanying her as well. From the get-go they'd become firm friends and although Clem married into wealth, you'd never know. She was so down to earth, and Ivy loved that. Even this holiday they were doing on a budget and staying in hostels. It's one thing to travel with the man who you pine after. Completely another to be travelling with a friend.

What? Was she really pining after Cameron? Oh hell, she was. Last night at dinner, her eyes couldn't help trace the contours of his handsome face. When he relaxed, she could see he was as gorgeous as sin.

Ivy walked into her bathroom, closed the door on that line of thinking and stepped into the shower hoping the tiny droplets could wash away her thoughts. The reality of her father's rejection seemed to make her more vulnerable to the pain of Cameron's disinterest. Was it true her battered heart was more a result of Cameron than it was Lamont? She ducked her head under the spray and focused on shampooing her hair, anything to wash away her pain of the past week.

By the time she stepped out of her room there was a cup of coffee waiting on the table and Cameron was dressed and working on his laptop. She stared at his broad shoulders as he tapped away on the keyboard. Swallowing hard, she rejected the urge to wrap her arms around him from behind. Instead, she walked to the other end of the table.

"Thanks for this."

"I got you a coffee, thought you might need a caffeine fix, with it being so early. That's what you have at home, isn't it?" Cameron kept his focus on the screen. He didn't even glance her way.

"You're spot on. Thanks."

"Now!"

Ivy looked up at him. Her jaw dropped, and she stilled at his opening line…no, word. It was only a word, but the high-handed way he said it gave her no alternative but to listen.

"Message or ring me every day." His tone was sharp.

"Was that an order, Cameron?" Ivy's hands found their way to her hips. "You're not my keeper." Challenging herself to remain reasonable, Ivy continued, "I thought we were friends." Abandoning her coffee, she walked over to her bag, trying to keep herself busy or more like working hard to ignore the tremble racing up her spine. Her head held in a threatening swell of pressure. Could your head really explode, because Ivy sensed hers could be in danger of doing so.

Passport? Check!

Phone and charger? Check!

And that wasn't so she could keep in contact with him.

Plastic money? Check!

Getting away from Cameron? Check! Check!! Check!!!

"What?" Cameron asked.

"What?" Ivy screwed up her face, had she verbalised the self-talk.

"You said something."

"Yes! I groaned. Why do you think I have to report in to you every day?" her fury rang out loud and clear.

"I wasn't asking you to report in!" A blush spread over his face as Ivy turned cold eyes on him. "I simply care that you're okay."

"Well, thank you for caring, but I can ring home to people who care and who won't order me around." Ivy's phone rang. She released a sigh. "Morning Clem," she tried to lighten her tone. "Okay, I'm on my way, see you in a minute."

Cameron picked up the room card and her bag and waited by the door.

"I can take that!" Ivy snapped, trying to get away from him as quickly as possible.

"What and give you more reason to think I don't care?"

Ivy stood in front of him, looking into the eyes she loved. The soft blue turned dark, and Ivy knew they were both angry now. Oh, what a fool! Ivy sighed, closed her eyes forcing the strain from her body. Opening her eyes again, she breathed through the tension and worked to drop her shoulders. Slowing her breathing she looked into his eyes.

"I don't want to leave with us fighting," she whispered the heartfelt words. A fight with Cameron was the last thing she wanted.

He reached out and carefully clasped her upper arm. The gentle touch gripped her insides with a vice-like attachment.

"Sorry, you're right. Have a great time. I'll be here when you get back and if you feel like ringing or messaging me to let me know how you're getting on…I'd appreciate that…a lot."

"Thanks, I will. And promise me you won't sit in here in self-inflicted solitary confinement while I'm gone."

"I won't. Phil and I are taking in a football match and there's plenty of work to keep us busy. Enjoy yourself." Cameron bent his head slightly and kissed her cheek. "Have the best time."

Ivy led the way out of the room, conscious of resurrecting some ease between them. Obviously, she was the one with the deep feelings, not him.

"Morning," Clem and Phil called as she stepped out of the front door.

"Morning," Ivy replied.

"Hi, you all set Clem?" Cameron asked, his voice gentle.

"Not sure how I'll cope without Portia and Phil, but I'm determined to have a good time."

"Not too good a time, thank you." Phil said in a teasing tone, throwing his arm around his wife but his eyes on Ivy. "Art galleries, cooking classes and the top Paris attractions, definitely aren't my scene."

"Sorry to hear that because workshops, good food and sightseeing, are my idea of a great time." Ivy turned her palms to the sky and shrugged, "What can I say, I'm a simple girl."

They all laughed as Cameron loaded her large backpack into the back of the car.

"Good. No leading my wife astray!" Phil added, pulling Clem closer.

"Loyalty is my motto, no straying or encouraging others to stray here, my friend." Ivy looked to Cameron. Would he read into her message of sincerity and care? She liked him and nothing would change till she was certain he wasn't interested. His cold and hot signals were confusing.

"Well come on, you ladies have a train to catch," Phil opened Clem's door for her.

Ivy turned to say goodbye to Cameron. "I'll be in touch. Make sure you get out a bit, promise?"

"I will. Don't worry about me. Have a great time. Oh, and if there's another performance you want to see before we head home, message me and I'll get us some tickets."

Ivy stepped away. "Umm, okay, I will. I'll be back in no time. Bye." Without realising she was moving, Ivy stepped back to Cameron once again and kissed his cheek. His arm wrapped around her and pulled her in for a hug. Their hug lingered, stirring her insides, she smiled up at him when they pulled away. "See you soon."

"Have a great time," as he said this, Cameron reached for his wallet, "Oh bugger!"

"What?"

"I wanted to give you money to buy some things for the kids, but I left my wallet in the room." He explained, still patting himself down.

"Just like what I got yesterday?"

"Yep, they were great."

"Come on Ivy, you'll miss your train," Phil called.

"Okay, sorry, coming." Turning to Cameron, she nodded, "Leave it with me."

"I'll pay you back."

She smiled, hopped in the car, and waved as Phil drove off.

A million emotions ran through her, watching Cameron watching her. Nothing stronger than the fact she was going to miss him. Maybe a bit of separation would do them good. Force Cameron to decide about her and maybe even a possible them.

Turning in her seat, Ivy saw Clem watching her, the grin more mischievous than Ivy needed. There were questions coming her way, she was certain.

DENIAL

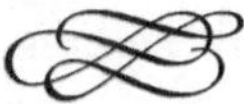

CAMERON

"Can we please go get lunch?" Phil said as he dropped into the chair in front of Cameron's desk.

"Since when were we going to do lunch?" Cameron asked, pinching the skin at his throat. What else had he forgotten? He tapped the ream of paper on the desk as he tried to remember any prior arrangements.

"Since the girls left yesterday," Phil said, leaning forward with his elbows resting on his knees. "By the way…what's going on between you and Ivy? Is there something there?"

"Nothing. Just friends," Cameron answered quickly and couldn't prevent heat creeping up his body. "Her second cousin is engaged to my mum. That's all."

"So, nothing?" Phil's eyebrows shot up high on his forehead, "Like you have no feelings for her, totally platonic? I think not."

Cameron closed his laptop and stood. "So, lunch, huh? I'm starving."

"Changing the subject, the first way of deflecting an argument?"

"No, because there isn't an argument," Cameron replied, walking around the desk. His voice was weak and hands were sweaty. He couldn't even convince himself.

With a chuckle, Phil stepped out of the office. "You really should face reality, Cameron. You're so into her and she's into you. Remove the blinkers, please."

Cameron released a nervous laugh as he followed Phil out. "So, when's this football match you're taking me to?"

"Sorry, we weren't talking about football." Phil said, as he reversed his father's car.

Cameron dropped his head onto the back of his seat. Talking about Ivy was the last thing he wanted to do. He couldn't believe how much he'd missed her last night. Spending time together was so good. "There was something going on between her and my brother, I think. I don't want to deal with the women he's rejected. Not now, not ever."

Phil looked across at Cameron and then back to the road. His mouth fell open and he slowly closed again.

Good, that stopped him talking.

Phil shook his head as he indicated and gently swerved into the right-hand lane.

Changing the subject again would be good right here, but Cameron couldn't think of anything to talk about.

Ivy hadn't mentioned Liam but the other night on the phone she told him she loved him so they were obviously still seeing each other, keeping it quiet and low key. On the drive in the car from Chester's Run to Melbourne, she hadn't really taken much notice of Liam. Cameron tried to recall the level of conversation. Oh, that's right, it was early in the morning, they were all tired and there wasn't really any chatting between any of them much at all.

Funny though, what Phil said was correct. Cameron was missing Ivy just as Phil was missing Clem. He'd never experienced this intense sensation about anyone else, well except his mother when she left for Chester's Run and though the level of pain with the separation was the same, the feeling was completely different.

Cameron looked over at Phil, who was smiling. He must have been watching and seemed rather amused.

"What?"

"This thing between Ivy and your brother, how serious is it?"

"I don't know, I didn't ask? Not sure I want to hear what either of them have to say about the other."

Phil pulled into a carpark and focused on finding a parking spot.

Cameron took in the puzzled look from his new friend. He sat quietly, watching as another car pulled out.

Once inside, Cameron found a spare table in the pub while Phil walked off to order drinks. In the few minutes it took to buy drinks and walk back to the table, Cameron's phone beeped with messages. Not just one, but a few.

<u>Ivy</u> — *Hi. Arrived safely and done heaps of sightseeing.*

<u>Ivy</u> — *Hostels fine, and Clem is a barrel of laughs.*

<u>Ivy</u> — *Nothing more to report on The Father Project, but didn't expect to.*

<u>Ivy</u> — *How are you doing?*

Cameron smiled while reading the messages. When he hadn't received word from Ivy last night, he didn't think he was going to hear anything.

His fingers flew over the keypad of his phone to reply.

<u>Cameron</u> — *Great to hear you're safe and sound. Spoke to Mum and Jack last night, they're all good. Try to forget about The Father Project and enjoy your time away. You deserve so much better than him.*

<u>Ivy</u> — *Thanks Cameron so much to deal with.* She finished with a sad face emoji.

<u>Cameron</u> — *Out to lunch with Phil at the moment*

<u>Ivy</u> — *Currently following Clem around the Louvre. This place is amazing.*

<u>Cameron</u> — *When does the first workshop start?*

Cameron was well aware it was the following day, but keeping this conversation going was his aim.

He watched the dancing dots on his screen, waiting for a reply, but nothing came. He looked up to see whether Phil reached the front of the queue. Only to realise Phil sat opposite him with his drink half gone and a smug grin spread across his face.

There was nothing to say or do. Cameron put his phone down and picked up the menu in front of him.

IVY

Getting away from London was the best medicine for her. Clem made a list of things she wanted to see and considering most of them matched Ivy's wish list, the two women ventured everywhere together. The places of interest were stunning up close, and Ivy's camera was permanently in action. Pointing this way and that as they shared some amazing experiences.

With Cameron's request to stay in touch constantly on her mind, Ivy decided to message him as she followed Clem through the Louvre. In between messages, Ivy would draw her attention back to Clem's comments or read something of interest. Her phone would buzz and her eyes ventured back to the screen, and she'd read Cameron's reply.

Reading his last message, she paused. She'd already told him when the workshops were, but it mustn't have been important if he'd forgotten. Was he really that self-obsessed to forget their conversations? Then a sudden thought hit her. He was trying to keep the conversation going, otherwise he wouldn't have asked. Ivy focused on releasing the tension in her body, she turned her attention to Clem while deciding whether to reply to his question or build another line of discussion.

Clem burst out laughing, causing Ivy to look around them.

"What?"

"I sent this picture to Phil," Clem showed her a picture of Ivy with her head down and fingers obviously typing something on the screen of her phone. The concentration on her face was intense.

"Then Phil sent me this."

Clem swiped and Ivy gaped. It was Cameron doing the same thing.

It was one thing to message him but completely another for others to realise, especially when Cameron was so hot and cold all the time.

"And?" Ivy tried to pretend it meant nothing.

"The blush spreading over your neck shows me I should be the one asking 'and?'." With her raised eyebrows and the corner of her mouth turned up, Ivy shrugged.

Clem linked arms with Ivy. "Let's go get coffee. I think we need to talk."

For the first time since Cameron closed down on her, she realised she'd like to talk. A world of pain was inside, and containing it was practically impossible.

The coffee shop was so overcrowded, they kept moving. "We'll come back later," Clem decided and headed for the exit. Outside, the two women shivered against the freezing wind. Still arm in arm, they walked until they spotted a little coffee shop. Clem found an empty table in the back corner and almost pushed Ivy into a chair, then took the seat opposite.

"Bonjour," the waiter greeted them as he stepped up to their table.

"Bonjour," Clem replied. "Two café crèmes and croissants, please?"

He smiled and in his thick French accent replied, "Certainly ma'am." He gave a slight bow and a lingering look at Ivy, turned, and walked away.

Clem held the laugh in only until he was out of earshot. "He was looking," she told Ivy, while still watching him.

"He was not!" Ivy replied, but she tasted the lie as it rolled off her tongue and also knew his smouldering gaze had no reaction on her. That stupid heart of hers was stuck on one man and one man only. And he didn't want her.

"Come on Ivy, you need to talk about this. There's something there between the two of you and this on top of your father's refusal to meet you," She shrugged, "Well, it's not healthy to bottle it in." Clem's gloved hand wrapped about Ivy's cold one.

Ivy dropped back into her chair and pinched her lips together, then threw her hands up in the air. What was the point of denying what the others could see? Her voice was strained as she spoke, "Yes, I have feelings for him, and I thought he did too but," Ivy shook her head recalling the day she'd gone to the Homestead for dinner and he barely lasted long enough to eat. "He just blocked me out, and I don't understand what I've done."

"Has he told you why?"

"Nothing. He's been so hot and cold since then I do not know what that man is thinking." Ivy's phone buzzed. She looked down at the screen. Cameron again.

She pushed the phone over to Clem as her stomach clinched when Clem's mouth dropped open. "He's missing you, you realise that, don't you?"

Ivy's hands flew into the air again. "I have no idea what's going on in his head, but it's difficult not to reply when he starts conversations like this. I keep hoping he wants more."

"Sorry, but a friend wouldn't be doing this."

Clem pushed the phone back, so Ivy read the message aloud, "How about Les Misérables? I can book tickets for the day after you return."

"Men," Ivy grunted as she threw the phone into her bag.

"What's stopping him from pursuing something with you?" Clem asked. "He's quiet but—"

"Sophie and Lindy have always been his rock. Cameron has always been the quiet one, but the time I've spent with him he's really come out of his shell. Maybe the idea of a relationship scares him."

"He's a man. Red-blooded male from what I can see," Clem's finger pointed to Ivy's bag sitting next to her. "How many messages has he sent you today?"

"Heaps, and I've replied to most of them," Ivy said, pulling the phone out again. "Not sure I can handle the pain of this over and over."

Their food arrived and Ivy focused on that and not on Cameron's messages, but that proved difficult when her phone buzzed again.

"Don't you dare laugh!" She hissed at Clem.

"You have to admit, it's hard not to." Clem closed her mouth around the crispy shell of the croissant putting a stop to any more of her laughter. A sigh left Ivy's lips.

GETTING A HANDLE ON HIS EMOTIONS

CAMERON

Hell, was it creepy Cameron was sitting in Ivy's room just to be close to her? She'd been gone four whole days, and he was useless. He scrolled through his phone, rereading the thread of messages between them. He'd booked the tickets to *Les Misérables* as suggested and yesterday he arrived at the office late, after stopping by Deb and Bert's shop to ask them out to dinner once Ivy returned. His shout at the local. They seemed a lovely couple and extremely sympathetic towards Ivy's plight. He listened to their pleasure at finally meeting Anita's daughter and to see how well she'd done for herself. The personal cost to Cameron to muster the courage was unbelievable. He'd almost returned home to change his shirt from the stress of the visit before going to the office.

"Lovely lass," Bert said in his British brogue.

Cameron couldn't help but agree with him. Any thought of her, sent warmth flowing through his veins, knowing he'd done something special for Ivy. Doing these little things with her in mind tumbled him into an unknown territory. The feeling sat well on him. But then his mind would spiral back to the afternoon he'd caught Ivy and Liam upstairs in her flat. Such a wake-up call. Liam wondering how to tell his brother about them. Well, he didn't need to because Cameron pulled away and his heart tore in two. Not to mention the phone call he'd overheard. Okay, eavesdropped on, 'I love you too' that stung.

She'd only ever see him as a friend. He got that. His relationship with Liam improved until that point, and he could still hear Liam dismissing Cameron's accusations of something going on between them. But seriously, he was all man, and he understood a connection when he saw it. He just wished it was him she could relax with, not his older womanising brother.

Cameron looked around her practically empty room again, got up off her bed and headed out to start his breakfast.

Today he and Phil were attending the football match. He looked at his phone again to check which teams they were going to see. That's right, Manchester United and Chelsea. He didn't really care about the game, but it relieved him to have something to occupy his day. A day spent without Ivy, was painful. He mentally ticked off another day until she returned.

As agreed, Cameron was making his own way to the ground and meeting Phil there. They'd put in a solid week of work and achieved so much. Cameron had everything he needed to finish the initial stage of the project. Being around people lifted his spirits more than he realised. Also, not having Ralph putting him down at every turn and belittling him, gave him self-belief and trust in other people.

He followed the hordes of supporters and boarded the train. He knew where he'd disembark and presumed it would be with the mobs in either red and yellow or blue and white. He found a seat tucked away in the far corner of the train, clutched his backpack to his stomach while he listened and watched the banter between friends and supporters.

He could honestly say he'd never joined a throng of people like this for a sporting match, not even in Melbourne where he'd lived. Especially considering Melbourne was dubbed, by Melbournians, as the sports capital of the world. Yes, his hands shook slightly and if he had to speak his voice would probably squeak, but hey he was out here doing this. He smiled to himself, pulled out his phone and began texting his sister, adding a photo, and waited for her reply.

Sophie — *No way, is Ivy with you?* Sophie's reply bounced back.

Cameron — *Nope! I'm doing this all by myself. Ivy's still in France.* Cameron's nervous fingers typed.

Sophie — *Where are you going?*

Cameron — *Stamford Bridge for a football match.* He added a funny face.

Sophie — *Shut the door, are you kidding me!*

He took a photo of the train full of passengers in football kits and sent it to her.

Sophie — *Okay, so you're not kidding. I'll stay on the line until you arrive safely.*

Cameron — *Thanks, but I'm fine. You have better things to do than babysit me via a series of messages.* Cameron laughed at that line. He was getting good at this messaging thing.

Sophie — *Fine. Everyone sends their love. Missing you heaps. Hope you're having fun?*

Cameron — *Work's going well. I'm enjoying the travel and Phil and his family have introduced me to many new things. I feel almost worldly.* Before pressing send he included a laughing emoji.

Sophie — *Who are you and WHAT have you done with my brother?* She replied with a laughing face with tears.

Cameron — *Mum won't recognise me when I return.* Cameron looked up from the screen and realised this was the last stop before his. *Must go. Will message again soon.* He ended the conversation with a purple heart.

Sophie — *Enjoy your day.* Sophie sent him a kiss.

Cameron smiled as he locked his phone, and put it away. He liked the person he was becoming. He'd heard the line of thinking that people grew and changed every day. At the moment he was changing more than most. This new Cameron sat well on him, but the heartache of wanting Ivy was a bugger.

A DISTANT LONGING

IVY

Stretched out on her bed, Ivy was exhausted from the two-day workshop they'd finished three hours earlier. They were returning home tomorrow, catching the afternoon train back to London. Ivy's phone buzzed again, and she cackled to herself as she replied.

"Who are you messaging now?" Clem asked, her own fingers flying over her screen.

"Sophie and Susie, the two women who work for me."

"Sophie is Cameron's sister, isn't she?"

"That's the one." Ivy answered while switching to a second conversation. Capable fingers typed another message. She read it, re-read it. When she was confident, it sent just the right amount of interest while remaining distant, she pressed send.

The number of messages which travelled across the channel for the last six days between her and Cameron were astounding. She put her phone on aeroplane mode so she could read through his messages without interruption. It confused her. What did Cameron want? He'd obviously missed her, which was pleasing to know because she'd been lost without him. The way they would chat about things, like the current conversation about travelling, they spoke about where else in the world he was interested in seeing. The musical proved a great hit, and they looked up what was playing back home and promised each other they would take Lindy to see something when they returned.

They messaged at length of the harsh winter in London and how they'd avoid that at all costs if they ever came back again. Ivy was speaking of an impossible meeting with her father and Cameron was referring to his contract, but at the time it sounded like together they were making plans.

Tonight, her end of the conversation was all about the workshops, where Clem and Ivy learned to bake a range of speciality breads. The idea of baking them back home meant an opportunity to expand her range for her customers. Ivy had an urge to sing.

Ivy — *I could make these new breads and sell it to other bakeries in the area. This is what your mother has been trying to get me to do. I could look at starting a wholesaling arm of my business with these products and Sophie's new creations as well.*

Cameron — *You sound so excited about this. I'd say this was just what your business needed, fresh energy.*

Ivy — *I'd need to plan carefully, but I'm sure I can do it.*

Cameron — *How about I do a computer program for you to track purchases and sales for the wholesale side of the business.*

Ivy — *You have enough on your plate.*

The fact he offered meant the world to her.

It made her laugh to read Cameron's excited view of the English Premier League football match. He spoke of the crowds, the chanting, and the raw devotion the English had for their teams. They were packed like sardines into the stadium and there was the exorbitant cost of the ticket, not that he'd paid.

Cameron — *I thought Aussie Rules back home is big. This here is huge. I still can't believe the crowd and the passion for the sport.*

Ivy — *Are you hooked?*

Cameron — *Well, more like interested, not hooked. Not yet, anyway.*

When they said goodnight, Ivy squirmed as something shifted inside. The tension eased the more they communicated. And the feeling was refreshing.

She hoped when she returned to London, they could be this relaxed in person. Taking her phone off aeroplane mode Ivy grinned when it buzzed.

But it wasn't who she hoped to hear from when she looked. Sophie had sent another message.

<u>Sophie</u> — *Mum's doing well. The bruising has almost disappeared. She still gets headaches occasionally, but less frequent nowadays. They all send their love.*

<u>Ivy</u> — *Wonderful news about Lindy. Sending my love back tenfold. Time for sleep. Talk soon, take care.*

CAMERON

Cameron jumped from one frozen foot to the other, waiting for the train to pull in. He looked at his watch. They, no, she was only about five minutes away. Phil was in the car with a sleeping Portia. According to Audrey, Portia had a big day with her Aunty Nancy, and she looked totally exhausted when Phil dropped by to collect her.

Cameron paced the waiting area, trying to keep the blood flowing all the way to his toes. He'd swear his feet were blue in his thick boots and socks. The train sounded in the distance. A couple of long toots of the horn blasted out as it pulled into the station. He couldn't wait to see Ivy. He drew in a breath as the train crawled past. Would she be as keen to see him? He could sit and listen to every detail of her trip, even though they'd messaged the whole time she was away, and still not be bored. Especially if she was describing the trip in her animated way. The thought of her hands flying haphazardly, her face flushed and her elongated words such as lovely, unreal, unbelievable, and awesome the way she does when she's excited.

He paused by the wall, watching for them to disembark. At the sight of Ivy's sandy blonde hair swaying as she walked, he couldn't hold back his smile. Both women looked tired but happy. Ivy hefted her carry bag higher onto her shoulder, repositioned the wheeler bag and followed Clem towards the exit.

Cameron appeared in front of them.

"Welcome back." He kissed Clem first and then Ivy. Taking in her vanilla scent as he did. "Here, give me your bags." The girls eagerly handed them over, hoisted their packs again and followed him out.

Phil saw them coming and jumped out of the car. "Cameron, you better jump in the front, someone is asking for mummy."

Cameron worked hard to hide his misfortune at not being able to sit next to Ivy.

"Right you are," he said as he loaded the cases, and waited for Ivy to throw her carry bag in. Then held her door open, waiting for her to settle herself in the backseat. Climbing into the front seat beside Phil, he turned to watch the interaction between mother and daughter. He twisted his neck further to see Ivy watching them too. In that moment, he imagined it was their child. His and Ivy's. And Ivy's face would glow the way Clem's was to see her daughter again. Before allowing himself to run away with those thoughts, he tamped them down. That and the jealous ones of the way Clem and Phil shared a cuddle before she jumped into the car. For the first ten minutes, Portia and Clem chatted away in baby talk and laughed together.

"Mumma, Mumma," Portia's little hands were beating out a rhythmic tattoo at having her mother home again.

Cameron turned to face the front. He wondered right there and then if Ivy wanted children. The thought never actually crossed his mind before. Well, why would it? He never thought he'd ever wanted them. Well not until he became a primary carer to Jack's family while his mother recovered from her ordeal. Watching Ivy now, he longed to know the answer to that life-changing question. Jack's mob really were a great bunch and since looking after them, Cameron considered a couple of times the possibility of being a father one day. Mind that would only happen if he had a loving and caring partner by his side. He held in a rising chuckle. The idea of a partner never crossed his mind before either.

"So," Phil asked, "How was it?"

Clem answered her husband, recounting all the things they managed to fit in, including the cooking workshops which both women were overly animated about. A few minutes later Phil pulled into the driveway of the hotel.

IVY

"Thanks for coming with me," Ivy told Clem as the two friends hugged each other. "I'm glad I got to share that experience with someone else."

"No. Thank you for allowing me to tag along."

"Yeah, thanks, Ivy. Hopefully, she'll stop hassling me about a holiday for a while," Phil teased as he leaned in and kissed Ivy good-bye. Turning to Cameron he said, "See you tomorrow."

"Will do," Cameron accepted Clem's kiss, with Ivy's pack over his shoulder and her suitcase in his hand. He stood beside Ivy as they watched their friends drive away.

Ivy's mind was on repeat. The words Clem said to Cameron, "Take care of her, she's rather special." Had not only caused her own cheeks to flush, but also his. The things Ivy and Clem shared while being away together cemented an understanding and care between them. Was that connection similar to what her mother shared with Deb when she lived here all those years ago?

Once the taillights disappeared, Cameron began walking towards the entrance and Ivy automatically fell in step behind him. She watched the rounding of his shoulders and the tension in his posture. It didn't take a genius to see if they were to have a conversation deeper than 'so you enjoyed the trip', Ivy would have to be the one to start it.

"How's the programming going?" she asked as they stepped into the elevator alone.

"Great. I could seriously return home tomorrow. I've seen everything I need to. The rest I can do from Chester's Run. So, I was wondering…" his voice trailed off in thought.

"You want to leave?" Ivy wasn't ready to return home just yet.

"Actually, no. I thought you and I could head off to Bath together."

"Really? You'd like to see it?" Ivy's voice rose, as did her mouth at the corners.

"I spoke to Phil today. He's fine with me coming and going. He's even going to give us his car for the trip. He only uses it on weekends anyway, and said he could do without it this weekend if we're not back." Cameron's smile was captivating.

Ivy didn't underestimate the effort he'd gone to in organising this for them. "Thank you, Cameron. I'd love to come." She dropped a kiss on his cheek and leaned onto the wall, hoping the thrill of what he'd done wouldn't lead to another let-down. Well, if it did, it meant Ivy wanted too much from this man. "So, when do we leave?"

"Well," Cameron's brows danced, "The thing is, tomorrow night we're having dinner with Deb and Bert—"

"What?"

"I popped in to extend an invitation for dinner, I thought you might enjoy chatting to them beyond the questions about your father. They were delighted. So, that's tomorrow night."

Ivy met his searching look and she smiled. "That sounds wonderful."

"Good." The tension in his body eased slightly. "So how about after that? Phil can drive his car to work tomorrow and I'll bring it back here, we can leave first thing Wednesday morning."

"You're full of surprises." Ivy said as they stepped off the elevator and headed down the corridor to their room. Next thing her stomach rumbled, making the loudest noise possible due to hunger. "Excuse me!" Her cheeks were hot, and a giggle escaped.

"Haven't you eaten the whole time you've been away?" Cameron teased.

The thread of messages between them had enough evidence of how much she'd eaten.

"On the contrary, I've eaten way too much," her silky laugh made him smile.

"Good, because I have ordered a light meal of soup and toasted sandwiches for dinner." A shadow suddenly passed over his face, Ivy didn't underestimate how open to her aversion he must have been in that moment.

"I...I...I hope that's okay?" his stammer was so cute and heart wrenching at the same time.

"Of course, it is. I really appreciate you organising dinner." Ivy explained as she flashed her card in front of the scanner and opened the door to their suite.

The smell of toast and something savoury hit them as they entered.

"Good, it's here." Cameron said, walking past the table to Ivy's room. He dropped her bags inside the door and headed back towards the table.

Lifting the silver lids from the dishes, she breathed in the aroma. She looked at the card beside the dish. "Country style chicken soup with pasta. Yum it smells delicious."

Cameron dropped a pile of papers on the table, picked up a bowl and began ladling soup into it.

"Come on, let's read through these brochures while we eat and decide what we're going to visit in Bath."

CAMERON

There was a slight shake of his serving hand, so Cameron clutched the ladle tighter. Maybe Ivy had been too preoccupied to notice. Tonight, he'd gone out on a limb, making decisions he'd never considered doing before. Perhaps a trip with just the two of them might be exactly what they needed. Cameron pushed the full bowl of soup towards Ivy and dished up his own.

When he sat opposite her, he saw the subject of her gaze. Ivy was trawling through the brochures he picked up for the trip to Bath.

"Oh, this looks lovely," Ivy said, tapping her finger on the glossy page.

Cameron leaned over the table to see what took her fancy.

"Sorry, come sit here," she said, patting the seat beside her.

The opened page showed the Bishop's Palace and Gardens.

"This place looks stunning," she told Cameron after he perused the page.

He pulled out his pen and circled the title. "Right, what else?"

"Oh, awesome. Look at this," Ivy held up the brochure a few minutes later. "The Bath Brew House, my shout dinner and drinks. It's got its own microbrewery."

"You don't need to pay."

"I know, but I want to," Ivy nudged his shoulder playfully. "Where are we staying?"

"Never you mind. That's all organised." Cameron took in the silence which now engulfed them. "What?"

"And what about payment?"

"My idea, my shout!"

"Is that so?"

They both laughed at the silliness they were partaking in.

Cameron's heart stalled when Ivy spoke again.

"Thanks for this. I know I shouldn't be so bummed about my father, but there's only one man in your life who should rightfully have the honour of being called father. And when he rejects the offer to meet you," Ivy sighed out the last words. "It not only stings, but closes the door on any chance of meeting other members of your family. At least I can go home and have Jack and Tessa and their families in my life."

At least she could talk about this without crying. Cameron bumped her with his shoulder this time and smiled. "You know you have us as well."

Ivy's face scrunched up as she stared at him for a few seconds. Pulling her gaze away, she replied in a quiet voice, "I know, thank you."

Cameron watched her as she continued to read the travel brochures, her playfulness vanished along with the beautiful smile that had warmed him from the inside out.

Why, oh why was this so difficult? He met a woman, liked her, well, like probably wasn't a strong enough word, but he wasn't going there. And between them they seemed to distance themselves more than open up and discover how well they'd coexist. Not that coexisting with Ivy was his intention. In fact, just the thought of his brother reminded him this was meant to be nothing other than friends.

An hour later with all the food demolished, and dishes stacked at one end of the table. Cameron gathered the brochures with the selected pages marked for future reference and stretched his arms over his head and yawned.

"Yep, I'm beat too." Ivy agreed, pushing back from the table as she stood. "Thanks for dinner, I enjoyed staying in."

"My pleasure."

"So, Bath on Wednesday morning, then?" She was obviously looking for confirmation.

"Let's head out early, the trip is about two-and-a-half hours," Cameron added, he'd checked the route and knew where he was going.

"Sounds good. Thanks Cameron," Ivy's hand rested on his shoulder giving a slight squeeze.

Would she bend down and kiss him? That never eventuated. Forcing his mouth into a smile, he worked hard not to allow his feelings to show. Man, he was all over the shop tonight. One minute he only wanted her friendship and the next, he wanted whatever she would offer him. Shaking those thoughts from his head, he looked up at her retreating figure, "Night Ivy."

"Night."

DINNER WITH DEB AND BERT

IVY

The day passed with Ivy washing and packing for the trip to Bath, while tossing the idea of dinner with Deb and Bert around in her head. By four o'clock she'd decided any mention of her father, would have to be raised by others. If Lamont Thornton was mentioned, she'd reply, but when it came to conversation, he was off limits from the moment he refused to meet with her.

For whatever reason, she would not force a stranger's hand. Although knowing she wouldn't meet the other half of her family, Ivy would accept Lamont's rejection in time. Checking her suitcase again, she made sure she'd packed everything. All Cameron's clean clothes were on the end of his bed, ready for him to sort out. The gifts she acquired for the children were lined up on her bedroom floor. She'd purchase something else for them from Bath and pack them away in separate bags when they returned. She and Cameron had been keen to bring home something for each of them. The trinkets from London sat on top of the T-shirts from Paris. They were all touristy things, but isn't that what kids enjoyed?

The door to the suite opened and Cameron stepped through, looking relaxed. His smile seemed to stretch to almost the full width of his face when he looked up and saw her standing there.

"How was your day?" he asked.

"Good. Got the washing done, your things are on the end of your bed. And I'm packed."

"Thanks for that. Have I got time for a shower?" Cameron dropped his bag inside the door of his room.

"Sure."

When Ivy was ready, she dropped onto the couch and waited for Cameron to join her. She could hear him rummaging around in his room before the door opened, and he stepped out. Knowing he had no sense of style, the combination of clothes he wore tonight delighted her. The classy look sat well, and Ivy couldn't draw her gaze from him. Their eyes collided. She coasted over the lavender shirt sitting snuggly across his broad shoulders. The shirt, his grey cargo pants and R.M. William's boots revealed another man. One that enhanced the man she cared so much for.

Neither spoke for a minute. The connection right there was beyond anything Ivy had ever experienced. Forcing herself to her feet was her excuse to break the intense eye contact between them.

"We should…um…we should get going," Ivy said, making a show of checking the time.

"Ummm, yep. That's…good." Cameron was still watching her as she stood up from collecting her clutch off the floor.

A couple were exiting the restaurant as they arrived, Cameron held open the door for them and then waited for Ivy to walk in ahead of him. After scanning the room, they spotted Deb waving to them.

"Hope you haven't been waiting long?" she asked with a kind smile. "I was so pleased when Cameron said he'd arranged this."

Cameron took Bert's offered hand and leaned over to kiss Deb. "Thanks for coming."

"Thanks for the invite. Seeing Ivy last week brought back so many memories," Deb said to Cameron as she struggled with the emotion of it all. "Most of them wonderful. I like the idea of having time to tell her about her mother." Deb covered Ivy's hand in hers. "You're so much like her, but there's a lot of your father in you as well."

Ivy swallowed hard. Talking about Lamont wasn't on her agenda for this evening.

IVY

The news she shared some of his features was comforting. "Thank you."

Cameron poured two glasses of beer from the jug on the table for himself and her before flagging down the waiter for another jug.

"So, these memories of my mother, can you share any of them with me?" Ivy's elbows were on the table and her hands clinched beside her left cheek as she rocked forward, waiting for Deb's response.

"I remember this one time when the boys were playing football," she looked up at her husband and smiled. "Your mother and I were there to cheer on the locals, well in our case the locals meant expats. We all hung out together, even though Australia was far away. There must have been a comfort in knowing other Australians. Anyway, this one day we were cheering from the sidelines and the expats were up two goals to nothing. Anita, forgetting herself as she sometimes did, called out—"

"Come on, you Pommy bastards at least make a game of it," Bert recited the line and Ivy saw it must have been a significant memory. He squeezed his wife's hand, "Sorry love, I'll never forget it for as long as I live."

Deb smiled at his interruption and simply eased back into her recount. "Two of the Poms stopped playing and headed over towards her. One was your father and the other my Bert and well the rest as they say is history."

Ivy wanted to laugh along with them, but no, they spoke of a man who rejected her, which somehow stung. Instead, she managed a small smile and dropped her eyes to the table.

"He loved your mother so much. In fact, he still does," Deb said.

"Not enough to stand by her when everything happened or to meet me now. Sorry, Deb, but I'd prefer not to talk about Lamont. Please don't think me rude."

At that moment the waiter cleared his throat, Ivy looked up.

"Are you all ready to order?" he asked.

"Just a few minutes, thanks," Ivy said and dropped her head to take in the gold gilded menu while hiding her reddened cheeks and the burn behind her eyes.

Once the waiter took their orders, Deb started again describing the work her mother did and the flat they shared. Ivy knew her mother was a funny woman, Jack and Tessa often remarked of her sense of humour when they were young children.

After they finished their meal and each rejected the offer of dessert, Ivy turned to her mother's friends and asked, "I'd like to ask about what happened to my mother. The attack I mean. I've tried to understand what occurred from her letter, but it's vague and such a contrast from the story my grandparents shared with me as a child."

Deb and Bert exchanged glances. It seemed neither of them would rehash that awful time in their past.

A man standing to the side of Ivy cleared his throat. He was a tall man with grey-brown hair and of slight build. Ivy looked up at him and stared.

"Gabe, what are you doing here?" Bert asked as he stood to greet the stranger.

"You said you were meeting Anita's daughter and let's just say curiosity got the better of me." As Gabe spoke, his eyes didn't move from Ivy. He seemed to study her intently. Who was he and what did he want? Hairs on the back of her neck stood and prickled. She knew him. But she'd never seen him before. Surely…

This man was her father.

He showed no delight in seeing her and failed to introduce himself.

Cameron's hand landed on her shoulder. Must have been his show of support and comfort. She reached up to cup Cameron's hand gently, hoping he understood she was okay.

Without looking at Bert, Ivy asked, "You called him Gabe, but my mother said his name was Lamont?" the question in her voice was clear.

"My name is Lamont Gabriel Thornton. I was engaged to your mother." Gabe replied, his eyes transfixed on hers.

"The truth of what happened to your mother is not Bert's or Deb's story to share. That cross alone is mine to bear." Lamont, or Gabe as his friends knew him, dug into his pocket, and pulled out a card. "I'll share the events with you if you'd be kind enough to meet me at this address, say tomorrow morning at ten. If that doesn't work for you, I'm prepared to make another time, though I understand you leave for Australia again soon."

Ivy didn't bother to get into a conversation with Gabe Thornton, but she planned on having her questions answered when they met. Turning to Cameron she asked, "Would you mind if we stop by on the way out tomorrow?"

"Not at all. Ten's fine with me. You sure you still want to go? I can cancel our trip if you'd prefer." Cameron's eyes combed her face closely.

"No, we have plans, we'll leave straight after I meet with Mr Thornton." Turning back to the man she should have had the privilege of calling Dad, Ivy smiled and confirmed, "Thanks. Cameron and I will be there tomorrow morning at ten." Trying desperately to control the sarcasm in her voice, Ivy added, "And thanks for your time."

Gabe nodded and without another word walked away. Ivy focused on the drop of his shoulders as he left the restaurant. She couldn't hold back the grunt as the door closed behind him.

"Now love," Deb said, patting her hand again. "Here's your chance to understand everything. Please don't be too harsh on him and promise you'll hear him out."

Ivy nodded, her eyes on Deb now. "Thank you for having dinner with us. I won't lie to you and feign exhaustion, but I think I just need some time to prepare myself for meeting Mr Thornton tomorrow."

"We totally understand," Deb gripped Ivy's fingers as she pulled back from the table. "Are you still happy to stay in touch once you head back to Australia?"

"Absolutely. Whatever happens tomorrow won't have any bearing on us being friends." And Ivy meant it. Surely there were many more wonderful stories Deb could tell her about her mother.

THE TRIP TO DEVON

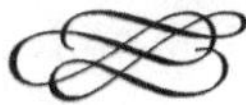

CAMERON

With the car packed, Cameron stood just inside the door waiting for Ivy. She'd been in a weary daze all morning. After returning to their suite last night, Cameron asked Ivy if she was all right with this news.

Her only reply was, "Let's just see what tomorrow will bring."

He'd watched as she walked to her room. Dejected probably wasn't the correct word, but the dictionary would be pushed to find a word describing how Ivy felt. Cameron was struggling as well.

He played with the key ring in his hand and only looked up when Ivy walked towards the door.

"How long did you say it will take to get to Devon?" Ivy asked, stepping out ahead of him.

"Three and a half hours. Then about two hours to Bath."

"How about we stay the night in Devon? That's a lot of driving for one day." Ivy suggested.

"Let's see how we feel after Devon and go from there." What

Cameron wished to say was 'see how things go with Lamont Gabriel Thornton' but he wasn't game.

They drove much of the way in silence. Ivy switched on the radio when they first hopped in the car, once they left the city, she seemed agitated by the sound and turned it off. Cameron wondered what was worse, the noise of the music or the blaring silence.

Nearly two hours into the drive, he pulled the car over when he spotted a little cafe. "How about a coffee?" he asked, pulling the hand-brake on.

"Do you think they'll have anything stronger?" She asked with a forced smile.

Cameron chuckled. "How about we save that for later? You might need it."

Ivy raised her brows, turned, got out of the car, and followed him into the shop. Ten minutes later they exited into the frigid air with coffee and a paper bag of sweet goodness each.

Cameron opened her door and waited till she dropped into the passenger seat, he safely secured the Classic Victorian Sponge Cake Ivy selected to give as an offering when they arrived. He hurried around to the driver's side and jumped in, shivering as he did.

"Okay, let's trade a bite before we take off, or I might not get any of that," Cameron pointed at the strawberry eclair in Ivy's hand with one third already demolished.

"Fair enough, but where's my macaroon first?" He couldn't hide his smile at the amiable nature of their banter, even though he accepted it was only temporary. The closer they got to Devon, Ivy would over think the situation all over again. He handed over the macaroon and took a bite of Ivy's treat. "Ummm, that's good."

Ivy snatched it back. "And it's mine. Paws off."

He took a quick sip of coffee and pulled back onto the road.

Devon, here they come.

IVY

The washer wipers flew noisily over the windscreen as Cameron's phone directed them to the address he'd typed in earlier. They followed a tree-lined road which seemed to lead to nothing. The rain hampered the view. Well, there was nothing to see except a large building up on their left, which looked more like a country estate than someone's home.

"I think we've missed it." Ivy said, checking the address on the screen against the one on the card in her hand.

Cameron pulled over and checked it again for himself. "I don't think so. That's what it says up there," he pointed to a large grey stone entrance barred by double gates. The heavy rain still falling steadily.

They looked at each other and then back at the entrance.

"Surely not," Ivy spat out.

Cameron slowly approached the gate and pressed the intercom.

"Can I help you?" A male voice with a strong English accent asked.

"Yes, I have Miss Ivy Masters to see Mr Gabe Thornton?"

"Enter the gates and continue up the drive. See you in a few minutes," the voice replied, confirming they had the correct address.

Ivy's raised brows remained hidden in the low sweep of her long fringe until they arrived at the building they saw from the road.

"Oh, my God! Is he a butler?" she hissed just before her door opened.

Cameron didn't have time to respond.

"Miss Masters and Mr…"

"Kemp," Ivy quickly added.

"Do come in," he held an umbrella over head for Ivy while Cameron jumped out and dashed up the stairs behind them.

They shook themselves off, as Ivy remembered the cake. "Oh, I left the cake in the car."

She was talking to Cameron, but the butler chimed in. "How about I fetch it on your behalf, miss?" He didn't wait for a reply, pushed the umbrella back up and walked out when Cameron unlocked the car and told him where to find it.

A few minutes later the butler escorted them into a large sitting room, Ivy stared out the window at the view beyond the fence. Through the rain they could see for miles. Green and trees and rock walls. It was beautiful.

"Sir, Miss Masters and Mr Kemp to see you, sir."

"Thank you, Higgins." A desk chair turned and Lamont Gabriel Thornton stood.

He was a tall man, which Ivy had noticed on their first meeting. She and her mother were rather tall, so it wasn't definite that the height genes were her father's. But the eyes, oh how those same eyes stared back at her in the mirror for her entire life.

"Welcome," he said, holding out his hand to Cameron first and then Ivy. They held on for longer than necessary as they took each other in.

"You look like her—"

"I have your eyes—"

They both spoke at the same time. After a small chuckle, he offered them a seat.

"Why wouldn't you see me?" Ivy said, determined to have a lifetime of questions answered.

Gabe released a sigh that seemed to spring from the tips of his toes, gaining momentum as it went, ending in a rush of breath. "There are so many reasons, some good some bad, but I suppose the most important one for me was my promise to your grandmother after Anita, err…um your mother died."

"What promise?" Ivy swallowed forcefully.

"How about I start at the beginning and go from there? Otherwise, we'll be going in circles." Gabe answered and pulled out what looked like a photo album from the table beside his armchair and placed it on the larger coffee table in the middle of the room.

"These are photos of your mother."

Ivy picked up the well-worn album and cautiously opened the cover. Even though Cameron was sitting next to her, he somehow gave her the space she needed to study her parents' history. Her hands trembled as each page became another in the story of her past, one that until this point no one had shared with her.

When she reached the end, she looked up and gave Gabe a sad smile.

"Thank you. I wish I'd seen some of those pictures on the lonely nights I spent without my parents. Please tell me everything." The demand came out even, but the intent was clear. Ivy was old enough to know what really happened.

Gabe pushed back in his chair and rubbed his hands down his thighs as if looking for some traction to tell Ivy possibly the most difficult thing she'll ever hear in her life.

"This whole sorry tale is hard to revisit, even after all these years."

As he drew in a breath, Higgins appeared at the doorway with a tray of morning tea, including the offering Ivy and Cameron had bought. The three of them took the cups and Higgins distributed the plates with the cake, then turned to leave the room as silently as he entered.

"Perhaps the best option is to start from the beginning," Gabe explained. And that's exactly what he did.

GABE AND ANITA'S STORY

GABE - 1990 - AUGUST TO EARLY DECEMBER

The afternoon was dark as I watched the heavy grey clouds rolling above me in early spring. I stood mid-pitch with some of my teammates, hands on hips and sucking in each badly needed breath. The first game back was always hard, but today was worse than normal. The expats were putting up a real challenge. Thirty minutes in and we were already two goals down.

Our goalie booted the ball back to the centre, and we took our starting positions, again. There was a holler from the sidelines that made my blood boil. I turned as an Australian accent rang out. It was so true what they said about the loud-mouthed Aussies. Though this was the first outspoken female I'd encountered.

I was intending to return her dig when the sentence stalled in my throat. I coughed to clear my airways. I couldn't believe my eyes. Standing there was the most beautiful woman I'd ever seen. Never had I seen the complete package. The looks, that mischievous smile and those piercing eyes. I rubbed the centre of my chest, not from the breathing thing, something else was causing a ruckus. A slight discomfort distracting me in that moment and would remain in my heart forever.

"You boys coming to the pub?" One fellow called as we stood in the change rooms discussing our dismal performance.

"Sure," Bert answered. The corner of his mouth hitched. "Which pub?"

"The Traveller's Arms."

Bert and I didn't say another word. Our aim was to get showered, changed and meet the boys at the pub. The Traveller's Arms was known as the expats pub. Just maybe I'd get another look at the woman who mesmerised me into submission earlier. And besides, shouting a round for the expats was the least we could do after they'd played a great game. From their point of view, a win against the locals, five to nil, would have been something worth celebrating.

Precisely eighteen minutes later, Bert and I sat down at the end of the bar with all the lads, though I was searching for one particular woman.

"And one for my buddy, Gabe," Bert said.

Beers were placed before us at the same moment as the woman I was hoping to meet walked behind the bar with a tray full of empty glasses.

"Hell, it's a busy one tonight, Deb."

I looked around and saw not only a couple of soccer teams but also a large group of people dressed up. Were they really wearing outfits from the Rocky Horror Picture Show?

"Could you pour thirty-six pints, please?" The woman asked, ringing up a sale at the register.

Deb poured, and the other woman walked off with the first full tray. I realised this was my chance to meet her.

"Shall I follow her with this tray, Deb?"

Eyeing me through squinted slits, I could feel her sizing me up.

"Anita," Deb directed her words over my shoulder, "This lovely young man has offered to carry a tray for you."

"Thanks, that would be great. Deb, keep pouring they want one more round before the play starts next door."

Not having to be asked twice, I picked up the tray and followed the woman who was addressed as Anita. Together we ferried another three full trays to the men in drag and I helped her carry the empties back after the crowd left.

"Have you ever seen the Rocky Horror Picture Show?"

Anita's chuckle was so sweet. I was lost at the sound of it. "No, not really my thing," Her face relaxed and her smile looked totally at home, "But they are a lovely bunch, that lot." She said nodding to the closed door. "They do the same thing every week. This week there seems more of them though."

"Do they always get dressed up like this?"

"Some do, others just enjoy the social scene."

"Have you ever been to a performance?"

"I work Saturday nights," she shrugged, "So, I couldn't even if I wanted too."

"Fair enough." I took my seat with the lads and watched her for the next couple of hours.

Just before closing, the lads dispersed. "See you next week," Bert called, but didn't move an inch.

"We going?" I asked, nudging Bert's shoulder with mine.

"No. We've been asked to escort these lovely ladies home. Warren normally does it, but he had a hot date." A thought crossed my mind, why was Warren out on some hot date when he could be with Anita? Maybe she'd just arrived.

"So how long have you been in London," I asked Anita as I fell into step beside her.

She pulled her winter coat tighter around her, which seemed unusual as it wasn't at all cold. Maybe that action was more from nerves as we walked beside each other. At least I hoped it was.

"Eight months on Wednesday, to be exact," came her reply.

"That sounds like an anniversary worth celebrating, I'm heading back home to see my family tomorrow but I'll be back for class Wednesday morning, so what do you think?"

The blonde looked up and gave me one of those smiles that could melt a North Pole ice cap. "Where do you recommend that will be cheap? Pub wages don't stretch very far."

"My invite, my shout," I added. Was she really considering my offer?

"Sorry, no can do. You're studying, so there's no way you're paying for me. We go Dutch or it's fish and chips." Anita shrugged.

I watched her closely, intrigued by the way she was considerate of my budget. Maybe her life had been a struggle. Or better still, maybe she was this respectful of everyone. Being me, my social life was full of women throwing themselves at me, wanting me to buy them the world. Anita presumed nothing and discussed everything.

That really appealed.

Without a reply, Anita presumed, "Fish and chips. Excellent. Deb, are you available for fish and chips on Wednesday night?"

Deb lent forward. "Yeah, sure. Why?"

"We're celebrating my eight-month anniversary of arriving in London." Anita told her friend, leaning past Bert's large frame to see her.

"Are you in, Bert?" I asked, holding back a grin. A communal dinner wasn't quite what I had in mind, but it would do for now.

Wednesday evening at precisely six o'clock, I raised a fisted hand to knock on the girls' front door. I turned up the collar of my black leather jacket and waited.

When Deb opened the door, Bert and I were greeted with, "Evening, come in. Anita just got home, she won't be long."

As I stepped inside, I looked around the shabby three-room shoe box and instinctively understood the girls' financial position. I, on the other hand, bunkered down in my parents' city dwelling with three other guys from uni. We had the best of everything because, well, my parents could afford it. As for the three other guys, they were surviving on a meagre trust fund which would buy the girls' hell hole a few times over every year. Bert wasn't wealthy, but he was clever with his money. I helped him set up a small nest egg. Every month he would put a bit aside from his part time job in his parents' shop just off Hyde Park. He was studying in London.

When Anita stepped out of the bathroom a few minutes later, she looked dressed to dazzle. I was speechless for a few seconds. It wasn't her clothes, her short flowing skirt held up by a wide elastic belt, her brightly coloured floral shirt or hairstyle, though they were lovely. It was more her...charisma. The woman made everything seem bright and warmer when we were together. Take the shoebox of a room. It appeared to double just because she was there.

The fish and chip shop around the corner was only a short walk away. As we strolled along, Anita greeted everyone. Other Aussies, a French woman older than Anita who gushed over her with a smile. She shook hands with an Indian man and his wife, nodding as she did so, and then laughed and waved when another woman across the road called out a friendly greeting. In that moment, I was drawn to the miracle that was Miss Anita Masters.

I was experiencing the most amazing time I'd spent with anyone. I discovered Anita was a hard worker. She studied, saved hard, invested her money. Spending beyond her means was never a consideration. She was very careful and smart financially. There was no nonsense with Anita. From that point on, we were inseparable. Days turned into weeks and then months.

We'd been dating for nearly four months when I arrived at Anita's and she answered the door with red-rimmed eyes. It was the first time I'd seen her upset.

"What's the matter?" I stepped inside and wrapped her into my arms.

"I spoke with my parents this afternoon, they asked when I'm heading home."

"Do you have to go?" My hands trembled as I caressed her long blonde hair.

"My initial intention was to only stay a year," she looked up at me with tears in her eyes, "But you happened."

"What did you tell them?"

"That I'd met someone." Anita looked at me again. She paused and sighed, "Someone very special." She smiled while playing with my fingers, as she often did.

We sat in silence for a few moments, "Can you get the weekend off and come with me, I want you to meet my family?"

"Really?"

I'd spoken about my family but never hinted at introducing Anita to them. "Absolutely, they'll love you."

We spent the evening cooking a meal of creamy herbed chicken and rice. That seriously was the best part of my day. After dinner had been demolished and dishes were done, we sat opposite each other, at the small dining table and studied. Looking up occasionally, I could see Anita hard at work, but not with her usual vigour.

"Okay, so we are doing this?" I asked to get her attention. "You're coming to Devon to meet the family?"

After class on Friday, I stopped by Anita's place where she was running around packing the last-minute things. "Sorry, I stayed back to speak with the lecturer after class."

"That's okay," I laughed as she rushed around frantically, "How was your day?"

"The best, as always." Anita gave me the beginning of a smile. There was always a silver lining with Anita.

"What did you need to speak to the lecturer about? Are you struggling with something?" It amazed me how we spoke about everything. Absolutely everything.

"We were discussing the movement in my stocks. He thinks I'm playing at this, he doesn't know I've invested for real." Anita groaned, "My earnings are increasing, and I suggested another stock to him today, and yet again he canned that possibility as well. You'd think by now he'd realise I actually understand the market and its volatility." She shrugged her left shoulder with her head favouring that side.

It was so cute.

"Exams next week and I'm done. Completing my Masters in Investment is more than Mum and Dad ever thought I'd do here."

I realised maybe she'd decided, "Are you going home?"

"No. Sorry I didn't mean to suggest that. At least now I can show them what I've achieved." She played with the jumper she was folding. "But..." she stammered.

"What?" The thought of her deciding to leave was like a punch to the gut and a knife in my heart.

"I'm their only child. If I choose to stay…" her voice trailed off. She shook her head and sighed. "How about we cross that bridge when we come to it?"

Her normally calm voice was anything but, I could see this decision was hard for her right now. Taking her to meet my family this weekend was the best idea I'd had.

"Okay, I'm packed." Anita announced, shredding the funk of a minute earlier.

"Well then my lady, your carriage awaits," I bowed low before picking up her bag and following her out to the car.

GABE - 1990 - EARLY DECEMBER

"Oh, Gabe darling, you made it, I was getting worried."

"Hello Mother," A kiss from my mother was like a warm blanket wrapped around me, I couldn't hold back a smile when we both lingered on the hug. "We just got away later than we hoped. Mother, this is Anita."

I watched as the two women appeared to study each other for a few seconds. My mother was a lovely lady, respectful of everyone she met until they gave her cause not to, and Anita was so positive this could only go one way.

"Anita, how lovely to meet you. I'm Bridget, welcome to our home."

"Thank you for having me this weekend, Mrs Thornton" Her voice was shaky and her normally composed posture appeared to wane. I looked from my mother to my girlfriend trying to understand what was happening. The two women shook hands and mother cupped her spare hand around Anita's already clutched one. It was such a friendly gesture.

Next thing I heard was my little sister's shouts. "Gabe. You're here!" She practically launched herself at me.

"Scarlett," as always, I picked her up and swung her around. Both of us laughing at the absurdity of our actions as Anita watched on with a grin.

"Where's Father?"

"I'm coming," he called from the boot room. "Just feeding those dogs of yours." I loved that my father was never short of a hug either.

"Father, Scarlett, this is Anita Masters," I announced with my arm still wrapped around my father's shoulder.

He turned to Anita and pulled her in for a hug. "Welcome young lady, please make yourself at home."

Anita swallowed hard. "Thank you, sir."

"And none of this Sir or Mr. and Mrs.," Mother scolded. "This is Monty and I'm Bridget, and that's what you're to call us."

Anita finally smiled. "Okay, thank you…Bridget."

"Much better. Now dinner will be in half an hour, so please take Anita into the study to ring home. And please call me to say hello to your mother, darling."

"No…no…no." Anita's hands waved like paddles on a tarmac, "I don't want to waste your money. It's fine."

"My dear," Mother began, "Gabe explained you only manage a brief call home every week and asked if you could call your parents for a proper chat when you arrived. Monty and I thought that was a wonderful idea." Now it was Mother's turn to wave her hands, but in a shooing motion. "Go on. Then Gabe can show you your room for the weekend."

In the study, Anita pulled out her little red address book and dialled. She held out the phone so we could both listen. First there were the beeps, then her father's voice.

"Rod Masters."

"Hi Dad."

"Oh, hi love, how are you?"

"I'm good. Just wanted to let you and Mum know that we arrived in Devon."

"How was the drive?"

"Long. It's nearly four hours from London."

"That's not long," her father chuckled.

I wasn't sure what the joke was, but Anita waved it off, laughing with her father. There was a click of an extension and Anita's mother spoke.

"Hello love. Was there any snow?"

"Hi Mum. No, nothing yet, but Gabe tells me we'll probably get some in the next week or so."

I ducked out the door and called down the hallway to my parents. I heard them pick up the phone in the lounge room.

"How was the last exam?" her mother asked.

"Hard, but finished. They're all out of the way now."

"Well done, love, I'm so proud of you," Rod praised.

"Thanks Dad."

"Hello," Mother's voice joined the conversation.

"Mum, Dad, this is Bridget and Monty Thornton, Gabe's parents." Then to my parents she added, "These are my parents, Judith and Rod Masters."

We listened on as the four adults chatted. Scarlett arrived at Anita's side and settled onto her lap, listening patiently. The conversation began a little stilted, but our parents were so open and friendly before long they fell into a comfortable rhythm. My mother assured Judith and Rod that their daughter was looking well and happy. Anita and I grinned at each other as my sister occupied her knee and our parents chatted and laughed for the next ten minutes until finally Anita's father said, "Well, we better stop wasting your money. It was so lovely to talk to you all. Thanks for the opportunity. You fine people go off and have dinner. Anita, we'll talk to you again soon."

Judith's voice called out a farewell and then to Anita she added, "Take care darling, thanks for calling," she finished the call as I soon learned, the way she always did. "Love you and speak very soon."

"Love you both too. Bye." I didn't miss Anita swallowing hard when she hung up.

"You okay?" I asked, my tall frame crowding her slender one while we sat side by side on the couch with Scarlett still cuddling into Anita.

"Yes, thank you. I often find myself emotional after hearing their voices again."

"You sure you're okay?" asked Scarlett.

"More than okay. Now come on let's clear our bags out of the hallway and then help your mother with dinner."

The meal of roast beef and Yorkshire puddings seemed to have done the trick. Anita settled in well and joined in the table conversation. This was the woman I was drawn to.

The weekend was spent with my family, and Anita went along with whatever my parents planned. Saturday morning, we all piled into Father's car and drove through the local countryside pointing out all the places the family would take Anita when she visited in the spring, summer, and autumn. Anita loved the coastline. As we drove to the English Channel at East Prawle, Anita observed, "The rugged coastline seems to work hard fighting back the angry sea."

"You're not wrong. Over to your right," Father pointed out, "Are wonderful walks. Come and join us in the summer and we'll do a couple of them."

Anita looked at me as if asking for my approval, I nodded eagerly. "Thanks, I'd love that."

"There's also Darlington Court, which you must visit," Mother turned to Anita as she spoke and saw Scarlett asleep with her head in Anita's lap. She gave Anita a friendly smile.

Scarlett and I have always been close, so it meant so much to see Anita and Scarlett hit it off so well. It made my heart swell with pride. I watched as Anita leaned into me as she gently ran her fingers through Scarlett's hair. Maybe a guy isn't meant to notice such things, but I did, and it meant the world.

When we pulled into one of the local pubs for lunch, Anita gently woke her new best friend. Mother and I shared a knowing look as we watched Scarlett slip her hand into my girlfriend's as they walked inside. They sat together and Anita lavished as much attention on my sister as she did on me. It was effortless, the way Anita cared for Scarlett.

GABE 2017 – FEBRUARY

Gabe sat forward in his chair with his elbows pressing hard into the flesh of his thighs. The retelling of this story proved excruciatingly harder than he'd expected. What an idiot! How could he think after all these years he'd be untouched by the pain of his previous life? He sat in silence, trying to stop the pounding of his heart against his ribcage.

He couldn't go on. Remembering living here with Ivy's mother, enjoying his life as they grew closer to one another. He glanced over at the small table beside his seat and noticed Anita's diary. The one book that managed to soothe and calm him when things cropped up. He stared at the leather cover and eventually reached over and picked it up. Opening the book, he fingered the pages and looked to Ivy. Yes, for now this was the only way to go on.

ANITA'S INTIMATE THOUGHTS

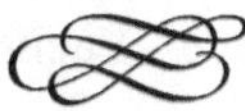

IVY - 2017 FEBRUARY

"Sorry, Ivy," Gabe gulped as he stood with a beautiful leather book in his hand. Was he stopping? Finishing his story there when she could tell there was so much more to learn.

"This is your mother's diary, could you just give me a few minutes?" He opened the book to where a frayed slip of material poked out the bottom. "This is when your Mother and I would travel to and from Devon on weekends to visit my family."

He dropped the book into her lap and Ivy watched him as he walked over to the window. Settled his legs hip width apart, crossed his arms over his chest and stared out to the world beyond the sitting room.

Ivy read aloud to Cameron, but hopefully it wasn't loud enough to upset Gabe.

ANITA'S DIARY ENTRIES – 1991 FEBRUARY

Evening my dearest companion, though you are slowly losing that title, as I discover perhaps the sweetest family in the world second to my own, of course.

Oh, how I miss everyone back in Chester's Run. I wrote a letter today to Tessa and Jack. I can't wait to receive their reply. Well, it's Tessa's reply with Jack's scrawl attached to the bottom of her letter. But I must admit, he says the sweetest things for a twelve-year-old boy. Oh gosh, I've just realised both he and Scarlett are about the same age. How cute!

Well, I make my entry this evening filled with joy and a sense of achievement. Now that I've completed my Masters in Investment, and Gabe's heading home every weekend to help his father organise things before their big skiing trip, I was fortunate enough to tag along again this weekend. While the men locked themselves away for hours on end, I spent time with Scarlett and Bridget. We braved the elements and bundled up against the chill of the morning flurry and headed down to the stables and arena. I watched on as Bridget schooled Scarlett in her riding lessons.

"That's it darling, keep your back upright. Feel the horse beneath you."

"She's very accomplished, isn't she?" I asked Bridget as we stood side by side watching Scarlett taking her horse, Willow, through its paces.

"Do you ride?" Bridget's face screwed up. "I'm sorry. I never asked before. I'd presumed not."

I'll never forget Bridget's dismay when I let out a chuckle. "Yes, ever since I could walk, apparently. Both my father and uncle are prolific riders. Well known for their talents with quality horses back home in Chester's Run."

"Oh Anita, let me get you a horse. Why didn't you say?" Bridget called their groom over, "Mitch, could you saddle up Toby for Anita, please?"

"Certainly ma'am."

Ten minutes later he led a bay stallion out. He stood nearly sixteen hands. "Would you like a leg up?" the groom offered.

"No thanks," I replied with a smile as I took the reins in one gloved hand and mounted Toby with an effortless stride. I smiled down at the pair of onlookers, "Where shall I go? I don't want to disrupt Scarlett."

"How about you lead her, she'll follow you?" Bridget called out to her daughter, "Follow Anita, love."

"Okay, Mother." Scarlett called back and waited for me to trot ahead of her.

Bridget and Mitch stood dumbfounded as we ran Toby and Willow through their paces around the arena. Scarlett working hard to mimic my every move. We rode together for at least an hour, a dream come true for me, with Bridget barely having to say a word.

Oh, dearest diary, you have no idea what it was like to feel the power and strength of a horse beneath me again. And what made it even more special was I shared that experience with Scarlett. We are becoming so close. It's times like these I realise what it would have been like to have a sibling. Especially a sister.

"Well, I think you have just found your new instructor," Bridget announced to Scarlett as we both dismounted.

"Where do we wash them down?" I asked.

"Oh, don't worry about that love, Mitch will do it," Bridget explained.

"Would you mind if we did? My father and uncle always taught us to wash and brush our own horses, so we'd know if they were uncomfortable or sore. Uncle Tony says the best way to know your horse is to be one with him," I said as I patted Toby's long neck.

Mitch looked over to his boss, a frown settling on his face.

"Sorry if I've overstepped," I quickly added when Bridgett failed to comment. I was sick to the stomach thinking that I could have undermined Bridget, it was never my intention. She's been so welcoming to me.

"Oh no dear, you haven't overstepped, you've opened my eyes to an oversight. Thanks Mitch, could you please lead the ladies to the washing station and find all the equipment they'll need? Anita, can I leave you in Scarlett's safe hands? I have to begin lunch."

We busied ourselves with the horses while Mitch looked on. As I was taught, I took delight in teaching my charge. There was an unexpected thrill in teaching Scarlett about horses the way I'd been taught.

Together we ran our hands over Willow. The buckskin pony stood stock still, only his ears flickering. As I guided Scarlett's hands over the silky coat of her horse, I sensed a deeper appreciation for her connection to riding and all things horses. I must remember to get her a jigsaw puzzle of a horse, just like Willow. We started doing puzzles together when we're not busy doing other things.

I spoke to her the way my dad and Uncle Tony did with Tessa, Jack and I, "Go gently, let the horse know you care about him." It brought back memories of riding at home.

I don't think I've really been able to describe the warring factions inside of me before. But today I have really fought hard to hold in the tears of missing home. I love my parents and extended family, especially Tessa and Jack, who have always been the closest thing to siblings I've ever had. But I think my love for Gabe is stronger. I have never believed in soulmates before, but I can't help but think I've found mine.

Scarlett's hand continued the exploration as I watched on in silence. She followed the backbone before tracking down each leg alternately. Finally, looking up at me, she asked, "Willow didn't move, does that mean she's not hurt?"

I couldn't help but laugh. "It means that she knows you care about her. Now watch Mitch as he checks the horse's hooves."

When the two horses were back in their stalls, feed and water topped up, we snuggled back into our wet weather gear and ran through the sleet back to the house.

"Can we do that again?" Scarlett begged.

"If your parents don't mind?"

After washing up, we went into the kitchen to help with lunch.

I listened as Scarlett told her mother everything. "Mother, I got to run my hands all over Willow and she just stood there patiently. She seemed calmer when I did that." Scarlett gushed. "And Anita let me watch while Mitch checked her hooves. She said that if you know your horse then you'll both be safer. They'll tell you what's wrong with them, she'll trust me more."

Bridget ran her hand over her daughter's cheek, "I think Anita is a hidden gem. Now set the table, good girl. Anita, could you please go down and get the men, lunch will be ready in five minutes."

I loved knowing Bridget treated me as she did her daughter, giving me jobs to do and errands to run. These people were so amazing and friendly. Being in Devon is just like being at home with my own folks.

IVY – 2017 FEBRUARY

Taking a moment to gather herself, Ivy looked around the sitting room, a place her mother apparently called home, and closed her eyes. Could she feel her mother's presence? There was something familiar about being here, but logically the whole notion was just ludicrous.

Opening her eyes again, she sought out Gabe. He was motionless. The man looked lost in his own misery.

With no movement or interaction from Gabe, Ivy fingered another fraying length of ribbon and flipped to that page. If her father would not talk, then she'd read on and give him some more time.

ANITA – 1991 MARCH

Greetings, my trusted friend. I thought I'd write today to remember the simple and sad days here in Devon. I have so many wonderful memories, but today was rather different from normal. But before I get into that, Monty and Bridget spoke with my parents again today. It wouldn't surprise me if they chatted every week whether or not I'm here. Anyway, on to my memories of today.

The family sat down to breakfast, with travel brochures strewn across the unused end of the long wooden dining table. I listened as they spoke of Austria, skiing, accommodation, hotels and all the touristy things they'd been entertaining as possibilities for Monty and Bridget's three-month trip away.

Bridget sat fiddling with her pearl necklace, looking from Gabe to Scarlett and back again. "Will you two be okay? I think I've remembered everything you need to know. It's all in the note pad on my desk."

"Don't stress, Mother," Gabe lowered his voice and smiled. "I'll be home Friday night and return to London on Monday for Tuesday's classes. Scarlett will be fine with Mrs Dyer. You and Dad have been looking forward to this for a long time, don't go getting cold feet now." I loved listening to his crisp English accent.

"Will Anita come up and give me horse riding lessons?" Scarlett asked, practically bouncing in her seat.

"I'm sorry, that's not possible," I said, and breathed through the squeezing of my heart. I hated saying no to Scarlett. "I have a job in London and I think I've pushed my luck enough coming up for the last three weekends in a row."

The pouting bottom lip from Scarlett told everyone what she thought of that outcome.

"Scarlett," Monty admonished in his eloquent voice, which gently scaled up as he spoke. "Please don't pressure Anita. She has to earn a living, though I hope she knows she's welcome here anytime."

I couldn't hold back a smile at that comment. "Thank you, I'll try to come up every few weeks. I am looking for another job, so my weekends are free. If I can find something, then if Gabe will have me, I'd love to visit."

Scarlett expelled a rushed breath. "You can give me riding lessons and we can… Oh, I can't think of what we can do, but we can do…everything."

We all laughed, knowing Scarlett hated to sit idle.

The doorbell rang, and Monty excused himself from the table.

The rest of us continued to chat, well until we heard Monty's voice, "Bridge, love do you have a minute?"

After Bridget left the room, Scarlett urged me to plan an activity for after breakfast.

"Sorry we can't spend more time together," Gabe cut in, taking my hand in his. It was common knowledge the men would retire back to the study and Bridget had notes to write up from Thursday night's fundraising meeting. She was president of the local hospital's fundraising committee.

"I have a jigsaw puzzle with 3000 pieces," Scarlett's eager voice exclaimed.

I grinned at Gabe. We were both amused by Scarlett's persistence to be by my side.

An idea to bake something jumped into my head. As a child I would work side by side with my mother in the kitchen, she was a wonderful cook. She turned meal times into something memorable. How we all kept our figures probably had more to do with working the property and the horses than it did with under eating, which was never a possibility when Mum and Aunty Darla got together to cook.

So, I suggested, "Or we could bake a pie for dessert tonight."

"What about a cake? Could we please bake a cake?" Scarlett's body bounced with the idea.

"Only if you make a chocolate cake with ganache," Gabe's brows lifted.

Scarlett's little mouth screwed up. "Which one?"

Gabe released my hand, stood up and left the dining room. He was a man on a mission. He returned a few minutes later with a cookbook. When he opened it, the spread displayed the best-looking chocolate cake I'd ever seen.

"Have you made this before?" I asked, swallowing back the threatening drool. No one needed to see that.

"Mum has twice," Gabe said.

"Yes, this one. Please?" Scarlett begged.

IVY – 2017 FEBRUARY

"Do you believe me when I say your mother loved it here?" Gabe asked as he turned back towards them.

"Yes. I know her handwriting anywhere and to read her words," Ivy pressed her hands to her cheeks, "I feel like she's right here with us now."

"Don't think me stupid, but I'm not sure she ever left." Gabe said as he came over, took the diary, and closed it. "Time for me to continue."

ILLNESS OF A FRIEND

GABE – 2017 FEBRUARY

"You okay?" Cameron whispered.

Ivy gave a small nod.

Gabe headed back to the window, looking out over the lush green acres of his property. The same view that had known the laughter and fun of Anita's presence.

"Scarlett tried to get me to reupholster the couch you're sitting on, but I couldn't. The memories of sitting there with your mother are still strong. We'd sit together and discuss everything. Nowadays that's where I connect with her, I ask her forgiveness." Gabe dropped his head, "Actually, I beg for it." He reached up with his right hand and cupped the back of his neck.

He breathed through the pain of remembering his beloved girl. How desperately he wanted his past to still be part of his future. He turned back towards his daughter. How he wished things were different. But after today, this woman, his daughter, for her own safety, would never be a part of his life. He had to tell her everything, regardless of the pain it caused him. He watched as she leaned into Cameron.

He sensed a connection between these two, but it wasn't one of ease. Closing his eyes, he prayed she'd find a strong man to protect her. Shaking his mind clear of how he'd failed Anita, Gabe began again.

GABE – 1991 MARCH

We all watched as Father led our mother back into the room and helped her into a chair, her face ravaged with pain.

"What's happened?" I couldn't imagine.

"That was Sylvie, Mrs. Dyer had a heart attack early this morning, she's in hospital, they're not sure she'll pull through." Mother's hands shook as she clasped them in her lap. The pain etched into her face. No one could process what this poor family was going through yet again.

"No way."

"Go get your mother's bag," Father instructed Scarlett. Turning to my mother he added, "I'll take you to the hospital and then we'll call around and see what we can do for the family."

"What about Johnny?" Scarlett cried, her delicate chin wobbling as tears tracked down her face.

"You get your things, too," he told us, "Let's see how we can help."

As Father drove, I sat contemplating the magnitude of the situation. Anita squeezed my hand and gave me a questioning look.

"My family really loves this woman." I whispered to Anita. Right then, I could see Anita was happy to be with us and to help. It was the mark of who she really was and everything she stood for. "She has five children, the eldest was the daughter who shared the devastating news, she's married and has a small girl. Next are the two boys close to my age. Then there were twins, a year older than Scarlett. A disabled boy and his twin sister." I paused when Anita turned her attention to Scarlett. She struggled with the news. Anita pulled Scarlett into a hug as I continued, "Her husband died of cancer about five years after the twins were born. Mum gave her jobs around the house to help her financially and they became firm friends."

"Will your mother be okay?" Anita asked. Mother had lost her usual carefree way.

How could anyone cope with another family tragedy like this? It was unthinkable for them to lose both parents.

At the hospital I stopped in the waiting room with Anita and Scarlett, while our parents made their way to Mrs Dyer's room. A few minutes later Father joined us and took a seat next to Scarlett. He wrapped an arm around her shoulder and kissed her head. Tears in his own eyes.

"What about when you go away?" Scarlett's shaky voice asked. "Mrs. Dyer was going to look after me."

"I know, sweetheart," Father pulled her closer. "Your mother and I will work something out." The strain on his face indicated he had no idea what they'd come up with at this late stage.

It broke my heart to watch on as Scarlett leaned further into Father's chest and cried. Even Anita wiped away a tear and she'd never met the woman. The whole thing was heart wrenching.

An hour later, when we arrived at Mrs. Dyer's house, the neighbours were gathered around the dining table of the small but spotless home. They were trying to help sort out a roster for looking after Johnny. He just sat in his wheelchair, looking out the window in silence. As far as intelligence went, Johnny was bright, but he was a quadriplegic, so doing things for himself were impossible.

Folks around the table shuffled along and made room for my mother as they listened to Johnny's eldest brother Markus, "We'll get him dressed of a morning, but if someone could organise his meals that would help. Stephen and I change him for Mum. But we must get to work."

"What care does he require?" Mother asked, entering the discussion. Her tone was one of the head of the fundraising committee now.

"Well, with Mum," Markus began, "He does his exercises, she won't give up on that."

Mother reached into her bag and pulled out her trusty notebook and jotted things down as Markus continued.

"He's also doing a course by correspondence in investments. Mum helps him three hours a day. They have built up a tidy nest egg between them." It was easy to see Markus was proud of his family.

They were all rather smart kids, but the opportunity didn't present itself after their father died.

"Mum takes him out every day unless the weather prevents it. Oh, and he has a couple of standing appointments every week." Markus took the diary Stephen held out for him.

"Thanks," he said to his younger brother. "Monday afternoon at two and Thursday morning at ten. Everything else happens around them," Markus said before shutting the book and handing it back to Stephen with a small smile.

GABE – 1991 — MARCH

"Thank you for joining us," I watched my father closely as we both entered the small reception room, which looked as if Mrs Dyer kept only to receive visitors. The trimmings on the couch and chairs were pristine and the rich colours set off the room. "Anita I've had this idea but if you don't think it's right for you please say so."

"Okay," Anita replied slowly, her eyes widening.

"We need someone permanent for Johnny, the stability is important to his progress. And for Scarlett once we've gone. I was wondering if you'd consider a paid position. You understand finance, which Johnny needs, and Scarlett loves you, so for us we'd know she was in good hands."

Anita's eyes bugged out of her head. "Me?"

"I know it's a bit to take on, but if you're interested."

I studied Anita's face, willing her to say yes and knowing for my parents this was their best option. Trying to get anyone at this late stage that they trusted and were qualified would be practically impossible.

"Umm, well." Anita swallowed hard. "I'd have to go back to the pub and give notice."

"Of course, I wouldn't expect anything less from you." Father nodded, his eyes locked on Anita.

"And pack up my stuff from the flat," she added, thinking on the fly.

No one commented. The only movement was my father rocking back and forth slightly, waiting for Anita to accept or reject his offer.

Anita ran a trembling hand over her golden hair and turned to me. "Gabe, what do you think? I don't want to push myself into your family." Her eyes shone, and I didn't miss the hidden message.

"I'm finishing up soon so we'll be here together," I said with a shrug, as I tried to reassure Anita without forcing her hand.

"If you just give me accommodation and food until you return, that would work. I'll find a job when you guys get home," at first she looked to my parents but as her sentence continued Anita turned back to me.

There was an undercurrent of questioning, I could see it in her eyes. Squeezing her hand, I added, "When Mother and Father get back, we can sit down and work out our next move, together." I wanted to make her understand this option would be perfect for everyone, but I didn't want her to feel forced into accepting the position.

"Okay. I'll do it." She agreed, nodding thoughtfully.

"Thank you," my mother sighed, pulling Anita in for a hug.

I chuckled as Father also stepped in and kissed her cheek. "You're a lifesaver, but I also know you're perfect for both jobs. Oh, and by the way," Father added as he pulled back, "There's a wage with this. A decent one."

Anita went to reply, but my father held up his hand. "This is not open for discussion, young lady," and with that my parents walked back into the dining room to put the option to the others.

Five days later Anita arrived back in Devon with me, my car full of her things. We talked all the way home. I could feel her bouncing in the passenger seat as we discussed options after my parents returned. I loved how we talked about our future together. There was an enthusiasm for our relationship and Anita's unconventional new position.

As Anita settled in, it was easy to see how much she loved the job.

She took hold of the opportunity to work with both her heart and her head, giving it everything she had. Driving back to London, my mind pondered how she'd taken it all in her stride. It comforted me knowing how well she fitted into our family.

Her work with Johnny began the following day. Mrs. Dyer was on the mend, but her progress was slow. Anita took the car my parents made available for her and headed over on Sunday afternoon to collect Johnny's workbooks. Her intention was to study the system his mother had in place. I remembered Anita marvelling about the woman's neat script filling pages and pages of a thick notebook. They were onto their third. The notes dictated by Johnny were in blue, and Mrs Dyer's added thoughts were in green. The system Johnny and his mother created was impressive, but instead of using green for her own additions, Anita decided purple would be her colour. Later they could distinguish between her notes and Mrs Dyer's.

Johnny's study was well over a week behind when Anita finally began. They tried to work longer than three hours to make up the shortfall, but Anita was respectful of Johnny's limitations to concentrate for longer periods. Together they discovered a satisfying balance which ensured lots of small breaks. During the breaks, Anita learned more about Johnny's family. The respect shone through for his mother and siblings. Johnny didn't carry on about his own situation. Though he did occasionally clinch his jaw and turn away from others, as they participated in things he couldn't. Anita found those times tough to experience.

GABE – 2017 FEBRUARY

Gabe blinked a few times, and smiled as he focused on his daughter, "You would have been so proud of the strength your mother showed. Not only with Johnny but with everything, especially you." Giving a slight shake of the head, Gabe added, "Anyway, where was I?"

"You were talking about Johnny," Cameron told him.

"Oh, that's right."

GABE – 1991 LATE MARCH

"How was your day?" I asked when I phoned Anita one night.

"Oh Gabe, he's such a pleasant young man. He speaks well despite his impairments, but his knowledge is beyond that of a normal thirteen-year-old. Though he holds some resentment at not having his mother with him, he has accepted my help and is becoming more respectful of my time." I could hear the delight as she spoke. "My days are full, working with Johnny during the day, and the evenings are spent helping Scarlett with her homework. It's great practice for when your parents go away." There was mention of how Anita would sit in the lounge and discuss finance with my father, they were tracking particular stocks and Anita shared her exceptional knowledge of the activity within the market. Shares were heading skyward, and she was tapping into the money being made from the short-term market.

I loved our weekends. We spent time together, Scarlett joined us so our parents could organise themselves for their trip.

Our parents never experienced a holiday like the one they'd planned to Austria, but with me finishing my studies they saw it as the perfect time for skiing in Europe. The plan was always for Scarlett and I to join them during the semester break for ten days. Now knowing Anita remained at home working with Johnny, I wasn't as keen on making the trip without her.

"Would the neighbours be able to pitch in for the week, just come for seven days," I'd begged.

But her only response was gentle, "That can't happen, Gabe, and you know it. Go with your parents and enjoy the time away. I'll be fine here." Though the words were kind, we both knew what she said was true.

When I arrived home that final weekend and pulled my car into the garage, Scarlett was there with a massive *'welcome home'* sign and balloons lining the back wall of the large garage.

"Surprise," she yelled when the garage door opened and I drove in.

"Hey squirt. What's all this?" I asked, putting her down after a hug.

"You don't have to go anywhere again," she gushed.

"No, that's right." I clasped her chin with my thumb and forefinger, "But you do," I couldn't hold back a laugh when she pouted.

This was her last year at home, boarding school was awaiting her in the fall.

The last week came and went and before we knew it the five of us were driving up to Heathrow where our parents were flying out.

"Look after yourselves," Father said, pulling Scarlett and me in for a hug.

Anita stood with her arms around Mother, who couldn't hold back her tears.

"Oh hell, I hate saying goodbye," my mother muttered into Anita's ear.

"Fine, then I'll say, see you in three months and have a wonderful time."

"Oh, we will." Mother agreed. "And thank you again for everything. Look after our babies," her gaze locked on both of us and we listened again to last-minute instructions.

"See you when we see you."

GABE – 2017 FEBRUARY

"But it wasn't to be," a pacing Gabe mumbled through roughened hands as they coasted the length of his crumpled face. On a sigh he continued, "Our parents were killed in a car accident in Austria. Six weeks later Anita and I stood either side of Scarlett as we buried our mother and father."

Ivy's hand rushed to her face as she gasped aloud.

Gabe didn't look at her. He couldn't. It would be like looking into

Anita's shattered eyes all over again. Instead, he did the only thing he could right then. He returned to his past and dragged out the sorry tale.

"That's when the roller coaster began. I barely understood what was happening. Anita kept both Scarlett and I going. The extended family stepped up to help us, but when they all returned to their own lives, it was Anita who held us together. She no longer worked for Johnny as Mrs. Dyer was better, so instead she took on the two devastated offspring of Monty and Bridget Thornton.

I met with my father's land manager and the lawyer, insisting Anita be by my side with everything. Luckily I did, because they were dipping into the family money. Anita picked up on things I'd missed. My father would have been so proud of her." Gabe came to sit down opposite Ivy. "I didn't deserve her, she was too good for me. We sorted it out, and they remained in my employment. That," Gabe said with his finger shaking in Ivy's direction, "Was my first mistake." The burden of his story clear in his voice as he clasped his hands together and gripped them tight. After a minute of trawling through unspoken memories, a harsh breath escaped, and he released the last bit of control. Gabe closed his eyes and forced himself to continue.

GABE – 1991 – SEPTEMBER

"You ready?" I looked to Scarlett as she stood in the hallway with her bags packed, ready for boarding school. This was our parents' plan for Scarlett, just as they'd done for me.

"You sure you still want to send her?" Anita's words were gentle, guiding and hopeful that I would back down. I was fully aware she didn't agree with my decision to follow through with my parents' wishes.

"I do." I answered with a nod and kissed Anita's cheek. I turned back to Scarlett, tears in her eyes pleading with me, but I had to see this through. Become the man my parents expected of me.

GABE – 2017 – FEBRUARY

Gabe stood again, unable to remain seated. "Anita's intuition was spot on. Scarlett gave the school and us absolute hell, it was left to Anita and I to deal with Scarlett's rebelliousness. At first her jeering was directed at Anita. In Scarlett's opinion Anita was trying to be her mother. The yelling from Scarlett soared to unexpected levels, Anita held her temper when I would have lost it. I looked on, amazed how much Anita cared for my little sister." He paced the length of the couch, turned, and stopped.

"The path was a long one, but she finally came around. Anita remained in contact with the school and counsellors, she was exceptional. During this time, the two of us became so close. After living side by side through all this, I knew your mother was the one for me. One night I took her out for dinner and asked her point-blank if living permanently in Devon would be possible. I still can see the shimmer in her eyes and her reply, 'If it's to be by your side forever then definitely.'"

"A year later, I proposed to Anita. She said yes. She and Scarlett were planning the wedding, the bridesmaids were going to be Deb, Scarlett, and Tessa if they were going to make it over. We found out they couldn't come to England. So, we were considering a change of location. Having the wedding in Chester's Run became a real possibility. We'd have a celebration back here for our friends and the local community. It would have been a thank you to the people who supported us through everything."

Gabe paused, rested his elbows on his knees, and steepled his fingers in front of his face. Lost in his memories, he slid into an abyss.

GABE'S DEEPEST REGRET

GABE – 2017 – FEBRUARY

"Iknow I'm skipping through so much of our lives, which was wonderful. I truly loved the time your mother and I spent together," Gabe said when he forced his eyes to connect with Ivy's. "But these are the parts you must know. The parts you need to understand. The hardest parts for me to live with."

He expelled a breath, leaned back in his chair and continued.

GABE – 1991 – OCTOBER

The phone in the hallway rung and Anita got up to answer it, I rubbed at tired eyes and strained my ears to hear who she was talking to.

"Gabe!" Anita shouted. "Come on, we have to go."

"Where? What's happened?" I jumped to my feet, still a bit dazed from my nap. I spread out the coals and returned the fire guard to its spot in front of the fire.

"They've rushed Scarlett to the hospital."

I led the way into the hospital, only stopping at reception because we needed directions to Scarlett. When we walked into recovery an hour later, Scarlett was unconscious and pale, she looked so slight against the hospital bedding.

"Apparently, she complained about a sore stomach to her dorm supervisor," the nurse explained. "Unfortunately, the woman thought it was period pains. When she went to check on her an hour later Scarlett was in a great deal of discomfort. They called an ambulance, but her appendix ruptured as they were racing her in. At this stage, all we can do is wait and see," the nurse with Cas on her name tag finished. "The doctor will be in to see you shortly."

I dropped into the empty chair by my sister's bed and sensed the moment I was shrinking into myself. First, I'd lost my parents, and now Scarlett was at death's door as well. I wasn't certain I could take any more.

I looked up to see an extremely pale Anita leaning in and talking to Scarlett. Sweet words of encouragement and reminding her of her role in our upcoming wedding.

"Hey beautiful girl, you must get better quickly, we have to pick out your dress. You'll be the most beautiful young lady in the town of Chester's Run. Your brother will be fighting the boys off with sticks." Her shaking voice was trying to be positive, "You'll finally get to ride my horse and see my father's stallion, Duke. Remember, I told you he was nearly seventeen hands. He's such a beautiful boy," Anita swallowed hard, looked up at me as she sucked in her top lip.

Anita continued this routine for hours until she finally got a response.

"My mother has found all my old jigsaw puzzles for us to bring back and…" Scarlett's hand gently squeezed Anita's. Her other hand brushed my sister's fringe off her forehead, "Hey darling, Gabe's right here." Just the change in Anita's tone told me that Scarlett was conscious.

"Hey kiddo," I jumped to her bedside, one hand clasping at my heart. "What are you trying to do to me? Worried me half to death." On the word death, Scarlett's eyes fluttered and I couldn't miss Anita's harsh stare. "But you're back with us now," I rushed on, "You just relax and get better. We're right here."

Scarlett stared at me as tears leaked down onto her pillow. "Your brother and I aren't going anywhere," Anita told her, "You rest darling."

For the next twenty-four hours Scarlett floated in and out of consciousness, leaving me at a loss. Surely if she came to, she was going to be okay? I sat with Anita's head in my lap as we waited for Scarlett to show more signs of improvement.

"How's she doing?" a male voice asked, waking us both from sleep.

"Smyth. What are you doing here?" I asked my land manager.

"My wife's sister works downstairs. She saw Miss Scarlett had been sent in and let us know, so I thought I'd check on how you're all doing."

I waited for Anita to sit up, then stood to speak with Smyth.

"She's in and out of consciousness. But according to the doctors, her vitals are all good. Her body needs to repair itself."

Smyth looked over at Scarlett. "What can I do for you?"

"Nothing, really. It's just a waiting game. Actually," I said, seeing Anita's still pale features, "Could you drop Anita off home. She needs a decent sleep."

"I don't need to go home," Anita countered.

"We don't need both of us wrung out, and besides, you look really pale. Head home and sleep, come back later this evening." Turning to Smyth, I added, "That is if you don't mind?"

"No, that's fine, I'm going that way." He looked over at Anita. "I'll wait for you outside."

"Thank you," Anita practically whispered.

I pulled her into my arms and kissed her. "You are an amazing woman." My hand cupped her cheek, "You're looking really pale. Go home and sleep, I'll ring if there's any change. I promise."

"Good or bad," she was insistent.

"Yes. Good or bad. Now go on and drive back only if you're up to it," I ordered.

I gave Anita a lingering kiss and as she walked away, our fingers were still touching until we could no longer reach each other.

IVY – 2017 – FEBRUARY

Sniffling at the door had Ivy spinning around to see who was making the noise. She gasped at the sight of an almost perfect match of herself standing propped against the doorjamb, a mere twenty feet away. The hair length was the same, but the colour was more like Gabe's in the photos Ivy saw earlier. Oh, those cheekbones. Ivy tilted her head. The shape of the woman's eyes was identical to her own.

Gabe stood and held out his arms. "Why did you come early?" he attempted to admonish.

"Could I lie and say I haven't spoken with Deb in months?" a sad laugh escaped her lips.

"Well, come and meet Anita's daughter." Gabe walked her around to the front of the couch. The woman was stunning. An older version of herself. Though this woman held herself well, she'd obviously attended some sort of finishing school.

"Finally!" she gasped out. "Ivy Bridget Masters-Thornton." A few tears leaked out as she smiled. "I always believed Anita, and now here's the proof." She clapped her hands for emphasis.

Ivy didn't have time to stand, she was pulled to her feet and into a hug, reminding her so much of her mother. At last someone from her father's family was happy to see her. The two women held on tight.

"Hi." Ivy croaked out when they released one another. The words 'Aunty Scarlett' wanted out, but Ivy didn't want to presume. "I can't believe it's only just clicked, but Bridget, my middle name, I'm named after your mother, wasn't I?" Ivy looked between her father and her aunt.

No one answered. What was there to say when the truth was plain to see?

The two women stood holding hands and swiping at tears.

"And who may I ask is this?" Scarlett asked, drawing in a deep breath as she took in Cameron.

Ivy looked down at an uncomfortable Cameron who sat quietly on the couch taking it all in. "This is Cameron Kemp, a friend, a good friend."

"Well Cameron Kemp, good friend of my niece's, welcome to Devon." He also was hugged. As awkward as it was, he didn't protest. "I understand the hard part is yet to come," Scarlett said, taking the third spot on the couch beside Ivy.

Aunty and niece clasped hands tightly as Gabe continued.

"What happened next was a blur and nothing I'm proud of."

GABE – 1993 – MARCH

The echo of the courtroom resounded as I sat there, Deb to my left and Bert on my right. My former land manager and lawyer in the dock, and Anita sitting between her parents behind her lawyers. My eyes switched from Anita to my former staff. I still couldn't believe the last year and a half and how it panned out.

"All rise," the clerk of the court announced.

Everyone stood except Anita, her wafer-thin body too fragile to obey.

The judge looked down at the Masters' family and then to the two men in the dock. "Councillor, I take it your client can continue?"

"She can, Your Honour. Ms Masters will be back in hospital directly after this." Anita's representative explained, I saw Anita's pale, strained face and hands clasped in her lap. I watched as the man nodded to the judge.

"As you wish. First, let me say, before I pass sentence on the men here today, I wish to say greed is a wicked thing. The injuries inflicted on Ms. Masters were not only cruel but despicable. Two men who took matters into their own hands when this woman realised their thieving and underhanded tactics to pilfer from Mr Thornton's estate are unforgivable. The means by which you treated her the afternoon she came into your care, Mr Smyth, is a crime against justice and humanity. All because you men looked to repay gambling debts to save your own necks."

I watched the judge as he spoke the accusing words to the men my father had trusted for years.

"You may justify your actions any way you wish, but your intent was to murder this young woman and make it look like suicide. Succeeding on getting her out of Mr Thornton's financial situation, leaving the way open for your deceit to continue. According to the reports from no less than three doctors, the rest of Ms. Master's life will be one of ongoing pain, not to mention the heartache of leaving behind the people she'd been so determined to protect. That she refused treatment trying to save the life of her unborn child will result in her premature death. May her final passing from this life be on your conscience till the day you die."

The judge dropped his gavel after he sentenced both men. They'd be released from prison eventually, but as very old men.

When the judge turned his attention to Anita, so did I.

"Ms Masters, I commend you for the choices you made at the time for your unborn baby. I wish the outcome could have served more in your favour. And the determination you showed to bring these criminals to justice, ensuring they can never commit a similar crime against another living soul. I wish for you peace and improving health."

The judge stood, his eyes roaming the courtroom until they landed on mine. "And as for you, Mr Thornton, the victim may have forgiven you for your rejection of her, but I suggest you, young man, study your own conscience extremely carefully and understand where you went wrong. Your sister is in your custody again now, but we will be watching you carefully."

I couldn't help dropping my head in my hands as the constabulary ushered the now convicted men from the courtroom. My lack of faith in Anita when Smyth accused her of attempting suicide after they had a supposed affair could have broken her spirit, but her strength to see justice done was the mark of this amazing woman.

IVY – 2017 FEBRUARY

"I'll never forget the last time it was just the two of us," Gabe said to his small audience as Ivy took in the truth of her existence. "We'd been together the day before while her parents sat in the next room of the hotel." Ivy squeezed her hand, forgetting she still clasped Scarlett's hand in hers. The two women shared a small smile. Both drawing from their connection. Gabe didn't seem to notice. He pushed on with the tale of his painful past.

GABE – 1993 – MARCH

"Why did you pursue them instead of worrying about your health and little Ivy's?" I begged to know…

"Because if it wasn't you next, it would have been Scarlett and in all good conscience, I couldn't live with myself knowing they would hurt either of you." Anita's shaking hand gripped his tighter.

"How's Ivy?"

"She's good, very good. Our little girl is growing up, and she's happy. I can guarantee that." Anita gave me a warm smile at the mention of our beautiful daughter. "How I didn't lose her in the fall will be forever a mystery to me."

"It was one of life's miracles. If only God would grant us another and keep the four of us together." I scrunched up my face, fighting back the pain of knowing it would never happen.

"Having Ivy is the only miracle I'll ever need. Our little girl will always be loved and free from danger." Anita shook her head and didn't continue.

"There's no more risk. Anita, you've taken care of that. Please, won't you reconsider? What about after you've gone? Can't I raise her? Be a father to her. I've missed so much already. With her and Scarlett, we'll be okay. I won't need anyone else in my life."

"Oh, my darling." Anita's head shook slightly again. "I must do this for my parents now. They can't lose me and Ivy, I won't let that happen."

Mopping at my tears, I nodded, "Why can't you agree to stay with me? I know I let you down, Anita. But I love you with all my heart. Can you ever forgive me?"

"You're a young man, Gabe, with enormous responsibilities. When Scarlett ended up in hospital, you seemed to close in on yourself and then this," Anita pointed to her ailing body, "This incident proved too much. You did what you thought was right for you and Scarlett. There's nothing for me to forgive." Anita now swiped at tears, first mine, then hers, "Promise me one thing?"

"Anything," I promised, clasping her hands tighter.

"Always remind Scarlett of how much I love her. And know I'll be guiding you both forever."

I could only nod. My heart seemed to constrict at her words.

"Please understand my need to keep Ivy in Australia with my parents," Anita squeezed my hand. I couldn't answer. "You need to put both of us behind you now, my darling, and begin again. Be happy, my love."

We sat in silence, hand in hand for a few minutes longer, until Anita spoke again. "Once this trial is over, you won't hear from us again. Well, not until my father has news for you. He promised to be in contact as you asked."

"Will they permit us to travel to Australia? To be there." I couldn't say the word. Her funeral sounded so definite. So painful. The end of everything we shared and meant to each other. Anita gently pulled my hand to her lips, the dampness of her wet tears tore at my heart. I expected her soft lips would leave an indentation in the back of my hand forever. I pulled her into a hug. A mix of tension, pain and emptiness mingling inside me. I had no one to blame but myself.

Till the day I die, I'll remember our last moments together.

I watched as her father wheeled her out of the courtroom, her mother by her side. Her parents displayed no pleasure at the outcome of the trial. How could they? No matter what the result, they'd lose their daughter forever, one day soon.

Anita's eyes locked with mine, both of us in tears. She was going back to hospital and then Australia and I'd lost my future wife and my only child. I wasn't ever going to marry. I had nothing more to give to another living soul. Except Scarlett.

THE ULTIMATE REJECTION

IVY

Silence engulfed the room. Ivy heard the tale which robbed her of both her parents. She was numb. How could…? Shit, why did…? Her mind spun. The one thing she'd hoped for was to meet her father, now she had. More and more questions bombarded her.

"I can feel you spinning," Scarlett said, giving Ivy's hand a gentle squeeze.

Ivy stood abruptly, breaking the connection. The need to pace was pressing on her. The weight of their stares settled around her. But there were too many unanswered questions. Reality hit as her thoughts raced, she clasped her chest and doubled over…all thoughts and stabbing pain was for her mother. The woman who loved her unconditionally. Given her life…at the expense of her own.

She was treasured and loved. She was so loved by the Master's family and now she stood in a room with her closest blood relations and realised after today her father would cut her out of his life again.

Cameron's gentle touch helped her focus. "Come and sit down."

His voice was so caring it made her want to cry. But right now, there were other things requiring her time and attention.

She went willingly. He sat her on a chair which looked out over a vast land, her father's property.

Ivy drew in a deep breath. Her aim was to clear her head in order to make sure they answered all her queries. Once she'd stepped back over the threshold, that would be the end of her only visit to this property. With that realisation her heart plummeted to the ground.

"Where was my mother plunged to her intended death?" That was one question she wanted to know as soon as Gabe spoke of the court findings.

"The property had a manager's cottage," Gabe's even tone replied. "We sold the land off just after your mother passed away."

"So, this is the house where she visited and lived?" Ivy smiled despite her sorrow.

It was Gabe who gave a small chuckle. "That chair right there," he pointed to where Ivy was sitting. "She'd sit there and plan her classes for Johnny and Scarlett, read, stare out the window lost in thought…"

"Jigsaw puzzles," Scarlett cut in, "Anita and I would spend hours doing jigsaw puzzles together, talking about everything. Including him," she added, her finger pointing to her brother. Now Scarlett grinned, though it was through reddened eyes.

"I still see her everywhere," Gabe said. "There isn't one room in this house which doesn't remind me of the woman I loved."

"In her letter," Ivy said, "Mum hoped that you'd moved on with your life. Settle down, have a family?" Ivy recalled.

"There was a woman," Gabe began and bit off whatever was coming next.

"And?" the question hung between them. Time passed and tension built.

Ivy turned to her aunt. But saw that Scarlett's eyes were focused on her brother's back.

"She was never the wonderful woman your mother was. In fact, I still suffer nightmares of my poor decision." Gabe turned to Ivy. The weight of his crossed arms pulled his shoulders down. He stared at the floor and eventually looked up again. Something like darkness seemed to surround him. He took on a hallowed look which almost convinced Ivy to let all this pain go.

"Do you know, since your mother, no other woman has ever turned my head and made my heart dance?"

"Do you say that out of guilt?" Ivy asked sincerely.

Gabe stared out the window, looking just over Ivy's head. He released a sigh, "No. Out of the deepest love and loyalty. The type of loyalty she deserved when I should have stood by her…and you, but by the time realisation dawned, I'd unwittingly given up that right."

"But she forgave you?" It was a question, although Ivy had read her mother's thoughts on the matter.

"Aye, that she did. Though your grandparents never did."

The twist of his lips sent a jolt through her. Ivy gently placed the pads of her fingers to her lips, as if his action caused her physical pain.

"And I haven't forgiven myself either," he replied eventually.

IVY

"Well, that's about all I have to share with you," Gabe said as he stood up.

There was no way she'd misinterpreted his meaning. The conversation was over.

Forever.

Ivy tracked his movements, her heart pleading against the inevitable. This was it, he'd kept his end of the bargain and now she was, dismissed. Her mouth formed the words and her voice projected, though she had no idea what she'd just said. But the looks from her father, her aunt and Cameron told her of mortification.

"I. Beg. Your. Pardon." Gabe spun on his daughter, his eyes told of his scarcely contained fury. "I told you how this was going to be and you accepted my terms."

His flaring nostrils didn't go unnoticed. Ivy tried to think fast, but her thoughts circled back to what she had said to upset him.

Oh, hell. The words now rolled around in her head, almost too heavy to keep her standing. Had she really finished the conversation with '*So you're rejecting me the same way you rejected my mother?*' No wonder Cameron and Scarlett could only stare.

Gabe picked up an almost pristine document case. Though the style screamed ancient, the brown pouch with its soft leather was feminine. Not matching Gabe's other office accessories.

"Here, this is yours, and the diary. Take them and leave." A vein in his neck bulged.

But Ivy didn't take the offering. Was it something to appease him? Well, any memory of him would only cause more pain and heartache. She wanted no part of his offering, as she attempted to move forward with her life.

Willing her body to cooperate and her knees not to buckle, Ivy walked to the couch and collected her bag and her mother's diary. Those words belonged to her now. There was no way she'd leave such a precious connection to her mother behind. She flung the strap of her bag over her shoulder and proceeded out of the room.

Cameron reached the car ahead of her, he held the door open and she climbed in, oblivious to the heavy rain and lightning in the distance. The only thing she was conscious of were the tears tracking down her face. Ivy stared into the abyss. No words shared, and she had no recollection of Cameron driving her away from her father's Devon home.

THE AFTERMATH

CAMERON

Muttering and pacing began once Cameron led Ivy into the suite they shared in London. He'd cancelled their trip to Bath and taken her back to the city. An idea formed as he drove home. He messaged Clem for help when he stopped to fill petrol just outside of London. His experience with stressed out women was non-existent. Sophie always comforted him growing up, not the other way around. Before Clem arrived, Cameron phoned his mother. Any help was better than none, and if he was honest, his mother was the best in the business at looking after others.

He expelled a loud sigh when her sleepy voice greeted him. "I'm so sorry I've woken you up, haven't I?"

"Something's wrong, Cameron, so just tell me," she encouraged in her soft, caring tone.

Cameron dropped into the chair near the door, his eyes on a pacing Ivy while he explained to Lindy what happened. He spoke, and she acknowledged with an 'aha', or 'yep', occasionally an 'oh no' dropped into the conversation as well.

Once Cameron finished the tale, Lindy was silent for a time. He waited with uncharacteristic patience. "You need to bring her home, Cameron. Ivy needs the people who love her by her side, that won't happen there."

For the first time, Cameron wanted to scream 'but I love her with all my heart, if only she loved me and not Liam.' In fact, right now he would even forgive her for the attention she'd showered on his brother. But this wasn't about him, it was about Ivy, and he'd remain focused for Ivy's sake.

Cameron looked up when the sound of Ivy blowing her nose brought him back to the present.

"Okay Mum, I'll organise it."

"Is she there, love? Let me speak with her. Put the phone on loud-speaker."

Cameron did as his mother directed and when Lindy's voice called out, Ivy stopped and stared as if the contraption was a deadly missile.

"Ivy honey," Lindy began, "Come and talk to me."

Ivy dived for the lifeline. Her shoulders seemed to lift ever so slightly, enough for Cameron to understand he'd done the right thing.

"H—hi Lindy," Ivy replied, "I'm h—here."

"Okay darling, I want you to listen to me," Lindy began her gentle persuasion and soothing. Her words were like a caress on his soul, he watched on as Ivy responded to the intervention. Slowly but surely Ivy joined the conversation and together they analysed and planned.

Cameron stood from the chair by the door when a knock rang out. Grateful for the extra support Clem's presence would provide.

IVY

"Thanks Lindy," Ivy repeated for the fifth time. "Yes, I promise. Now get some sleep and we'll ring again in a few hours." She'd taken the phone off speaker and held the handset to her ear. More grateful than words could say to have Lindy's soothing advice. An invaluable resource reminding her of the love which already surrounded her. Unconditional love.

"Okay, thanks, guys. Talk soon." Ivy disconnected the call and fell into Clem's waiting arms. Her tears began again because Clem understood the turmoil of Ivy's life. Not everything, but a huge portion. Phil hugged her next and Portia pushed from her father's embrace into Ivy's arms and squealed with delight, unaware of the tension in the room.

After a while Phil stood up. "Portia, come with Daddy and we'll go for a walk. Let's take Cameron to the playground."

The little girl clapped her hands with delight and chirped her approval.

"You'll be okay?" Cameron asked Ivy.

"Yes, thanks." Her eyes locked with his. "I think Lindy's right, it's time to head back home." There was a distant look on Clem's face, but being here now was useless. She needed to get back to the bakery and try to put all this behind her.

"Okay, we'll arrange it all this evening." Cameron leaned in and kissed her cheek, "Just ring if you need anything. Clem's much better at this stuff than I am."

She didn't miss the scarlet blush invading his cheeks. "What you did was wonderful, I'm here and I'm fine. Go clear your head." Her hand itched to caress his stubble spattered cheek. Instead, she used the movement of her fingers to play with one of her rings. Nice diversion tactic.

"Talk to me," Clem said once the door closed.

"Oh Clem, I can't believe what happened. He finished his tale and then that was it. He tried to hand me something, but I refused it and we left."

"What was his reasoning, this Lamont character?"

"He promised to explain and showed me the door and that's exactly what happened," Ivy grunted, "That and the fact that I landed a parting blow," she admitted.

"What parting blow?" Clem's furrowed brows seemed to clench further.

"I announced I was being rejected just as he had done to my mother."

"So, he can't handle the truth." Clem shrugged her shoulders, "He's not worthy of you, darling. Go home knowing you tried but failed because of his shortcomings, not yours."

Ivy huffed out a sharp breath.

"Knock, knock" a voice called out while the owner of the voice physically knocked. "I know you're in there, Ivy, open up."

The two women looked at each other.

"That's…" But Ivy didn't get to finish.

Clem jumped up and said, "Scarlett?" as she walked to the door.

Through the opened door the three women looked at each other surrounded by an uncomfortable silence. Clem's head swinging from Scarlett, her husband's relation, to Ivy?

"You two know each other?" Clem asked.

"You know Ivy?" Scarlett questioned simultaneously.

Ivy couldn't speak.

Scarlett took control. "What's going on here?"

"I'm here to console Ivy. Her father has just rejected her, and she's devastated."

"Hang on, let me get this straight," Scarlett frowned. "How do you know her?" This time her words were for Ivy.

"Cameron, the guy you met this morning was coming over for work and when I told my family I wanted to find my father, they decided this was the perfect opportunity, so I travelled with him," Ivy's voice came out soft and strained. "Cameron is working for Phil and Thomas's engineering business."

"So, you didn't know each other before you came over?" Scarlett asked, digging further.

"What are you accusing me of? And how do you both know each other?" Ivy's voice rose. This morning she had sat next to this woman listening to the truth of her mother's time in Devon and now, well now she didn't know what she was being accused of.

"Your father and I are Audrey's cousins, Phil's family." Scarlett's brows rose as she spoke.

"Gabe is your father?" Clem's focus shifted from Scarlett to Ivy. "You said your father was Lamont." Ivy saw her friend's eyes widen. But why?

"Lamont Gabriel Thornton." Ivy explained. "I only found out his full name last night at dinner."

"Oh, shit!" Clem exclaimed as she fell onto the couch. Her face paling as her hands pattered the cushions blindly searching for her phone.

She typed out a quick message.

Clem — *You need to be here for this!*

Phil — *What's wrong???*

Clem — *Come back now!*

Ivy couldn't take it in. Her mind raced with so many questions.

Why was Scarlett here?

Could she really believe Ivy planned to use Cameron's connection with the Anders family?

Amid all the confusion of the moment, one question would haunt her for the rest of her life. Why had her father rejected her?

CAMERON

Cameron and Phil burst back into the room. Once Phil received the text from Clem, Cameron's heart contracted with a vice like grip. Blood pounded in his ears as he tried to maintain a steady pace back to their suite. All he really wanted to do was run back to her as fast as he could. What in the hell had Clem meant by her words?

"Aunty Scarlett?" Phil's puzzled expression distracted Cameron as the fraught air swirled around them. "What in heaven's name are you doing here?"

"I just asked your wife that very question," the youthfulness of earlier was replaced by a menacing look, one that lacked trust or compassion.

"Hang on a minute. What's going on?" Phil asked, settling Portia on the floor, and watching as she tottered to Clem.

Clem pulled her daughter into her arms. "How about you take a seat and we'll start from the beginning."

Phil nodded and sat next to his aunt, and Cameron took the space on the other couch beside Ivy. His leg brushing up against hers and his eyes locked on her face. She looked lost.

Silence closing in for a long moment before Clem took control. When Portia was drinking contently from her bottle she said, "Ivy, explain to Scarlett how you and Cameron came to be here," Cameron sensed a shift in loyalties. However slight it was, it was still clear.

"Well, how about I tell you my side," Cameron offered, still not understanding the interrogation in progress.

He explained what happened with his father and how his mother encouraged him to branch out on his own. Phil supported his analysis of the events leading to his trip to London.

Somehow Scarlett's nod was important. And Cameron paused, waiting for it.

Cameron rested his hand on Ivy's thigh. "Now, it's your turn," he said, his teeth clenching as he forced a smile.

"After Cameron and his sister Sophie moved out of my flat above my bakery, I decided on cleaning up the spare rooms as I'd been planning on doing for a while. I was cleaning up when I found a box of memorabilia my mother left me. I remembered seeing it when I first moved back to Chester's Run but I wasn't ready to return to the past as I'd just lost my grandmother." Ivy shook her head and continued, "Anyway, I found the letters, one for me and one for my father." Ivy's hand flashed through the air as if the name was displayed proudly along an enormous banner, "Lamont Gabriel Thornton."

"At the same time there was this guy I was interested in but he'd just cut me out. I was down and needed to move on," Ivy fiddled with her ring again, one that went everywhere with her if she wasn't at work in the bakery. "Anyway, I decided it was time to find my father."

"Who was the guy?" Scarlett asked, her eyes bulging.

Cameron wanted to answer for Ivy when she didn't say but it

wasn't his place to throw his brother under the bus but hell, he wanted to. Because of Ivy's interest in him, Cameron backed off and gave her space, he found it difficult to do the friend thing with her but since this trip their connection was deepening.

"That doesn't matter," Ivy told her, shaking her head, "I've accepted where I stand with him."

Cameron caught a glare from Clem. What the hell? Why should he suffer for his brother's sins?

"Anyway, my cousin Jack and Cameron's mother, decided we should travel together. You know, safety in numbers and all that crap." She gave a dismissive wave of her hand.

"So, you're telling me you two knowing Phil and Clem are a total coincidence?" Scarlett asked through narrowing eyes.

"Absolutely." Cameron replied. "I'm the one who has a business connection with Phil."

Cameron looked at his new friend. "So you two know each other?" His hand hovered between them.

"Scarlett and her brother Gabe are my mother's cousins."

Phil took his wriggling daughter from his wife and continued, "The woman in the photo on your wall, she looks like Ivy. Is that her mother?"

"How do you remember that photo?" Scarlett asked.

Phil smiled. "That's easy, I've never seen Uncle Gabe as happy as he was in that picture."

IVY

Tears tracked down Ivy's face. She wished seeing her father smiling was a joy she'd experience, but it wasn't and by what Phil had just mentioned he hadn't been happy in a long while. Wiping away the tears and attempting to school her voice before speaking, Ivy asked, "So, how did you find us?"

DISCOVERING HIS ERROR

CAMERON

Cameron found himself a little on edge as he walked back to the suite after seeing Clem and Phil off. Ivy stood staring out the window overlooking the city of London. In the distance, the green of Hyde Park reminded him of Chester's Run. Oh, how he wished they were both back there right now. The leaves on the deciduous trees would be slowly turning to shades of autumn, getting ready to fall. He hadn't experienced autumn in Chester's Run. At this moment, he longed for home. He could picture it, walking the horses through the trails with the children, and maybe Ivy might even join them.

He studied her for a moment. Pain oozed from her, and he suffered on her behalf.

"Are you okay?" he asked.

Ivy didn't reply but her hands balled into fists as he looked at her.

"I'm so sorry Ivy. Come and sit down," Cameron suggested.

"What have I done to deserve rejection?" Ivy looked as if she expected an answer. Well, he didn't have a clue. Her eyes pierced him, her face transformed from a blotchy red to an enraged purple. "Men!"

She hissed the word out as if it was poison. "Never again will I allow a man to reject me."

Why was she angry at him? Her father, Ivy could change that but Liam. She should have chosen better, especially when Cameron was there waiting for her.

Ivy pushed past him to go to her room, but for some stupid reason he reached out and stopped her.

"Don't blame all men for the sins of the two who hurt you," he whispered.

"Why not? When one of them is standing right here." Each word came out as if they were the last words she'd ever speak to him. He was glad she couldn't breathe fire because in that moment he would have been burnt to a crisp. Though the heat of her accusation still seared him.

"What was it I did that made you treat me that way?"

"What?" Cameron's voice rose. "How did I treat you?"

"You rejected me just like my father did. One day we were the best of friends and the next day you wouldn't even join me at your family's table."

"You'd made your choice."

"How? Who? What the hell are you talking about?" He could see Ivy had been pushed to her limits. Cameron never witnessed her emotions getting the better of her like this before.

"My brother! Or don't you remember?" Cameron was matching her octave for octave now. "I dropped by the bakery to get my toiletries bag. The day after I moved out, I saw and heard you and Liam together. Your arm around him and his hand on your knee."

Ivy's eyes widened. "You think I'm interested in your brother?"

"I heard him say, 'what would I say to him. How would I tell him this after everything else we've had to endure over the past few months? Cameron's been doing so well. We've become so close. Ralph hasn't been there to manipulate us against one another. This could send him reeling.' I don't do my brother's rejects. And if you were smart enough you would have realised, he was going to reject you."

"Are you serious?" Ivy's arms flew high into the air. "I was being a friend just like I am with Jack's kids. Well, not even, with Jack's kids, I hug them and kiss them and spend time with them. I treated him like part of the family."

"I saw how close you were sitting to one another."

"You saw him struggling with a tremendous weight. Something he couldn't talk to any of you about. You've been so caught up in yourself you haven't even realised Liam is suffering at the moment." They were only millimetres apart as she spat the words at him.

Cameron's mouth fell opened. Oh hell, had he really got all this wrong? "You don't like him?"

"Me, like Liam?" Ivy's face seemed to elongate further with each word. She let out a sardonic laugh. "No." Ivy stepped around him and dropped to the couch, pulling a nearby cushion into her chest. "The idiot I liked, rejected me. Retreated to his bungalow and treated me like rubbish. No explanation. Nothing!"

"So, let me get this straight. You haven't kissed Liam."

Ivy's groan echoed through him. "A hello and goodbye kiss. Is that what you mean?" Her sarcasm grew.

"So, you don't like him?"

"As your brother, yes. As anything else, no. I was foolish enough to fall for the other one. The idiot who pre-judged a woman for helping his family."

Cameron stood there, his mouth agape.

"I'm desperate for a drink," Ivy stood, gathered her purse from the hall stand and walked out. Slamming a door for the second time that hour.

Cameron dropped to the nearest seat and stared at the pale blue wall ahead of him. There was only one way to find out the truth. He picked up his phone and dialled.

A sleepy voice answered, "Cameron, what's wrong?"

"You said there was nothing between you and Ivy. Do you mean never?"

"Cameron, it's four-thirty in the bloody morning."

"Liam, I have to know!" Cameron all but screamed.

Cameron heard a voice in the background. "Well, you've obviously moved on."

"Enough Cameron. Stop right there." Liam snapped, "There has never been and will never be, anything between Ivy and I. Even if I liked her that way, she's too special to my idiot brother for me to make a move." The person in the background spoke again.

"Who is that?" Cameron pressed.

"What's the matter, Cameron?" Sophie's voice called to him. Liam must have put the phone on speaker.

"Sophie, why are you in Melbourne?" Cameron questioned, he shook his head trying to clear it, there was too much going on.

"I'm not, Liam's in Chester's Run."

Cameron couldn't think which question required an answer first.

"Why? What Happened? Is everyone okay?"

"First things first," Liam spoke. "What happened with Ivy?"

A sigh escaped Cameron's lips. "Her father has rejected her, and she accused me of rejecting her as well."

"Which you did!" Liam clarified in case Cameron hadn't caught on yet.

"I didn't." Oh hell, he'd stooped to the strategy of a twelve-year-old. No, make that a six-year-old. That's something Caleb would say.

"Cameron, let me clarify something here,' Sophie chimed in, "She took us in without question. Then you scarcely lasted long enough to share a family meal at the same table as her. And conversation was practically non-existent until the trip became a thing."

"But I had my reasons!" Cameron snapped. This wasn't looking good.

"Unfounded and a figment of your imagination. But okay, they were your reasons." Liam deadpanned.

"You promise me there was nothing between you two."

"Cameron, I can't even think where you conjured something like that up." Liam's irked voice hit back.

"The afternoon you were at Ivy's and she had her arm around your shoulder and your hand was on her knee." Cameron thundered.

"What?"

"I saw it all. I came back to get my toiletries bag."

Both men were practically yelling, and Cameron couldn't believe Sophie hadn't stepped in to tell Liam to stop it.

"Are you for real?" Liam went silent for a few moments, "A woman we all love and care about takes time out of her day to allow me to clear my head and you judge her for her generosity?"

The silence stretched out between the three of them.

"So, you don't have any interest in her?"

"Cameron. Stop." Sophie never used that tone with him, and he didn't like her using it now.

"I've stuffed up, haven't I?" His voice only a whisper.

"Yesssss," Liam let the silence linger for a bit.

It was a while before any of them spoke again.

"But we can fix this." Liam's now calm voice was attempting to reassure him. "Cameron, take a deep breath, and let's sort this whole thing out."

HEADING HOME

IVY

Still numb from the events of the previous day, Ivy dropped into her economy seat towards the back of the plane. Cameron stowed her luggage, leaned over and squeezed her shoulder, and continued down the aisle. His seat was three rows back. They'd barely spoken since the fight yesterday afternoon.

Her thoughts circled back to the previous evening at the bar. Sitting with a sparkling water in hand, her phone pinged with a text. She read it to see Cameron changed their flights and explained they were leaving the following morning.

<u>Cameron</u> — *New flight 9am via Singapore*

<u>Ivy</u> — *Thanks*

Thirty minutes later, Deb and Bert walked in, their faces mirroring her own.

"So, you've heard," Ivy said, but didn't expect a response.

"Cameron just phoned us to say that you're leaving in the morning. How're you holding up?" Deb asked with overwhelming sincerity.

Ivy waved down a waiter going past, ordered flavoured mineral water for herself, and waited as Bert and Deb placed their orders.

"I came, I failed," she shrugged, "And now I'm going home to people who love me." She sucked back more tears.

Deb leaned in and hugged her. "Well, for what it's worth, we're so glad to have met you. Gabe would fill us in occasionally on what you were up to, but to have met you has been wonderful beyond words. Will you stay in touch?"

Ivy's head was spinning. How did Gabe fill them in on her progress? She stared at her glass for a moment, watching the condensation drip down the side. She raised a shaky finger to follow the trail, drawing in a deep breath, desperate to find her equilibrium. Feeling her heart rate slow, Ivy formed a calm string of words.

"How did he know what I was up to'?" Ivy's eyes pierced Deb's.

The mental slanging continued as Bert and Deb exchanged a look. What the hell? The look they shared wasn't one of realising that they'd let the cat out of the bag, but more one of knowing they couldn't say more.

Bert shrugged his shoulders. "Gabe's a lovely man. He has a big heart."

They were talking about a different man, not the one who banished her from his life earlier today. Drawing in a sharp breath, Ivy let the comment slide. Her father, no, he didn't deserve that title. The sperm donor she was unfortunate enough to be genetically connected to, wasn't getting any more of her time. And neither was Cameron. There was a fierce determination to start over, without either of them.

Gabe would be here in London, and as for Cameron, Chester's Run was a big enough place that they wouldn't have to see each other much.

Ivy didn't watch as the cabin crew went through the safety spiel before the flight. She donned her head phones and closed her eyes, not bothering to wipe away the errant tears. This trip was the worst idea of her life, both heart crushing and soul destroying. In that moment she thought of her mother. Would she have given up this easily?

CAMERON

Cameron removed his headphones as they landed in Melbourne. On the second leg of the flight, he sat in the row behind Ivy and because the child sitting next to her had his seat down to sleep, Cameron could see her for the better part of their journey. He lacked sleep, but he couldn't draw his eyes from her beautiful face.

The conversation with Sophie and Liam the other night made him feel so foolish. He'd wasted all this time when the trip could have been so much more between them. Well, he would rectify that. He hoped. If only he shared Liam and Sophie's positive attitude, that Ivy would forgive him.

Cameron pulled the last of their luggage onto the trolley and waited for Ivy to join him. She'd gone to freshen up before the drive home. When she emerged, Cameron gave her a smile and nodded towards the doors. "You ready?"

He only got a nod in response. In fact, if she'd said more than one hundred words to him since she stormed out of the suite in London, he was lucky. When they headed for the door, a man in a cap stepped in front of her.

"Miss Ivy Masters?"

"What?" Ivy's puzzled look crowded her face.

The man in the chauffeur's get-up appeared to school his features at her response. "Miss Masters, your car is this way."

"What car?" Ivy snapped. "We don't need a car. Do we, Cameron?" A combination of being sleep deprived and coming to terms with her father's rejection seemed to be guiding Ivy's reaction at present.

Cameron walked towards the doors as the driver led the way. "Good morning. Early start this morning, I see. Thank you for this."

"Cameron," Ivy shrieked.

But he only left Ivy to follow. And she would, because he had her backpack containing her money.

"Ugh."

He heard her groan and the squeak of shoes on the tiled floor. Yep, she was behind him. Cameron helped load the bags into the car and looked over to see a red-faced Ivy standing on the curb. He had to remain strong if this was going to work. Ensuring his backpack was over his shoulder, he watched as Ivy was ushered ever so gently into the back of the car and he joined her in the luxurious town car. The BMW was sleek and stylish. How Liam pulled this off, he'd never know. There was mention of a friend and a favour.

Once the doors closed, Ivy turned to him. "What the hell is going on?"

"Probably Liam's idea of a joke. I asked him if he could pick us up," Cameron said, fishing his phone from his pocket. He found the conversation and allowed Ivy to read Liam's response for herself.

Liam — *Sure mate. I'm on it!*

Cameron turned to look out the window, sucking in his bottom lip. Now it was all up to him.

The driver pulled out of the carpark and joined the throng of cars turning left and they were on their way. He looked over and saw Ivy's arms crossed tightly over her chest and her mouth turned down. Now it was time to put the next piece of the plan into motion.

"Have you ever seen Living Legends?" he asked, pointing to their right. Ivy saw the white-fenced paddocks neatly arranged and the sign to Woodlands homestead.

Her face softened as a small smile raised one corner of her mouth. Horses calmed her.

Cameron lowered the window between them and the driver and asked, "Would you mind stopping at Living Legends for a minute, please?"

"Certainly sir."

"The retired racehorses live here. Mum used to bring us here when we dropped Ralph at the airport. Over the years we saw some amazing thoroughbreds like Better Loosen Up, Might and Power and Sophie's favourite Paris Lane. She won some good money on that horse."

He could feel Ivy's tension from the past forty-eight hours ease.

"Might and Power won my Grandpa good money. I remember us going out to dinner to celebrate."

The car stopped, Cameron jumped out, and Ivy followed. He strode beside her to the fence which housed the legend, Might and Power. Liam really had done his homework, and Cameron was grateful.

They both leaned on the fence. Cameron turned his face up to meet the late February sunshine. He'd never thought he'd have missed the warm weather this much, but he had. He pulled off his jumper and noticed Ivy doing the same with her jacket. Together they leaned on the rails and watched the horse carelessly roaming the paddock, grazing on the grass surrounding him. His large body was graceful and strong. After a while he looked up and slowly ambled towards them. Ivy waited patiently for the horse to approach. She was a seasoned horsewoman and showed the animal the respect he needed to feel comfortable around her.

"Good afternoon," a woman called out to them.

"Hi," Cameron said, turning to greet her.

"We're actually closed today," the woman explained.

"Sorry. My friend is a horsewoman from up Mansfield way and I just wanted to show her Living Legends. We just flew back in from London."

"A horsewoman. Well, in that case you two come with me," Cameron and Ivy fell into step with the stranger and the conversation started about all things horses. Cameron listened to the chatter which lifted Ivy from her funk.

They followed her in through a previously locked gate and then into Might and Power's home paddock. As soon as he heard the click of the gate, the horse hurried towards them.

"He's expecting a treat," the woman told them as she dug into the large pocket of her apron and handed Ivy an apple.

He dropped his head towards Ivy's hand but didn't make a move to snatch the apple from her. Instead, he waited patiently. Nudging and whinnying, the horse became playful. Cameron watched the interaction between human and animal. He smiled at the sight of her rounded shoulders lifting and the tension in her face receding.

Liam was right, before he talked about them and a potential future, he had to make her comfortable around him again.

IVY

The smell of the horse and hay in her nostrils chipped away at the stress plaguing her. She wasn't home yet but being this close to a horse was invigorating, Ivy breathed deeply again. It cleared her vision and her thinking. But instead of allowing a hundred and one things to invade the previously closed space in her head, Ivy shut it all out for now and enjoyed the attentions of Might and Power.

Horses really were a cliché, they had the muscles and the power behind them to be a force to be reckoned with, but mostly, they were the most beautiful, gentle animals she'd encountered.

"So, Mansfield?" the woman asked.

"Actually, Chester's Run, a little nowhere place that's getting bigger and bigger every day." Ivy said.

"Horse country?"

"Yep, my uncle and grandfather were renowned in the district for their horses."

"I bet my father would have known them. He knew all the horse people around the state."

Ivy gave the apple to the horse. "You from up our way?"

"No, actually from the Western District, but Mum and Dad had contacts everywhere. Horses have been my life since I was a child. That and racing."

The woman talked and Ivy listened while noting Cameron was so close, he almost invaded her space. She took in his blue eyes as the woman talked about horses. This really was a chance meeting, so Ivy focused again and continued the conversation.

Ten minutes later they made their way back to the car. "Thank you so much for your time," Ivy said.

"My pleasure, here's my card and if you are ever in the area, let me know. I'd love to find out more about your Grandfather and his horses."

"Will do," the chauffeur opened the door and Ivy climbed in, followed by Cameron. She watched out the window as the car descended back down the driveway and out onto the country road towards home.

The window came down. "Excuse me."

"Yes." Ivy answered.

"There's food and drinks in the bar fridge there, please help yourselves."

"Thank you." The window closed and Ivy watched as Cameron opened the fridge and looked in.

"Okay, there's savoury croissants, sushi, or wraps."

"Yes, please," Ivy replied. Her stomach was empty. She hadn't eaten much on the flights. Cameron set up a little table and then set the food out and waited while Ivy chose. "I'm starving." She unwrapped the ham and cheese croissant and took a bite.

Cameron looked at the food and decided on a wrap.

"So, who organised all this?" Ivy asked, finally realising that a trip to Chester's Run in a chauffeured car wasn't going to be cheap.

"Sophie and Liam did it for me," Cameron answered shyly.

Ivy's brows furrowed. "Why?"

Cameron discarded his unfinished wrap and worked his jaw for a minute.

"Ivy," he said, drawing in a breath. "I was completely wrong and out of line about Liam."

"You think!" Ivy chastised, her voice rising with each word.

"No, I know. I rang Liam after you stormed out yesterday. Short of calling me a loser, both he and Sophie made me see sense."

"That would have been nice to know before we left," Ivy turned her face away from him, taking another bite of her food because she needed something else to focus on. "Cameron, I'm not a fickle woman whose attention can be turned by a nice smile and a compliment." She took the last bite, not enjoying the food anymore but desperate for a moment to think.

"I've never felt this way about anyone in my life." Cameron took her hand in his, making her turn back to him. "Liam verbally smacked me around the head, making sure I understood I was jealous of another man's attention towards you. Relationships and I haven't had a past, I've avoided the entanglement at all costs."

She couldn't help it, Ivy laughed. Sophie told her the stories of Cameron and his struggles with understanding people and their behaviours. Maybe that explained him jumping to conclusions about her and Liam.

"You're laughing, but I don't think it's a fair joke," Cameron squeezed her hand.

"So why the car?" she asked, changing the subject.

"Because we needed to talk, and Sophie suggested this time together. This way it's just the two of us and plenty of time."

CAMERON

The incredulity on her face stopped his heart. He saw the gamut of emotions caress and tangle as she watched him.

"We've been away for almost three weeks."

Cameron squeezed her hand softly.

Ivy whipped her hand out of his as if either his touch burned her skin or she'd forgotten he held her.

Silence echoed.

"You have questions or statements, so talk," Cameron said, but not really sure he wanted to hear what she had to say.

"I can't believe you thought I was interested in Liam, especially as you've based your opinion on that one occasion." She spoke to the window, but he heard the tension loud and clear.

Part of him knew he deserved her wrath, but still that didn't make this easy. "In my defence I couldn't believe that you'd actually like me and I think instead of being rejected I preferred the idea of having made a mistake."

He visibly flinched when Ivy took hold of his hand. Relaxing into her touch, he turned to her. "Sorry. I didn't mean to flinch."

"Did your father ever hit you?" Ivy's voice was low.

"Where did that question come from?" he asked.

"You flinched. If it's not what I'm thinking then it's me."

Cameron's emotions gathered momentum. He hadn't cried in front of anyone for a long time, not even Sophie, but then not even she knew this. Could that be his excuse to allow his emotion to pour free?

"Okay, so that's a yes," she replied for him when he was still deciding what to say. "Does Lindy know?"

Cameron was up with the conversation now, so he pivoted his head, signalling no.

"What about Sophie?"

Again, it was a no. He had told no one. Until today, he'd kept those painful memories to himself. "Nobody knows except you. And him, of course." Cameron ran his free hand over his face. "This is meant to be about us, to see if we have a future together, not about me."

Ivy's head drifted from side to side. "You don't get it, do you?" Her words were gentle, but there was some hidden force behind them.

"Get what?"

"For you and me, our pasts are our future. What your father did to you and what my father did to me is all mixed in with this. Cameron, I bear scars too but mine are different." Ivy paused, as if gathering evidence. "Both those men were our fathers. Meant to be there for us. Help raise us, love us, teach us how to survive in this world. As a parent, those were the expectations on both of them. And they failed us."

Cameron drew on everything he could, hoping to understand. He stared into her eyes.

"Are you saying we'll be no good for each other?" Please don't let it be that. He never thought he'd fall in love, now that he had, it meant everything to him. She, Ivy Masters, meant everything to him. The question was, would she want to become his world?

CONTEMPLATING A FUTURE TOGETHER

IVY

The car drove them straight to Lindy's place. Ivy was too exhausted to face the shop and everyone there. Midday rush was wonderful when you were working but not when you needed time to yourself.

"Take us around the back, please," Cameron instructed the driver. "Over to your left, the place up ahead."

Liam came out of the big house and ambled over to them. "Welcome back." He hugged Ivy and then Cameron.

"Where is everyone?" Ivy asked.

"Work and school. Mum's gone shopping, and I just put Bradley down for a sleep." Liam looked back to the house as if he'd hear his stepbrother if he cried. "You two look beat."

"Is my room clean?" Cameron asked. "Ivy and I need some sleep," Cameron held up his hands. "I know we should stay awake, but…"

"We've had a tough couple of days," Ivy picked up where Cameron left off.

"Sorry to hear that. Can I get you guys anything before you get some sleep?"

"No thanks. Oh, and thanks for the car, it was well-stocked with food and drinks so we're fine." Ivy headed for the bungalow.

"Yeah, what Ivy said. Thanks." Cameron followed Ivy into the house and walked her to his bedroom door. "You can sleep in here, I'll take the couch."

He walked in to drop her bags inside the door, and Ivy closed it. "How about we both sleep in here, it's your room after all, and this way we'll both have a decent sleep?"

Cameron gave her a lopsided grin.

"No Cameron Kemp, we've a long way to go before that," her cheeky grin matched his. She focused on her suitcase, found her pyjamas, and walked out to use the bathroom.

Cameron was in shorts and a T-shirt when she returned. He took his turn in the bathroom and Ivy was getting into bed when he walked back into the room. The blinds were closed and there were clean clothes on her suitcase for later.

"Hope I'm not on your side of the bed?" Ivy realised it might actually be a big deal for Cameron.

"Well actually, I sleep in the middle so any side is good for me," Cameron told her.

She turned onto her side and faced him. "Thanks for rescheduling the flight and sorting out the car."

"Thanks for listening to me on the way home." He reached a hand out and cupped her shoulder. Licking dry lips, he asked, "Would you like to go out for dinner later in the week? Maybe even the pictures? We could go to Mansfield."

"Cameron Kemp, are you asking me out, on a date?" Ivy teased.

"If you have to ask, perhaps I stuffed that up too." Cameron answered in a light tone.

"I'd be honoured." Ivy leaned into him and kissed him. After a delayed response, his lips quivered under hers, which further announced his lack of practice and his shyness.

"Sweet dreams, Ivy."

"Sweet dreams to you too…" but Ivy didn't finish her whispered sentence. She watched him through the diminishing gap as her eyelids slid closed and stole her thoughts as she drifted off to sleep. As she slept, images of her, her father and her aunt danced through her mind. They were clear, but the meaning was anything but.

CAMERON

It was after three in the morning the next time Cameron's eyes fluttered opened. Ivy was still lying facing him as she was when he drifted off to sleep early yesterday afternoon. They were both still in the same position, he must have slept for hours. He lay there listening to her breathing. His lamp was still on and he liked that he could see her clearly. She looked beyond beautiful, especially asleep next to him in his bed.

He was aware of the need to visit the bathroom, and he was thirsty. Cameron eased himself out of the bed and took care of business, visited the kitchen for some water and gathered some dip and biscuits as well. His stomach rumbled, but he wasn't cooking up a meal at this ungodly hour. In the fridge he noticed two plates covered in glad wrap. Bless his mother, she always thought of everything. They would keep till tomorrow unless Ivy woke and was hungry. Then he'd come out and heat them up, otherwise he'd try to get back to sleep. Being back home, he was ready to sink his teeth into the new project for Anders and Butterworth Engineering. He walked back into the room and snuggled into bed.

Next thing it was morning, the light coming in the window was warm and welcoming. He'd enjoyed the London winter, but seriously, nothing beat the heat of an Australia summer. He was happy to be home. Rolling onto his back, he saw the tray on his bedside table. The two glasses of water had gone and the biscuits and dip a distant memory. Though he couldn't actually remember eating them.

"Morning," a sweet voice greeted him. Ivy was sitting at his desk by the window. He could only make out her silhouette.

"Good morning, when did you wake up?"

"About twenty minutes ago," she walked over to the bed and sat next to him. "Sorry, but I drank your water and demolished your share of the biscuits and dip."

"Now that makes more sense," he laughed. "I couldn't remember eating them."

Knock. Knock.

They both turned to the door as Cameron called out. "Come in." He expected Liam, but it was Lindy standing in the doorway.

"Welcome back," she said, stepping into the room.

Ivy jumped up to hug her friend. "Hello."

"How're you feeling?"

"I'm okay. In a few months, I'll be content to know where I stand. But at the moment it's still raw," she would not hide her pain.

"I'm so sorry about that, love. You know we're all here for you," Lindy told her.

"You know, I think that's the only thing that got me through. Knowing I was coming home to you guys."

"Good, because I was a little afraid that he might try to keep you there," Lindy joked. "He clearly doesn't know what's good for him."

Ivy joined her laughter, but Cameron could see she didn't agree with his mother.

"How did you go, love?" Lindy turned her attention to him.

"Great. Ready to settle down and start working."

"Good on you for what you've achieved. Make sure you have a balance in your life now. It's not to be all work anymore."

Cameron grinned. "It won't be, I promise."

"Well, breakfast will be ready in fifteen, so head over and join the kids before school if you like. Otherwise, we'll bring something over to you later."

"Breakfast sounds great," Cameron said, rubbing his belly. "I'm starving," he turned to look at the tray beside the bed and Ivy laughed. Looking at Ivy he said, "You take the first shower."

"Thanks, won't be long," she kissed Lindy again and gathered her prearranged clothes and toiletries and headed out the door.

Lindy looked from the empty doorway to her son. "Will she be alright?"

"I think so, but it hurt me when the man told her to go, so I can't imagine how much it hurt her."

"We're all here and hopefully we'll get Ivy through it. We are proud to be her family, we have to make sure she knows that."

"I honestly think she does. Coming home to you guys gave her purpose. Now she hopes to find a new direction with the bakery." Cameron heard the shower turn off. "I'll have a quick shower and meet you over there."

FACING REALITY

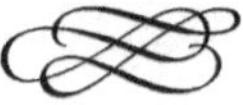

GABE

The crunch of tyres on the driveway had Gabe looking out his window. An image of his daughter walking back through his doors rolled his stomach. He hoped she took the leather pouch which belonged to her mother and headed home. Somewhere she was safe.

He couldn't have anything of Ivy in this house. His ex-wife's intent that her only son to Gabe would become his heir, still plagued him. Especially when she promised him she'd stop at nothing to get her hands on this house and any money to come with the family dynasty.

By God, he regretted the day he married her. She was a spiteful cow of a woman, and although the marriage only lasted ten months and they never were in residence at Thornton House, the woman vowed it was hers by right.

Still, to this day, the conversation that ended their marriage echoed in his head. She'd admitted to ordering Thornton House's land manager to remove Anita from Gabe's life.

The existence of his daughter, Ivy, had never been mentioned. Anita was so protective of Ivy. Even when she flew to London for the trial of her attempted murder, Anita was determined to keep Ivy safe with her Aunt and Uncle in Chester's Run.

Out of respect for Anita's wishes, Gabe only discussed his daughter with Scarlett, her husband, Deb and Bert. Violet accepted his story, Ivy was born prematurely due to complications following Anita's attack. He hated that he needed to create a lie to keep Ivy safe.

"Hello, darling," Scarlett said as she breezed into the room.

Gabe walked over and wrapped his little sister into a hug, breathing in her sweet smell of sugary goodness and drawing from her comfort.

"Hello Gabe," her husband Spencer greeted.

"You're back?" Gabe asked, giving him a hug also and a gentle slap on the back. "When did you get home?"

Spencer looked at his watch and made out he was thinking. He let out a laugh. "Straight from the airport, actually."

"Oh, so why are you here and not home sleeping?"

"Because old chap," Spencer said, "My beautiful wife and I have had enough."

Gabe looked from Scarlett to her husband and back again. "What are you talking about?"

Scarlett's stern face and clasped hands told Gabe he wouldn't like what she was about to say. "You, my darling brother, are moving to Australia."

"What?" His forehead furrowed with the strain of her words.

"Sit down and let's thrash this out," Spencer suggested. He pulled out a chair for Scarlett at the small table in Gabe's sitting room before taking one himself.

"Your priority is to get Violet off your back permanently," Spencer began.

"You think?" Gabe said, imitating his niece and nephews, making his sister laugh.

"Scarlett explained what happened." Spencer began, "Gabe, you and I both know what you want most in life is to have a relationship with your daughter. And you can't deny that she wants that as well."

Gabe swallowed hard. He still shuddered at the memory of Ivy's face when he practically banished her from his house and his life.

"Scarlett, you know what happened to Anita, I can't trust that Violet won't employ the same tactics which took her from me. If Ivy is injured, or worse, because of something I do, I couldn't live with that."

"Okay then let's face the elephant in the room. We need to remove the falsehood that your ex-wife believes. You must tell Ivy the truth. You're losing time with her, Gabe. Protecting her physically won't make up for the emotional pain you're inflicting on her."

"The way I see it," Spencer was a business man moulded by his brother-in-law. His no-nonsense approach was something which Gabe drilled into him over the years in his mentorship. "Getting you to Australia is our priority. Next you tell your daughter, our niece, the truth. It's her decision to accept or reject what's been bequeathed to her as your firstborn."

Though the room was silent, Gabe grimaced with the weight of responsibility resting upon him. Scarlett was pleading for his alliance, and Spencer was single-minded beyond expectation when he believed in a cause. Was he being over cautious? "You know Violet had a hand in what happened to Anita?" Gabe glared at Scarlett. She was asking way too much of him.

"I do," Scarlett's head tilted to one side as if trying to ease some pain. "But I also know if you and Ivy decide to do this, and as I'm the next in line to inherit, the courts will see you have my full support to bequeath the Thornton estate to Ivy."

"You have enough money to live off and you could train her up, if she's that way inclined." Spencer added.

"So, I just leave this place and head to Australia and drop this bombshell on my daughter. Is that what you're alluding to?" Gabe rubbed his calloused hand across the back of his neck.

"Well, what if we all move in? We'll rent out Wilton Manor and be here to look after everything. This place is enormous. We can have the west wing. Even when you're back, you'll be able to have your privacy from us." Scarlett offered.

"I tried to get you both to move in years ago. Of course, you can live here. As it is, you're too far away from me. Even if I don't agree to your proposal, I'd still love to have you all here."

"Oh, good try Gabe," Scarlett flashed a grin. "The deal is we move in if you tell Ivy everything."

Spencer laughed. "Well played, my love. We'll only move back if you promise to tell Miss Ivy Masters the truth. You agree to our blackmailing and I'll have the movers here by the end of the week."

"So, you admit to blackmailing me?" Gabe gave a harsh laugh.

Scarlett leaned across the table, took Gabe's hand in hers and squeezed gently. "When Anita left, you lost your fiancé, but I lost my best friend and sister. I hid my pain because I understood yours, but I missed her so much. Seeing Ivy again after all these years, I can't bear to walk away again. Seeing her and pretending she meant nothing, was like losing your amazing partner all over again. Do this for Anita and I, please?"

"Seeing her walk away, was actually more difficult than saying goodbye to Anita. This time I'm hurting them both. I want nothing more than to love my daughter. To get to know her and to make sure that the young man who couldn't take his eyes off her, endeavours to treat her right." Gabe stood and walked over to the window. "So, move to Chester's Run…you think this will work?"

"We have more than enough evidence that she's your daughter and we'll speak to your legal counsel now and build our case. By the time Violet gets wind of the existence of Ivy and your intention, we'll have everything in place to push through."

"What if she hates me for what I did? She's only just found out the truth about what happened to her mother, and anyway you know she could reject the offer," Gabe turned from the window to survey his sister's reaction to that thought.

"Sorry love, but that's a risk I'm begging we take." Scarlett stated. Her hands crossed over her chest.

Gabe sat pondering the possibilities. "Okay, let's start again from the top."

Spencer began, "First, we move in here to keep the estate going."

Scarlett grabbed a notepad and pen lying on the table and began taking notes.

"Secondly, you move to Chester's Run and form a relationship with your daughter."

"You won't mind if I go by myself, Scarlett?" Gabe asked, thinking she'd most likely want to be there with him.

"Of course not, and when the time is right, we'll travel over to meet and spend time with her."

"Thirdly, tell Ivy the whole truth and not the partial story you gave her the other day," Spencer paused, giving Scarlett a chance to write it all down. "Tell her about Violet and Jonah, not to mention her cousins."

Gabe nodded as he watched Scarlett's hand form such delicate, beautiful letters.

"Finally, speak with your council to get the ball rolling on securing the Thornton estate from that woman."

Spencer picked up his phone and made a call. "Tony, mate, I require your help."

Gabe and Scarlett put their heads together to sort out what else required his attention before he could leave. They discussed, wrote and by the time Spencer got off the phone, Scarlett declared, "Well big brother, you're going to Australia. Oh, I can't tell you how much this means to me!" There were tears threatening to spill, but Scarlett was fighting hard to prevent that.

Gabe smiled at her effort. His focus shifted from his sister to himself. Drawing in a deep breath, he realised for the first time in a long time, he had a reason to exist. A reason to smile and of course a chance to make everything right for his beautiful Anita and their daughter. Deep within, a small glimmer of hope bubbled up. He now had a sense of purpose other than making money and keeping his father's legacy going. The road ahead was bound to be steep and bumpy as hell, but if the outcome was as Scarlett envisaged, all would be worthwhile.

BACK HOME

IVY

Ivy and Cameron walked into the dining room, their hands full of gifts which had the children hollering with joy. Whether it was seeing them again or the presents, it was hard to tell.

"How was it?" Nate asked, hugging Ivy tight.

Tugging on her facade, which would be in high demand over the next little while, Ivy lied through her front teeth. "We had a great time, met lots of new friends, and did some awesome things." Nothing there was a lie, but if she kept going on the success of the trip, that would have been exaggerated.

"How did the programming go?" Jack asked Cameron once they took their seats.

"Fantastic, I might need one more trip down the track, but we'll see how that goes. Phil and Thomas were great to work with, thorough with the business and creative with their ideas." Cameron reached over and took two slices of toast and dropped them onto his plate.

"We both met the family," Ivy took over, "Oh, and I got to ride their horses. Oh Jack, you would have loved them, they were stunning specimens. Apparently, the entire family are into riding." A fleeting glimpse of the stables she could see out of the window at Thornton House entered her mind. They were something to be admired. But she shook that thought away.

Neither of them mentioned anything about her father as only Lindy, Jack, Liam, and Sophie knew of the real reason she headed for London.

Breakfast was full of stories of London, Paris, and the soccer match Cameron attended. The children listened to the tales as they studied their presents.

"We got your postcards yesterday, thank you." Evie pointed to the board in the dining room. The cards were lined up next to each other. Some had the picture showing while others displayed the writing.

"Can I take this to school, Mum?" Caleb asked Lindy after opening a model of the black English cab.

"Not today. Go up and wash your face and hands and brush your teeth. I'll be there in a minute to do your hair."

A few minutes later the table was clear of school children.

"Are you ready to talk about it?" Jack asked his cousin.

"Everyone was right, telling me not to get my hopes up," Ivy agreed. "He seems a lovely man, but there's no place in his life for his daughter."

"And you're okay with that?" Jack continued.

"No, but what choice do I have?"

"So, what shall you do now?"

"Not sure, but I know in my heart this is where I want to be. I missed you all while I was away," Ivy smiled over at Cameron, he blushed at the attention but held her gaze. She was grateful for his effort, they'd come a long way. "I'll start back at work maybe Wednesday and look into starting the new line of breads and continental cakes. The business is my future and I have Sophie and Susie who are relying on me to make this work. That will give me plenty to focus on for now."

"Well love, you know you're welcome here anytime, and let me know when you want your next mentoring session. You and Cameron are my pet projects right now," Lindy grinned and her eyes sparkled.

CAMERON

The front door closed, and a voice called out.

"In here, Liam," Jack replied.

Liam pulled out a chair, turned and straddled it. "Are the terrors ready?"

"Don't call them that and yes they should be, hang on, I'll get them," Lindy said as she stepped into the hallway.

"So big brother, you didn't tell me why you're up here on a weekday," Cameron looked at the disappearing figure of his mother as she left the room, turned to Liam and then Jack. It must have been something serious for him not to be in the office. He recalled the discussion with Ivy about Liam dealing with something he couldn't talk about. "And where have you just come from?"

Liam let out a tight laugh. "Curiosity killed the cat." But he didn't make eye contact with Cameron. "I actually stayed at the bakery with Sophie last night, so you guys could get a decent night's sleep."

"Thank you," Ivy said as Cameron looked from his brother whose focus was on the car keys in his hand to Jack who swallowed hard and shook his head.

Whatever was going on, Cameron wasn't sure. He and Liam were building trust and respect after years of tension created by their father, and then Cameron hampered their connection by his distrust of Liam and Ivy.

"After you take the kids to school, I was wondering if you could help me out?"

Liam's face split into a cheeky grin, "Always little brother. What's up?"

"Well, on the flight home, I thought, I'm going to need some office space here in Chester's Run. I'd like to set up my business properly." Cameron's left foot began bouncing, what would his brother think about his idea. "You know, have a shop front and maybe hire someone to fix computer problems and assist me with computer programming."

Cameron turned his phone over in his hands while talking, not making eye contact with anyone.

"I applaud your foresight, Cameron," Lindy said from the doorway.

It was difficult to hold back the grin spreading across his face, "You do?"

"Me too," Liam joined in, "In fact, I'll drop the kids at school and when I get back, we'll talk. See you in half an hour." Liam leaned across the table and fist pumped his brother. "Later dude," kissed Lindy and smiled at Jack, who followed him out of the room. Cameron picked up on the dark bags under Liam's eyes and the tension lines on his brother's face. Seriously, what was really going on here?

"I probably should head to the bakery, I suppose," Ivy decided, and Cameron immediately picked up that she wasn't going to intrude on his business.

"Not today. Stay with us, Liam and I'll take you out for lunch," he didn't miss her raised brow at the mention of her and Liam included in a joint activity. He was fully aware of how much pain he'd caused her by his presumption, so his priority was to show her of his trust.

"How about we drop in when we're in town later, then?" Ivy asked.

"Deal," Cameron agreed and looked up when Jack walked back into the dining room. "Is everything alright with Liam?"

"I'll let him tell you."

Cameron couldn't help it, he rolled his eyes. "Ralph, right?"

Jack grinned and looked at his watch. "I better head in, Ned was opening for me this morning."

"How's he working out?" Ivy asked.

"Great, hard worker, but there's still the issue of his PTSD. He's more settled first thing of a morning, some days he lasts to closing but others, Lindy comes in and I drive him home."

"Is there anything we can do?" Ivy questioned.

"He just needs friends right now, people around him who won't judge. I can't imagine what he's seen over there." Jack gathered his jacket from the back of his chair. "See you both for dinner?"

"You bet," Cameron replied and looked at Ivy.

"I think so." She gave a shrug, "Depends what Sophie says," Ivy paused for a moment, "She might have had enough of the bakery by now. And if that's the case, I should get an early night."

"Fair enough, well, hopefully I'll see you both later," Jack walked out, called to Lindy before the front door closed.

Ivy and Cameron headed into the kitchen to finish cleaning up the breakfast dishes.

"So, are you really thinking about opening an office in town?" The sparkle in her golden eyes delighted him. Just the idea of working in town meant one benefit would be lunch every day at the bakery, close to Ivy. Now who wouldn't want that?

AN IMPORTANT DECISION

GABE

Scarlett pulled her brother into her arms. Gabe was aware of the significance of their shared embrace.

"Call me every day," she whispered in his ear. "You know this won't be easy, but promise me you'll not give up. She's family, Gabe. Yours and mine. I don't want us to lose her again."

"I give you my word, I'll do everything I can to convince her to hear me out. After that I'll support whatever her wishes are. Look after yourselves and keep me up to date with everything here." Gabe kissed her forehead and pulled away.

"Time to go get my daughter."

Scarlett waved frantically as Gabe disappeared through the doors to customs. He watched until the doors closed and he could no longer see her. This was it, the next chapter of his life. It was twenty-five years later than it should have been, but don't they say, *'better late than never'*?

Sitting in the waiting area at Heathrow Airport, Gabe double checked he had all the important paperwork for when he arrived in

Melbourne. He had hired a chauffeured car to Chester's Run where not only was a new vehicle waiting for him, but also the keys to his new home. By the looks of the place from the agent's walk through, the house would require a great deal of attention and time of which Gabe could devote both to while getting to know his daughter.

He had the name of her bakery from the agent, Michael Evans. The man had been more than helpful, in setting up his new life in Chester's Run.

Gabe cringed at the recollection of meeting Ivy at Thornton House. His thoughts were only to tell her his story. He failed to ask about her and her life. The lad with her, was he her boyfriend? What was the connection between them and his cousin Audrey's family? An air of scepticism was raised when Scarlett explained Clem and Phil were visiting Ivy's suite when she'd arrived.

The whole thing sounded coincidental, but Gabe admitted to a slight doubt. But he could investigate things further once he got to know his daughter better. He could only pray she would meet with him. The truth of the situation was he had time on his hands and if Ivy was going to be as inhospitable as he was, he had the upper hand. He now owned a place locally, so there was no need to rush out of the country as Ivy did. He was prepared to wait her out if need be.

GABE

"You made it. Gabe Thornton, I presume? I'm Michael."

Gabe took the offered hand. "Pleased to meet you. Thanks for doing all this. I don't really know the area, but having eyes on the ground made this transition easier." Gabe looked around again, he'd taken in the views of the tree-lined driveway as the car approached but now standing in front of the house he got more of a sense of its grandeur. "Wow, this place is breath-taking. Amaroo, I like it. I like it very much." Gabe spun on his heel, taking in the three-hundred-and-sixty-degree view of his new home and surrounding property. When he studied the area and looked up this property online, the meaning of the Aboriginal word Amaroo was 'Beautiful Place' and how true that was. This indeed was a most charming spot.

"How about I show you through the house? As I explained and from the photos we sent, you understand there is work to do on the interior."

The men walked up the front stairs as the driver unloaded Gabe's luggage and carried it onto the veranda.

"Thanks for the lift," Gabe said, turning to the man when all three cases were deposited just inside the door. He opened his wallet and settled his account. "Have a safe trip back to Melbourne."

"Much obliged."

Michael and Gabe stood on the large veranda and watched the car disappear down the long driveway. The dust rose and dissipated on the slight breeze that danced around them.

The interior of this once grand house told of a bygone era. One that, on first glance, bore some attributes of Thornton House. Large rooms, high ceilings and brightly coloured wallpaper. Wide hallway with a chandelier, though smaller, reminded Gabe of home. The property had seen better days and as the house stood vacant for the last few years, Gabe wasn't deterred by what he saw.

"You said the bungalow is in a better condition?" Gabe asked, walking from room to room.

"Much. The family lived there when they no longer had the money to do this place up. I contacted a few local tradespeople in the area, but the one I recommend has recently moved down from Sydney. He's done a bit of work for me at home. One of the local tradies did a runner and left us high and dry. Family break up apparently. So, Owen took over and honestly, the outcome was first class."

"When do I get to talk to him?"

"This afternoon if you like. I mentioned it to him and he seemed happy to have a conversation with you."

"Would you mind making the call? I'd be happy to chat and see what he thinks about this place."

Michael called Owen from the hallway while Gabe kept touring the house.

"She must have been lovely in her day?"

"Absolutely. I have all the original photos from the previous owner. They dropped them off when they brought the keys in. Oh, that reminds me," Michael pulled a bunch of keys from his pocket. "These are for the house, bungalow, shed and these are the car keys."

Gabe took the offering and clinched his fist around them. "Thanks, I'll take my suitcases over to the bungalow and then we can check out the car."

The two men lugged the cases over to the bungalow and headed for the shed next to the stable.

"Oh, I spoke to Jack Saunders, he's the man to see about horses in the area. He'll point you in the right direction."

By the time Michael helped Gabe with everything he could, he wished him luck and left. Gabe sat on an old wooden deck chair on the veranda of the main house, enjoying the warm March sun and the sweet breeze. The gardens were well planned, but the beds were weed ridden and dry and the grass area had seen better days. Gabe made a mental note to ask in town about hiring help for both the house and the garden.

There was one thing he wanted to do, visiting Anita's grave was the second most important task, after convincing his daughter to hear him out. He closed his eyes, enjoying the warmth of the sun after the blistering cold of an English winter. Absorbed by the peace and tranquillity of the Australian outback, he sat in quiet contemplation.

SHARING ACHIEVEMENTS

IVY

"Wake up boss," Susie entered the kitchen with stacks of empty trays from the shop. "Or were you daydreaming about a certain someone?" Susie's hip bump made Ivy laugh.

"Seriously Susie, I'm never telling you another thing." Ivy tried enraged, but it just turned into another bout of laughter.

"You didn't. Sophie told me."

"I did no such thing! Don't dob me in, you were the one eavesdropping." Sophie rolled her eyes at the other woman's blatant dishonesty, though it was all done in good humour.

Ivy could only manage a shake of the head.

"So, how is lover boy?"

"That's my brother you're talking about," Sophie reminded Susie.

Changing the subject, Susie added her latest bit of town gossip. "Did you hear Amaroo has finally been sold?"

"No, really?" Ivy asked. "That place has stood empty for over three years. The Dawson's must be over the moon about the sale."

"Apparently it was an overseas buyer. Probably a rich Asian."

Susie added while undoing her apron and pulling it up over her head. "So where are you going for dinner tonight?"

"You're terrible. Have you always been eavesdropping on my conversations?"

"There has been nothing to eavesdrop on before this."

"Are you saying my future sister-in-law is boring?" Sophie asked, re-joining the conversation, her hands full of more trays from the front.

"No, she's not that bad, but this is exciting." Susie pulled a face, making Sophie giggle as Ivy turned her reddened cheeks away.

"Leave me alone. Don't you have a home to go to?"

"Not yet, and I'll be in early tomorrow for the juicy gossip."

With her back to the door Ivy yelled, "There'll be no juicy gossip and even if there was I won't be telling."

"Oh, hi Cameron," Susie said in a voice laced with humour.

Ivy pushed back her errant locks with wet hands and dropped her head.

"Hey Cameron," Ivy heard Sophie's footsteps retreat as she slipped out of the room, leaving Ivy and Cameron surrounded by an uncomfortable silence.

A gurgle of laughter echoed from the front of the shop and Ivy wasn't sure who blushed more, Cameron or her. "I—I—I just came to tell you we have the keys to the office." Cameron watched the vacant doorway behind him. Ivy decided he was probably opting for a quick exit. He turned back to her, swallowed noisily, and asked, "I was wondering if you'd like to look at it."

Ivy washed her hands and slipped off her food splattered apron. "Absolutely. I'd love to." Cameron led the way out through the front of the shop, Ivy didn't even look at Susie or Sophie as she followed him out. They didn't deserve an explanation.

"So how was your day?" Ivy asked as they headed right up Park Road, walking side by side.

"Not as inquisitive as yours," Cameron said, looking back at the shop.

"Yeah, sorry about them. I'll deal with them later. Or maybe not at all." She could see Cameron was trying to hold back a wry smile, but he failed miserably.

"What about you? What did you get up to today?"

"Liam and I spent the day online ordering furniture and stationery for the office. Mum chose the style of furniture and I think it'll look great."

"What about Liam? Sophie said he was explaining everything about Ralph to you both this morning."

"I couldn't believe half of it. Mum was with us and made some things clearer. But it's all good, Ralph won't be a problem for much longer. He's been offered a job in the states with an old friend. So, he's flying out next week."

Cameron's shoulders tensed, and Ivy was sorry she'd raised the topic. "Sorry Cameron, I didn't mean to upset you."

"Nah, it's all fine. There's always a silver lining. Mum told us not to look at the money as being from Ralph's business. More a legacy Pa has managed for us over the years. Either way, it's a lot of money and I know when the time comes to purchase a house, that's what I'll use the money for. Oh, and a horse. Jack's on the lookout for more horses. For you, Mum, Sophie, Liam and I."

"Is he really? I meant to talk to him about it but we never got around to the topic." Ivy's hands dug deep into her pocket as they walked. "I'm excited about knowing that."

"Me too." They shared a smile that caused his toes to curl. "Anyway," Cameron continued, "Liam and Sophie are going to say goodbye to Ralph on the weekend."

"And you?"

"Mum understands I've got nothing to say to him. Maybe in the future," he shrugged one shoulder, "But right now," he looked over at her and gave a shy smile, "I have more important things in my life."

Changing the subject, Ivy asked, "Liam's serious about starting his own architectural business in town?"

"Yep. He, Michael, and Jack looked at the land opening up around here and Jack believes he can really make a go of it." Cameron stopped in front of the shop and withdrew some keys. "Here we go," he told her, unlocking the door.

Cameron ushered Ivy inside with a hand to the small of her back. Ivy forced herself not to sigh and revelled in the goosebumps from his touch.

Though the lights were off, the area appeared bright and roomy. Inside there was a main reception area with four offices and a work room out the back. They walked from room to room, Ivy listened as Cameron explained the layout.

"There's going to be a receptionist in here. That's my office, and the workroom out the back will be mine. The rest Liam will use. There's also parking for three cars and apparently the most delicious bakery in the entire world a couple of minutes' walk from here."

"Does that mean you'll be there every day for lunch?" Ivy grinned at him.

"That and morning and afternoon coffee, do you think the owner will let us run a tab?"

"Nope. I know for a fact she doesn't allow credit, not even to family."

"Good to know. I'll have to break open my piggy bank."

Ivy loved the banter and ease between them. Over the last few days they called and messaged one another whenever they had something to say. Cameron was keen to tell her about every decision for their new rental property. And as for Ivy, she kept him in the loop about the changes she and Sophie were planning for the bakery. He mentioned the offer to create a computer program for the wholesale side of the business again, and Ivy was actually considering it.

"This is great. Congratulations."

"Thanks, I'm more excited about working with Liam, than actually having a shop front." Cameron looked around the place with an appraising eye and nodded. "Well, I'd better get you home, I hear you have a hot date tonight."

"Hot date, oh damn, I thought it was just a friend taking me out," Ivy's smile stretched to its limits when they both joined in the teasing and gentle conversation. She hadn't smiled this much in a long time.

And the easy going look on Cameron's face made him even more attractive to her. If that was possible. Feeling happy and comfortable together again only proved to Ivy she'd made the best choice with Cameron. As for her father, no one mentioned him for a couple of days and Ivy counted her blessings. Every time she thought of him, a sharp pain pierced her heart. At one stage, she honestly believed if she looked down, there'd be a dagger protruding from her heart. Thinking of what happened between them still smouldered deep inside. Hopefully, that wound would heal. They walked side by side back to the bakery.

FIRST DATE

CAMERON

Turning the music down as he drove out of Chester's Run, Cameron asked Ivy. "Have you settled back into a routine again?"

"Almost. Still waking up too early, but I just get up and start baking. It's all good. What about you?"

"Same, so I work. Oh, that reminds me Phil said hi."

"So does Clem. She messaged me today. They're all well."

"Do you regret making the trip?" Cameron had to know.

"No. I did at first, but now I've accepted what happened."

Cameron didn't respond. What else could he say? Instead, he took her hand in his and continued the forty-minute drive to the restaurant in Beechworth while talking about the other things they did on the trip.

Cameron pulled into a parking spot on Ford Street. Ivy looked at the nearest restaurant and then at Cameron.

"Provenance?" she asked before her mouth dropped open.

The look on her face was priceless. That made it all worth it.

"Cameron, do you know how expensive this place is?"

"And it's worth every penny. Wait there," Cameron jumped out of the car, hurried around to Ivy's side and opened the door. He held out his hand, which she took with a nod and a smile, neither letting go as they walked to the door of the restaurant.

Inside they were shown to their table, choosing to sit beside each other. The decor was rustic, lots of pale wood on the walls and tables with old style captain's chairs in a rich mahogany matching the floor. Each table had a glass vase holding a single red rose surrounded by a spray of Baby's Breath. The contrast of the red and white stood out beautifully from the rich colour of the tables.

Cameron lent in and kissed Ivy's cheek. "Thanks for coming tonight."

Ivy returned the kiss, "And that's for finally believing that there was nothing ever between your brother and I," Ivy countered.

"That was foolish of me, but I suppose I didn't believe you could be attracted to me, thinking the worst was easier to handle."

"If you and I are going to have a future together, Cameron, we must promise to talk about things. Involve each other in our thoughts and ideas and even question each other more," Ivy turned the page of her menu but Cameron wasn't sure she was actually reading it.

"As I told you previously, I promise to talk everything out with you." Cameron raised his brows. "I'm new at the dating thing." The words were soft and uncertain, but at least he'd said them.

"How about we navigate this road together? I really like you," Ivy leaned in to kiss Cameron but pulled back harshly.

The pair of them exchanged puzzled looks, Ivy was now visibly shaking from the conversation they'd just heard behind them. Cameron squeezed her hand as they turned in unison to see if they were right. Could it really be?

GABE

As Gabe caught Cameron's eye, he could tell this man would move heaven and earth to avoid pain for the woman he cared so much about. He couldn't sit here and eat his meal with them at the next table.

He saw his daughter bend down and pick up her purse as Cameron stood to leave. They were in tune with one another. But he couldn't let this happen. If he was too stupid to see how much pain he'd inflicted on her back in England, that action alone proved how deep her pain ran.

Gabe signalled the waiter, "Could you ask Miss Masters and her partner to join me for dinner, please?" His hand pointing towards the couple in question.

"Certainly, sir." Turning toward Ivy and Cameron, the waiter repeated Gabe's request.

"What are you doing in Australia?" the fierceness in her voice hurt, though he knew he deserved it.

Gabe removed his napkin from his lap and stood indicating the seats which were being placed at his table, "Please join me, Ivy, Cameron. I need to explain why I've hidden the truth from you."

"Why, so you can justify your rejection of me? There are only so many times a child can be rejected, Mr Thornton, and I've reached my limit. Thanks, but no thanks." Ivy stormed out with Cameron hot on her heels. Something about the man's loyalty touched Gabe.

Even though the sensible thing was to let Ivy go and try again later, Gabe couldn't do it. Dropping his napkin onto the table, he followed them out into the street. Cameron held open the car door and was assisting Ivy into the passenger seat. Hell, she was nothing like her mother.

Trying to shake off the knot in his belly, Gabe approached the vehicle and spoke to them. "Please, I really would like to talk to you and explain. Ivy, there is so much you don't understand."

"You can say that again."

"Please come back inside and share a meal or let's go somewhere so we can talk," Gabe's pleading voice faltered. Although he was starving when he arrived, he lost his appetite, waiting to see what Ivy would do.

"Give me one good reason why I should give you another chance to reject me," Ivy's emotions echoed in her voice. Gabe glanced at Cameron, who stood beside Ivy almost as her sentinel, ready to protect her from further pain.

"Because I love you, Ivy, you're my daughter."

"Yes, and I was your daughter in England but look where that got me," her gritted teeth made him move towards her.

Gabe squatted down beside her and spoke gently. "I was wrong Ivy, your aunt and uncle made me see things more clearly. In order to fix this, I've moved to Chester's Run. To tell you what I should have shared when I had the opportunity. Please, give me a chance to make it up to you?" Gabe stood, held out his hand to her and he was certain the world stopped.

The moment she leaned towards him he believed she would hear him out, but she blinked rapidly before her hands twisted together and she sucked in a rush of air. Her face a measure of more questions than he probably had answers. He vowed at this point to do whatever it took.

"Come back inside and allow me to buy you both a meal and then maybe we could go somewhere and talk." His hand remained outstretched, the only hope of connecting his past to a likely future with his daughter. He'd never trusted miracles to be part of his life after he lost his parents and then Anita and Ivy. But right now, he begged for one. A miracle he probably didn't deserve.

IVY

With Cameron's nod, Ivy looked up at Gabe. Hesitating, she expelled a groan and eventually placed her hand in her father's and allowed him to help her from the car again. Her four-inch blue heels hampered the ease of getting in and out of the car. She stood and ran her sweaty hand down her thigh as if straightening her little blue dress.

"Thank you," Gabe said as he stepped back onto the footpath.

Ivy reached for Cameron's hand and they walked back towards the restaurant in silence. After a gentle squeeze of her hand, Cameron dropped it and pulled her into his side. She pressed into him and followed her father back to his table.

"Thank you for holding the table, Miss Masters and Mr Kemp are my guests."

"Right you are, sir."

Ivy took the offered seat and tried to smile as Cameron helped her settle into it. She knew what pain this might cause, so remained ever vigilant.

The waiter placed a beer in front of Cameron and moved to Ivy, giving her a red wine, which they'd ordered earlier, along with another red for her father.

"When did you arrive here?"

"A couple of days ago." Gabe looked around the restaurant. "I came here last night with one of the local tradespeople in the area who's accepted the job of renovating my new acquisition."

"You've bought a house?" Ivy asked, her voice rising as she spoke. Having a house in Australia surely meant he was serious about being a part of her life.

"Amaroo, actually." Gabe's smile was warm and kind.

"You purchased Amaroo Homestead. The place is magnificent, though I heard it's been let go over the past few years." Why was the conversation between them so easy? She wanted to make this difficult for the man, but here she was talking to him like a friend. Not like the rejected daughter she had been in England.

"Yes, the place needs some repairs and lots of refurbishment, but I see a grand future for it."

"Where are you living if the place is in such disrepair?" Ivy wanted to be angry at this man, but she couldn't manage it. She remained on the safe topic of the property that had intrigued the locals for years. It was only fifteen minutes out of Chester's Run and had a grand history with the area.

Ivy sipped her wine and listened to her father and Cameron talk about general business topics, not getting too deep other than to speak of Audrey and her family, who now contracted Cameron to create their new computer system. He held her hand and encouraged her into the conversation. Their food arrived and Ivy devoured the wagyu beef served with a caramelised red wine sauce and a selection of vegetables. The food was divine. Cameron chose the fish and her father like her had the beef, all praising the meals with gusto.

When they finished their main meals, Ivy turned down the offer of dessert and instead made an offer of her own.

"Would you like to come back to the bakery, Gabe? I can supply you with coffee and dessert and maybe we can talk."

"If you don't mind, that sounds like a good idea. Cameron, would you join us?"

He looked to Ivy for guidance before giving his answer. When she nodded and smiled, he agreed, "Thanks, that would be lovely."

Cameron led the way back to Chester's Run under Ivy's guidance and parked the car around the back of the bakery with Gabe following them.

"Come through and have a look at the bakery," Ivy led the way into the kitchen first and watched as her father took it all in.

"This is wonderful." He walked around studying the equipment and setup of the kitchen. "You've used the space well."

"Thanks. Come and see the front of the shop," Ivy led the way and Gabe followed.

"It's a large area, how many can you seat at once?"

"Thirty comfortably. It's actually two shops in one. My grand-mother knocked the wall out here," Ivy stood in the middle of the large space, "And opened it up for her craft shop. The clientele keeps us busy."

They talked while Ivy turned on the coffee machine.

"You've done well." Gabe said, smiling at his daughter. "You must have a good business head on your shoulders."

"Well, I had help. Cameron's mother Lindy has mentored me and we've managed to draw a good profit in the last few months."

"You should be pleased with yourself."

Gabe lent on the counter and watched as Ivy chose a selection of slices for dessert and prepared three cappuccinos.

By the time she was ready, Gabe took the tray of sweets while Cameron carried the drinks and led the way upstairs. As Ivy followed them, she wandered what Lamont Gabriel Thornton had to share with her? Was it anything bad, hell she hoped not. Surely it couldn't be worse than what she'd already learned!

GABE

After setting the tray on the small dining table, Gabe walked around studying the photos on the walls. There was one of Anita, hanging pride of place. The photo was taken on an outing with Scarlett, Gabe couldn't remember where they'd been but he could never forget the fun they'd had that day.

There was another photo and on closer inspection and after he'd drawn his eyes from Anita, he took in the little girl with her mother. His daughter sat at her mother's feet, smiling as if she didn't have a care in the world. She was opening a present, Anita's gaunt figure brought back sad memories. Though there was a beautiful smile which caressed her lips. Those lips, Gabe remembered them better than he knew the back of his own hand.

He turned back and asked. "When was this photo taken?"

Ivy looked past him to the display of memories and smiled. "Mum and me, on my fifth birthday. She gave me a series of books, apparently they were very old books that were her favourite growing up."

"Enid Blyton—The Adventures of the Wishing Chair." Gabe replied with a grin.

"She told you?" Ivy asked, handing him a cappuccino.

"Told me," he let out an easy laugh, "Anita made me take her to

East Dulwich, where Enid Blyton was born. She read that series to Scarlett many times." Gabe's eyes became bright from such wonderful memories, he blinked away the unshed tears and forced unfulfilled dreams to the back of his mind. "In fact, if I remember rightly, this photo was taken on that day. Scarlett took Anita's camera and snapped this shot."

"Yes, I remember seeing it in your photo album." Ivy looked thoughtfully at the picture again. "I found it the day I discovered the letters from Mum."

"Oh, thank you for her letter. I don't think I would have listened to Scarlett and Spencer so openly if I hadn't received those beautiful words from Anita."

Ivy and Gabe stared at one another for a few moments. From the colour on her face, Gabe realised Ivy read his letter too. She understood what he was saying.

"I still have them, Mum's Enid Blyton books. My Grandma said they were too old for me at five, but Mum wanted me to have them before she died."

Needing to shift his focus, Gabe concentrated on Cameron as he picked up his mug and blew over the hot liquid, cupped his mug into his hands and sat back quietly.

"When Bert rang and told me you were in the country, I should have stayed away, but I had to see you again. You sat there in the booth talking to our oldest friends and all I wanted was to sit down and listen to you talk, ask you questions and…" His stomach gripped painfully as he remembered that day. This woman had come halfway around the world to meet him, and he just turned her away with little explanation. Even for him, the rejection proved harsh.

Ivy tilted her head and asked, "And?"

"Hold you and tell you from the moment you were born, I had loved you. There's not a single night I don't argue with your mother asking her to show me a way to protect you and have you in my life safely."

"Safely?" Cameron's tone was harsh considering the calm conversation between father and daughter. His arm snaked around Ivy's shoulder and Gabe smiled as she automatically leaned into him.

Grateful for a shift in focus, Gabe asked, "How long have you two been together?"

Ivy chuckled and looked at Cameron. "Would you believe tonight was our first date?"

"Oh, hell. I'm so sorry," Gabe looked between the two youthful faces as they smiled at each other. Oh, he remembered how that was with Anita. How he longed to have those times with her once again. He'd always wondered why their relationship raced from zero to one hundred in terms of intensity, but he learned the hard way there was only one such love in his lifetime. And he'd lost that and so much more.

"You mentioned having Ivy in your life safely?" Cameron prompted.

He was thorough, Gabe liked this young man.

He expelled a sigh, looked from one to the other and accepted that the time had come. "My estate manager, Mr Smyth," Gabe sighed, took another gulp of his cappuccino, and continued, "I mentioned I married," he waited for a response and when Ivy nodded, he continued, "The marriage lasted only ten months, ending the night she revealed she'd forced her second cousin's hand in Anita's demise. See, I dated Violet on and off for a few years before I met your mother, but there was just something not right. After meeting Anita, I knew immediately she was for me. Violet was my manager's second cousin and nothing but greed motivated her to pursue me."

Gabe shook his head, trying to shake off the pain he always experienced replaying these memories. "Smyth was up to no good, and Anita cottoned on. I'd forgiven him for what I believed was a poor lack of judgement and allowed him to stay on. In court, she told of the drive home and how he confronted her about sticking her nose in where it wasn't wanted. The man's greed was as evil as Violet's." Gabe rubbed the back of his neck. "Apparently that night, Anita begged for your life and was told not only would you die, but so would she. His efforts in a small way were successful because eventually your mother died of the injuries caused that night. But know this, everything she did from that moment on was to protect you." Gabe drank the last of his coffee and settled the cup on the table. He rubbed his hands down his thighs and met her gaze.

Expelling a harsh breath through his nose, he forced himself to continue. "I can't say I believed Smyth's story, I think it was more I questioned Anita's." Gabe sat forward in his seat. "That was my chance. My one chance to protect her, and you, but I didn't. There was doubt which plagued me as I sat by Scarlett's bedside. Everyone I loved was in hospital. I turned to Deb and Bert and they tried to convince me to believe Anita." With his head now lowered, he continued, "I couldn't conceive you were mine. An overactive mind formed enough questions to banish her from our lives and hearts. I don't believe Scarlett has forgiven me for my decision regarding you and your mother."

He looked over at her, finally forcing himself to gage her reaction. Twice in her life he'd rejected her, but now she'd hear the real reason he had to do it a second time. And prove there would never be a third.

"The night my wife and I split, she kept our one-month old son with her."

"I have a half-brother?" Ivy's mouth fell open and she waited for a reply.

"Yes, Jonah Lamont Thornton. When my lawyer became involved, Violet claimed the estate was rightfully Jonah's. She fought for him to have the house immediately and wait till I died, for her to claim his inheritance. But what she doesn't know, only because Anita begged me not to tell anyone, was the inheritance is willed to the firstborn which is you."

"Whoa! Hold on a minute," Ivy brushed her long hair back from her face and seemed to be challenging whatever her mind was saying. "Why haven't you told me this sooner? Because I would have told you I didn't get in contact with you for any money, my contact with you was purely personal reasons," Ivy gritted her teeth and then swiped at watery eyes. Hard. "I just wanted to know my father."

"Scarlett and I can't be sure what Violet would do if she found out you existed," Gabe paused. He had to get this right. "If you reject the inheritance, according to the will, I have to bequeath it to Scarlett and her family. But I need to prove you are mine. That way Jonah's mother realises there's no way she'll ever get her hands on the money."

"But what about your son?"

"I've been his benefactor, for all the years he attended school. The head of the school he attends is a dear friend of mine. Jonah and I see each other often, unbeknownst to his mother. Violet cares more for the money and power than she does for people." Gabe smiled when talking of his son. "Jonah claims to spend holidays with friends, but he actually comes with me, Scarlett and her family. Those times are amazing and I plan to get full custody next year when he can partition the court for his wishes."

"Scarlett's family. Do I have cousins as well? A brother and cousins?" Ivy sat forward on the couch and clasped her hands together.

Warmth invaded his heart to see the delight in her eyes. "Yes," he said, chuckling at the genuine pleasure of the truth, "Three cousins. Scarlett and her husband Spencer are dying to bring them all over to meet you."

"But how do you know I'm not as money hungry as Violet?"

Gabe noticed Cameron move uncomfortably as he let go of Ivy and pushed himself to his feet, "I should let you both talk in private. I know you're safe with your father, Ivy. This is between you two."

At that moment Gabe knew this man was the right one for his daughter. "Please don't go on my account. This was your first date, and I barged in and ruined it for you both."

"Ivy has some big decisions to make, she needs privacy and time to consider what you've just offered." Cameron smiled, but it was a sad smile that echoed the pain he must have felt.

"I'll only let you go if you promise me a do over tomorrow night. Gabe and I will sort this out, but promise you won't give up on us?" Ivy hoped Cameron understood her pleading.

"She's like her mother, Cameron. Ivy knows what she wants. Please don't turn away from her. I've caused her more pain in her short lifetime than anyone ever deserves."

"I have no intention of turning away until she tells me we won't work. But I just think Ivy needs to understand the entire tale before we can decide where we go," Cameron replied.

Ivy gripped his hand as he stepped away and followed him to the stairs. "Cameron, you know this doesn't change a thing, don't you?" she pleaded, "I care about you so much, remember, when you rejected me, I still couldn't stay away."

"I don't want to restrict you from knowing your family." Cameron reasoned.

"Promise me you'll trust me on this?"

Gabe got up and walked to the stairwell where they stood with arms wrapped around each other. "Cameron, could you do breakfast with me tomorrow? Give us a chance to thrash this out tonight and tomorrow I'd like us to talk."

Cameron looked from Gabe to Ivy and when she nodded, he agreed to Gabe's request. "Yep, I'll be here."

Ivy leaned in and kissed him goodnight, her body pressed close. "And dinner with me tomorrow night, promise?"

Lightening the mood, Cameron quipped, "Not sure I can handle so much food in one day. I might get fat, then you'll definitely not want me."

"I don't want you, Cameron," Ivy began and his face crumbled. "I need you in my life, by my side as a partner and a friend. Trust me, okay!" This time it was more an order than a question.

Gabe walked away giving them some privacy and heard two sets of feet on the stairs. The door opened, closed, and he heard a lock click into place. When Ivy appeared at the top of the stairs again, she was flushed and her face bore stress lines he hadn't noticed before. He blamed himself for that. Fancy landing this all on her on their first date.

A HUGE DECISION

IVY

In need of water, Ivy walked into the kitchen and poured herself a glass. What a stuff up her first date with Cameron had been. She sensed one thing always came at the expense of the other, and right now she'd hoped Cameron and Gabe would remain in her life. Cameron was her future, and Gabe and his family could be part of that, if they agreed on a path forward.

Gabe took a seat on the lounge chair once Ivy sat down on the couch. She'd placed a glass of water in front of him and smiled. "You know how to turn a girl's world upside down. That first date is definitely one to tell the grandchildren." Her tone was light, but there was a slight grievance.

"He's not only a respectable young man, he's a good one." Gabe said as if giving her his blessing.

"Thank you," her face flushed. "Okay, are you holding on to any other secrets? Tell me everything tonight, please hold nothing back."

Ivy sat in the middle of her grandparents' old brown leather couch, listening as Gabe explained the finer points of the will and all the options they could take. She understood for Gabe to bequeath the will however they decided, her parentage was to be confirmed.

"If you weren't born then I'd be able to draw up a new will but unfortunately the will states that if the firstborn was alive before the year two thousand then we had to adhere to the current standing document. Scarlett and I have spent the last few days after you left trying to understand what options we have."

"Does Scarlett want the inheritance?" Ivy asked, "I don't want to take away something she wants."

"Well, here's the thing, your clever mother had me set up an investment plan for her after your grandparents passed away. Just as Anita did for herself. You know that portfolio I gave you?"

The blank look was replaced with surprise. "That's my mother's investment portfolio?"

"Yes. Surely, you've read it?" Gabe gave her a look she couldn't decipher.

"If I'd opened it, I might have," Ivy said, hopping up from the couch.

When she returned from her room, Ivy untied the leather straps which secured the parcel and pulled out a large wad of paperwork and a USB stick. She flicked through the sheaf of papers and then returned to the front, which was a formal letter addressed to her. She looked to her father across the room with furrowed brows.

"Read it," Gabe instructed with a wave of his hand.

"Before I open this, I need to ask you something."

"Sure. What do you want to know?"

"When I first arrived at Thornton House, you mentioned a promise to Anita's mother, my grandmother. Can you explain what that was all about?"

"The promise." Gabe said, shaking his head. "After your mother's funeral. Our first visit to Chester's Run."

"You've been here before?"

"Scarlett and I came for your mother's funeral. Your grandparents were hurting so much." His face paled, and he sniffled as he reached into his pocket for a handkerchief. "The promise I made to your grandmother was I'd not try for custody of you. For all of us, you were our only connection to Anita and as much as my money could have secured you in my custody, I didn't dare do that to your grandparents. We all understood the pain of loss and as much as I longed to have you with me, they couldn't part with you. It would have broken them."

"You wanted me?"

"With all my heart. Scarlett and I spoke of it at length. We even proposed to pay for you and your grandparents to come to England for holidays as often as they liked. But they refused. I think they feared I would try to keep you there." Gabe gave her a sad smile. "Then after that I got tangled up with Violet and all contact with you was fraught with danger, so we severed all connection. I constantly wondered what you were up to, so I hired a private investigator to keep me updated. "

The room fell silent. What could Ivy say?

"I'm sorry if you feel violated but I just needed to know you were okay."

Eventually Gabe pointed to the pouch in her hand. "Are you going to open that?"

Doing as she was told, Ivy slowly began at the top and read, taking in every word. Once she reached the bottom of the page, she slowly turned it over and continued. The letter stopped halfway down the second page and she looked up at Gabe. "So, Mum started this and you've kept adding to it over the years?"

"Yes. Your mother was a wise woman, and she loved finance and investment. My father tried passed, but Anita had an uncanny knack of reading the market. After he died, she taught me so much more than he ever did. I set up a portfolio with Scarlett's trust fund and she is a wealthy woman and her husband is very stable as well." Gabe got up and came to sit next to her. "Scarlett wants you to have the inheritance."

BREAKFAST WITH GABE

CAMERON

The smell of coffee eased Cameron's butterflies as he arrived at the bakery for breakfast with Gabe the following morning. He'd tossed and turned most of the night with different scenarios swimming in his head. He kept seeing Ivy boarding a plane to England, never to be seen again. Those images sent a full-body shudder through him.

"Morning," Ivy called as he entered the front door of the bakery. "Come through."

Cameron greeted his sister and Susie and followed Ivy into the bakery kitchen. She leaned on the centre bench, waiting for him to join her.

"Gabe's just gone home to get a change of clothes, he should be back in ten."

"He stayed the night?" Cameron asked, flabbergasted.

"We talked till early this morning and I didn't want him out on the roads that late with the kangaroos."

Cameron knew of the pesky wildlife and nodded his agreement.

260

"Fair enough."

Ivy reached for his hands and pulled him closer. "Last night was a shock to me, I was wondering what you made of it all."

"It's not my place, Ivy. This is between you and your father."

"No, Cameron, it's not." Ivy's hand came up and caressed his face. "Please tell me you'll still give us a chance? Don't walk away from me after everything we've put ourselves through."

"I thought you might be the one to walk." He gave a sad laugh. "Or fly away."

She leaned in and kissed his lips, not the gentle kisses they shared here and there. This kiss rocked his world. There were so many messages in their connection. The ice that took residence in his heart overnight thawed. Maybe, just maybe, she'd not return to England with her father. He wanted a chance with Ivy. A real chance.

"When you two are quite finished," Gabe's teasing voice broke their connection.

"Sorry," Cameron said as the heat rushed up his neck and onto his face.

"I'll just get you guys some breakfast," Ivy said, leaning in to give him one last kiss before pulling back.

The two men were chatting when Sophie delivered a tray of food and coffee. Her raised eyebrows made Cameron want to burst out laughing. Never before had he put himself in a position like this. If Sophie hadn't already got it, she'd know now how important Ivy was to him.

"Gabe, this is my sister, Sophie Kemp. Sophie, this is Gabe Thornton, Ivy's father."

"Pleased to meet you," Gabe said as he stood and shook her hand. "You work with Ivy then?"

"Yes, I'm a pastry chef, Ivy offered me a job when Cameron and I moved up here to be closer to our mother." Sophie said, her eyes fixed on the man.

"Your mum and Ivy's second cousin Jack, is that right?" Gabe's finger pointed at her and bounced with each word.

"Yes," Sophie giggled. "Good luck keeping up with all that."

"Don't worry, I'll keep trying. I look forward to meeting all of Ivy's family and friends." Gabe looked at the spread Sophie delivered. "What did you bake here?"

"I did the croissants and the cinnamon scrolls and Ivy did the sourdough bread and banana bread," Sophie seemed a little more at ease now.

"Well, thank you and I shall enjoy this immensely, I'm sure."

Looking to Cameron, Sophie said, "The condiments are in the fridge."

"Thanks."

Once it was just the two of them, Cameron focused on the food, not that he could eat much with his stomach rolling and pitching. He was certain nothing would stay down. In the movies, wasn't this the part where the rich man made his demands and sent the penniless boyfriend packing? Cameron reached for his coffee, but his hands shook so much he changed his mind. He'd try again in a little while.

"Thanks for agreeing to meet me," Gabe began.

Cameron swallowed and nodded.

"Please don't misunderstand me, but Ivy told me a bit about the real you, or should I say in her words the man she fell for."

Cameron could only stare.

"You're an amazing person to have got through all this with your father and still move on with your career."

"I didn't really have a choice. My mother and Sophie," Cameron pointed to the now closed door. "Would never let me wallow."

"You and I are more alike than you'd think. Sisters can really be a pain or they can be our saviour. I think we both have wonderful sisters." Gabe took another bite of his croissant, which he'd lathered in marmalade. After wiping his mouth, he continued. "I'm not here to turn Ivy's world upside down, well not any more than necessary. She deserved the truth, and I need the peace of it all. I'm not getting any younger."

When Cameron chuckled, Gabe looked up.

"What?"

"I don't think you can claim you're not turning her world upside down. It's not everyday someone discovers they're an heiress."

"You know what, you're right. I'm sorry to land here with this when you're both starting out on your journey together."

As Gabe continued, he didn't give Cameron the third degree or question his intention. There was only talk about himself and the history of his family, Cameron appreciated the respect he showed and the ease in which they talked.

"Do you have questions for me?" Gabe asked, suddenly looking nervous.

Cameron's knife clattered to the plate. He slowly finished his mouthful and washed it down with a gulp of coffee, while deliberating the question before answering. But that wasn't hard, he still saw images of Ivy boarding the plane without him. "Does you coming into Ivy's life mean that she has to return to England?"

Gabe's mug paused halfway to his lips. "Thanks for your honesty. And no. This is Ivy's home, and I'd never ask that of her or you. Especially if you're going to be a permanent part of her life. The offer I made to Ivy doesn't have to change anything. You have my word. But let me ask you something?"

Cameron nodded, not able to speak.

"Would you accept me becoming a more permanent fixture in her life? You see, I have plans for Amaroo and most of it includes Ivy and this business."

Cameron watched Gabe closely as he mulled over the true meaning of his words. Ivy needed this man in her life, and they'd both experienced what it was like to live and grow up without a supportive father. He'd never deprive her of that opportunity.

"You'll be sucked into the Saunders/Kemp madness that has become our family over the last few months." Cameron grinned for the first time that morning. Feeling the weight of the world drip one small drop at a time from his tense shoulders, slowly easing the burden he'd allowed to take up residence there lately.

"You're on. Now let's finish this up. Before I allow you to head back to your computer and get working on Phil and Thomas's new computer program, I have something I wish to show you."

MEETING HER COUSINS

IVY

The next three weeks were hectic. Ivy and Cameron tried to spend as much time as they could together in the evenings. Lunchtimes were were devoted to working through the Thornton legacy with Gabe. Ivy not only inherited her mother's substantial investments but was now the heir to her father's inheritance. Her head spun, it was too much.

She'd asked Jack if he'd stand in as her personal adviser with the ongoing talks. He was always someone's rudder in times of need, and she trusted him unconditionally. He cared and loved her as a cousin turned big brother would. Jack and Gabe spent a lot of time discussion riding, breeding and all things equine. She was relieved Lindy and Jack accepted her father so openly. Tessa wasn't as quick to embrace his presence, but with Aunty Darla and Uncle Tony inviting him around for a meal, Tessa seemed to concede.

Yesterday when Gabe arrived for lunch, Ivy noticed he wasn't his normal, cheerful self. Something must've upset him. "Come on, a problem shared is a problem halved."

He smiled and said in his sweet English accent, "How right you are, love. That's why I spoke to Spencer and Scarlett. All shall be well."

Though his spirits lifted slightly, Ivy could see whatever it was, still weighed heavily on his mind.

He kept talking, "But I must tell you, as of yesterday, Spencer hired one of the top estate lawyers in London to represent you if you agree to what I'm offering. He and Scarlett decided using my usual lawyer, Jonathan Chadwick, wouldn't be a clever move. Especially when we can almost guarantee Violet would somehow catch wind of the proposal and try to veto it at the last minute. Even though we're not sure how she's managing that."

The complexity of the proposal had Ivy's head spinning. Gabe was such an exceptional businessman, and she wondered how her mother understood the intricate details of the stock market and investments. The whole thing seemed as if it was another language. At school she attempted Japanese, and being honest she could understand that more than what Gabe was teaching her.

The man was so encouraging and patient. If left to her own devises, Ivy would have given up long before this.

After finding out Gabe purchased Amaroo Estate, Ivy begged him for a tour.

"I'm sorry, but I can't even get in because the electrical and plumbing are all being redone. So, until Owen tells me the place is clear, it's a no-go zone."

"Could I come and see the property, at least?" she whined, making Gabe laugh.

"I'll make you a deal," Gabe finally relented. "You provide the picnic lunch and bring Cameron and the three of us will go exploring."

So here she was packing enough goodies to feed her men. She was fully aware Cameron was definitely hers, but Ivy had to pinch herself to accept she could claim Gabe as being a permanent part of her life as well. Cameron carried the picnic baskets, yes plural, to the car.

"Seriously, it's just the three of us. We won't eat all this," he'd admonished as he headed for the car, his arms loaded up once again.

"Ah-ha," Ivy laughed, wiggling her brows. "There's method in my madness. This Owen character might be open to bribery and let us have a sneak peek inside the house."

Cameron laughed as he continued as her pack donkey.

By the time they arrived at Amaroo Estate, Ivy was on a high. The house, no that wasn't a house but more a mansion came into view and she released a groan.

"They've barricaded it off."

"Yep, of course, haven't you seen that before?" Cameron asked.

"Yes," Ivy snapped, "In town, but I didn't think it would be an issue out here." She was fully aware of her sulking, but she was desperate to see inside the mansion. From all accounts, the place had gone to wreck and ruin.

Cameron followed Ivy's directions, and they stopped out the front of what looked like the manager's cottage. From there, you could only see the rooftop of the main house.

Gabe came out to the veranda and welcomed them. "I'm so glad you could make it," he said, pulling Ivy in for a hug and shaking hands with Cameron.

The two men grinned at each other, which Ivy thought was weird, but the fact they were getting along thrilled her so she ignored the tingling in her stomach.

"So, this is your home away from home," she said, following Gabe inside and stopped short. In the lounge area sat a man, a woman and three children. The only one she recognised was Scarlett, her aunt.

Scarlett was wearing a big smile and so was the man whose arm rested around Scarlett's shoulders. "Spencer, guys, this is Ivy, your Australian cousin."

Ivy's heart pounded. "You're here? In Chester's Run?"

"In the flesh," Spencer replied before pulling her in for a kiss and a hug. Next the children stood up and fell in beside their mother. "Ivy this is Charles, Lyle and Donita, guys this is your cousin Ivy and her…"

"Boyfriend," Gabe prompted.

"Boyfriend, Cameron." Scarlett finished.

After greeting the children, both Cameron and Ivy gave Scarlett a hug. The last time they'd seen each other, things were very strained and uncomfortable. But not now. All seemed forgotten.

GABE

As he clapped his hands together Gabe said, "Well come on you Aussies, show us how to picnic down under."

"Will we have enough food?" Scarlett asked as they walked out onto the veranda.

Cameron laughed. "We have one cooler bag and two picnic hampers for the three of us, even with you lot we'll still be bringing back leftovers."

"Cameron Kemp, are you sassing me?" Ivy retorted as she followed him down the front stairs.

"Ivy, can we come with you?" Charles asked, running after them.

"Sure you can, if it's okay with your Mum and Dad," Ivy agreed with a grin.

"Go on," Spencer encouraged, "We'll be in Uncle Gabe's car."

The boys let out a cheer and scurried after Cameron, excited and chatting about everything they saw around them. They climbed into the backseat and buckled up as instructed.

"How about we take the left track from the main house and follow it down to the river? There's a shaded picnic spot under the river gums." Gabe suggested.

"Sounds good," Cameron agreed.

Cameron led the way back to the main house and followed the track Gabe suggested to the river. The track was not only bumpy, but dusty as hell. The drive only took ten minutes and they pulled up beside the clump of river gums.

Spencer helped Cameron get the food out of the car while Scarlett and Ivy spread a couple of picnic rugs out. A soft breeze blew, and the sun was high in the sky.

"Donita, can you hear the birds?" Scarlett asked.

"Where are they, Mummy?" Donita's eyes scanned the trees, not sure what she was looking for.

Ivy dropped beside her on the rug. "See this big tree above us?"

Donita's eyes tracked to where Ivy was pointing.

"Yes," the shy little thing replied.

"Follow the branch to the end," Ivy's voice quietened and Donita followed the direction of her finger in silence.

"I can see a nest," the young girl declared in an excited whisper.

"Inside the nest are some babies," Ivy explained, "The mummy and daddy birds are finding food for them to eat."

Donita sat for the next few minutes with her head tilted back, watching as the adult birds flew away from the nest and returned with a morsel of food for their babies, who squawked with delight.

"Wow!"

Scarlett and Ivy opened containers and handed out a few plates for the adults and Donita while the boys snacked with their fingers while they ran off and explored, only to return a few minutes later for something else to nibble on.

Gabe watched as Donita attached herself to Ivy as the conversation flowed and ebbed and laughter reigned supreme. It reminded him of how Scarlett had befriended Anita whole heartedly. He looked over at the boys who were running around discovering the Australian bush for the first time. Donita was six years old, and the boys towered over her in height and confidence. Charles was turning eleven later this year and Lyle just turned nine.

Cameron extracted himself from the tangle of arms and legs with Ivy lying over him and Donita over her. "I'll get the football out of the car."

"You knew this was happening. I should have been suspicious when you had a football in the car. You're not a sports person," Ivy said, sitting upright.

"I wasn't a sports person, but Phil changed that," Cameron said, leaning over to kiss Ivy before he walked away.

"Where are you going, Cameron?" Charles asked, running up behind him.

"Just getting a ball out of the car, thought we might have a kick." Cameron said as he opened the back door.

Charles dove into the backseat to retrieve the ball. "What type of ball is this?" he asked, tossing it from one hand to the other.

"That's an Aussie rules football," Cameron couldn't hold back the laughter as the boys' faces screwed up.

Cameron spent the next half hour kicking the ball with the boys and trying to remember the rules. By the time they returned to the mat, Cameron was puffing and panting along with Ivy's little cousins. "We must introduce them to Jack's mob."

"What's a mob?" Spencer asked.

Ivy roared out laughing as Cameron explained a mob was actually a group of kangaroos.

"So, Jack's got a group of kangaroos?"

"Oh, I see why you're laughing at me," Cameron said as he tickled her, causing more laughter. "Well, we call a group of kids or people a mob, that's more an aboriginal term, but we've adopted it."

Gabe joined in on the explanation. "So, Jack's children are a mob."

Spencer nodded, but Cameron could see he didn't really understand.

"How about dessert?" Gabe all but begged.

The boys sat down next to their father, Lyle on the football and Charles on his knees sampling all of Ivy's delicious sweet treats. Once the boys had stuffed themselves silly, Spencer and Cameron took the children for a walk, leaving Gabe and Scarlett to spend time with Ivy.

"What's up?" Ivy asked as Gabe settled into a camping chair with a cup of tea.

"You're as astute as your mother," Gabe said, "An excellent trait to have."

"Look, we have to convince you to come back to London for the hearing," Scarlett began.

Gabe's head hung low, unable to look at Ivy. He'd hoped things wouldn't have come to this, but Violet was determined to move heaven and earth to get Jonah's so-called 'rightful inheritance'.

"What happened?" Ivy looked from one to the other.

"Violet happened," Gabe shook his head. "See, we've sort of set her up. From what we could tell she was always informed of what we were doing, but we could never work out how." Gabe puffed out a breath. "My legal counsel suggested we run one lawsuit out of his office, where we believe there's a leak and another with a well-regarded friend of Spencer's from London. Their so-called informant does not know of your existence. When Violet and her team rock up to the hearing, they'll be unprepared for Anita's child to claim the inheritance."

"So, who do they think will claim it?"

Scarlett grinned and wiggled her brows. "Yours truly," she announced in her upper-class British accent.

"What do you need from me?"

"Nothing other than your presence and your legal team. But," Gabe said, changing tact, "Jonah is also appealing to the court for me to be his guardian and not his mother."

"Why?" Ivy's eyes bulged.

"The woman has used him as a pawn in this game once too often. Though he doesn't know you'll be present, he just believes he will reject any claim to the inheritance." Gabe ran a rough hand down his face.

"How have you spoken with him?" Ivy asked, aware of the restrictions Violet tried to place on Gabe.

"Through the headmaster of his school. He will appear as a character witness for Jonah." Gabe told her.

"What's he like, my half-brother?" Ivy's head tilted in question.

"Like his dad, the spitting image of him, actually. At fifteen Jonah's lanky and a gentle soul who's been neglected."

"Okay, so my last question is," Ivy said, "When would we fly out?"

"On Friday, with this lot." Gabe shared, displaying a little hope that she'd agreed to come.

Ivy sat lost in thought for a while. "I'll purchase my ticket and arrive after you guys. If Cameron will come with me, I'll not have any contact with either of you until the hearing."

"Are you sure?" Gabe asked. "I'd feel like I'm abandoning you again."

"If we're going to do this, we'll do it properly. Cameron and I will be fine," she released a giggle before adding, "I might even book the honeymoon suite."

Gabe's features tightened, as Scarlett and Ivy burst out laughing.

ANOTHER TRIP TO ENGLAND

IVY

This time Cameron drove them to the airport and left his car there. Other than saying they were heading back to London, the family did not know what was happening. Except Jack. Who was sworn to secrecy. Cameron used an excuse of having an issue with the computer program as a reason for his return, and that Ivy was tagging along as well.

In the end, they travelled a day earlier than Gabe and Scarlett. Once they landed in London, they would hit the ground running. Ivy had meetings with her legal team.

Clem and Phil, unaware of their reason for the return, agreed to meet them for dinner that evening. Just a ploy by Cameron to keep Ivy busy before the hearing the following day.

After checking in to the honeymoon suite, as planned, Ivy and Cameron ordered a taxi and headed off to their appointment.

"Mr Salisbury, your twelve-thirty appointment has arrived," the receptionist hung up and escorted Ivy and Cameron down a long corridor to a meeting room where a short, balding man with a friendly smile stood waiting for them. "Miss Masters, Mr Kemp, lovely to meet you in person."

"You don't mind if Cameron joins us for this meeting?" Ivy asked, her voice rapid and scratchy.

"No, of course not. Mr Thornton phoned me just before he flew out of Melbourne, letting me know he would accompany you."

"Oh good," Ivy gushed, "I should have done that myself."

Mr Salisbury gave her a gentle smile. "Please, Miss Masters, relax. Take a seat and we'll get started." Mr Salisbury didn't stop. He kept talking as Ivy and Cameron settled themselves across from him. "If all goes to plan tomorrow, the judge will ask you a few questions then make his ruling. Mrs Thornton's council will be totally unaware of the true situation, but just in case, let's run through the other possibilities."

Ivy and Cameron sat and listened as Mr Salisbury stated their case and her legal entitlement to accept her father's offer. He spoke of the details of her wishes as she and Gabe drew up and then paused with a grin.

"Does that sound okay with you?" Mr Salisbury asked.

"There's just one change I'd like to make," Ivy said and smiled at Cameron when he squeezed her hand. They'd discussed this at length in hushed tones on the way over.

"Oh, and what would that be Miss Masters?" Mr Salisbury asked, looking at her over his spectacles.

"Could you include my half-brother, Jonah Thornton, in the settlement along with myself and our cousins? As with the rest of us, he can't access his trust fund until he's thirty. Or without a signature from two people, before that age. Either our father, Aunty Scarlett or myself."

"Are you sure about this, Miss Masters?" There was a smile on Mr Salisbury's kind face.

"Absolutely. But this is to remain private, Mr Salisbury. My wishes are not to be public knowledge at any stage." Ivy squeezed Cameron's hand, which she'd clung to like a lifeline.

"As you wish," he nodded his head and stood. "I'll need about half an hour to change the official documentation and get signatures from you."

"Certainly, thank you," Ivy added with a smile of her own.

"If you would wait here and I'll have my receptionist refill your cups if you wish," Mr Salisbury collected the required paperwork and headed for the door.

Ivy and Cameron exited the building nearly an hour later. She stretched her neck, feeling as if a weight was lifted from her shoulders. Nothing could chase away the unsettled feelings of going to court, but at least she was one step closer. "Now for tomorrow," she said, leaning into Cameron's embrace. "Thanks for being here with me, it means the world."

"For me also," Cameron leaned in for a kiss before directing them towards Hyde Park to enjoy the first signs of spring. It had been too cold during their last visit.

GABE

Checking his watch, Gabe called out, "It's time to go." They had an hour before the hearing started. Gabe, Scarlett, and Spencer kissed the children goodbye and left them in the care of their paternal grandparents at Gabe's city residence. After landing only a couple of hours earlier, they headed into court.

Scarlett suggested they arrive earlier than needed so they didn't run into Violet before it was necessary.

"Jonah messaged me," Gabe told his sister in the car, "Apparently Violet is on top of the world."

"She won't know what hit her when her case crumbles faster than a building detonated by explosives." Spencer chuckled. "Are you happy with your decision?" he asked.

"Very. Thanks for knocking me about and making me see sense. I can't tell you what it's like to have Ivy in my life," nodding as if approving of his last statement. "Here's my second chance to prove to Anita I'm worthy of being Ivy's father."

When they arrived, Gabe's new council ushered them into a room where Ivy and Cameron were sitting patiently. Ivy's golden eyes were round and uncertain.

Scarlett pulled her into a hug and kissed her. "Oh, dear girl, it will be fine. I've never seen Gabe take so much care with anything, and as a rule he's extremely thorough."

Ivy pulled back and accepted the same attention from Spencer and then Gabe. After greeting Cameron, they took seats and listened to last-minute instructions.

"It's a closed court hearing but the petition for Jonah to attend has just come in," holding up his phone, Mr Salisbury added, "I just received a text from my man. You had every reason to be cautious, Gabe."

Just then the door opened and Gabe's estate lawyer, Jonathan Chadwick, entered unaccompanied. "Morning, everyone," he said in greeting.

"Any news?" Gabe asked, desperate to know who the leak had been all these years.

"Funny you should ask. Mr Langford was chatting with Mrs Thornton's council when I arrived."

"Does he know you saw them?"

"No, not at all. I snuck past him and came in here. I have instructed my son to clean out his office. He won't be returning to Devon, that's for certain." Mr Chadwick confirmed.

"Well folks, it's time to do our thing," Mr Salisbury announced, looking at his watch. "We'll give it another five minutes after you, to enter the courtroom," Mr Salisbury reminded Gabe as he walked out.

Scarlett, Spencer, Gabe, and his lawyer, Jonathan Chadwick sat halfway down the row of seats on the same side of the court as Violet. She turned back, looking puzzled. Jonah slumped into a chair beside his mother. The boy did as Gabe instructed and never spared his father a glance.

Ivy and Cameron entered the courtroom five minutes later. They followed Mr Salisbury and sat in the front row behind her lawyer's table.

"What's going on here?" Violet bellowed.

But no one took any notice of her outburst as the judge entered the room.

"All rise," the clerk announced, and most of those present did as asked. Except for Violet, who tried to interrupt the proceedings by asking, "Who's that woman and what business does she have here?"

Turning to his clerk, the judge asked, "What's going on here? Don't we have a court petition to settle the Thornton inheritance?"

"We do, Your Honour. There's Mr Thornton and his sister," the clerk said, pointing to where Gabe and Scarlett sat with their hands linked. "And Miss Masters is there." This time the clerk pointed to Ivy with Cameron's arm wrapped around her shoulder as she leaned into him.

"Then who's that?" The judge pointed to Violet, her counsel and young Jonah.

Violet's counsel stood, "Your Honour, if I may. I'm here on behalf of Master Jonah Lamont Thornton. We are here to challenge the petition for Mr Thornton Senior to hand over his inheritance to his sister. Legally, the inheritance goes to his firstborn." The man turned and pointed to Jonah.

"What do you think you're doing?" The judge raised and dropped his gavel in one swift motion. "Counsellor, approach the bench." The man did as the judge instructed with papers in hand.

Violet turned to Gabe and Scarlett, her mouth twisted into a smile that would have any normal person running in the opposite direction.

"My client got wind of an underhanded attempt to undermine her son from losing his rightful inheritance."

The judge took the papers and studied them. He referred to papers stacked on his desk and then looked up at the counsellor. "Where did you get these?"

The man swallowed hard.

"Is Mr Jonathan Chadwick in the room?" the Judge asked.

"I am, Your Honour." Jonathan stood up and waited.

"Step forward please, and you too Mr Salisbury."

When they were standing before the judge, he leaned down and whispered something to the three of them. Gabe couldn't hear what he said but Jonathan took the papers the judge handed him and after studying each page he replied, "They are, Your Honour."

Turning back to Violet's representative, he asked, "Where did you get these papers?"

"From my client and her adviser," the man said, half turning to look at Violet, before nodding to her adviser, Mr Langford.

He flicked his hand at the three men, and they scattered back to their seats.

"Mrs Thornton?" Violet stood up.

"Could you please tell me where you got these papers from?"

"Of course, Your Honour." She blinked fast a few times and rubbed at her arms as she spoke. "Mr Langford got them from his place of work." The man fidgeted awkwardly in his seat before sitting forward with his hands on his knees.

The judge gritted his teeth and turned to Mr Langford. "Is that true Mr Langford?"

"I discovered a plot to do Mr Jonah Lamont Thornton out of his rightful inheritance."

The judge scratched his head. "When you got these papers, Mr Langford, what else did you take?"

The man swayed slightly and paled.

"When these went missing, so did extremely sensitive documents. Do you know anything about them?"

Violet looked at Mr Langford before turning back to the judge.

"What were you offered in exchange for obtaining all of those documents?"

"Your Honour?" Langford said, trying and failing to act the innocent party.

The judge spoke to his clerk while the court sat in silence. Ivy turned to look at her father. Her already wide eyes widening further. He gave her a wink and a small nod. "Mr Chadwick, do you wish to take further action regarding this theft?"

"Definitely, Your Honour."

"Bailiff, please remove Mr Langford from the courtroom, and have someone stay with him." The Bailiff nodded and escorted the man out.

"No wait, Your Honour!" Violet called out.

The gavel fell a second time, and the room hushed.

Once the door closed, the judge finished writing some notes and began again. "Is Mr Lamont Gabriel Thornton in the room?"

Gabe stood, "Yes, Your Honour."

"Ah, good. You have petitioned the court to invoke the clause of the family inheritance which allows you to name your successor to the Thornton estate?"

"I have, Your Honour."

"Who do you nominate?" the judge asked, glancing at the page in front of him.

"My firstborn, Miss Ivy Masters-Thornton, Your Honour."

"Miss Ivy Masters-Thornton, please rise."

"She's an imposter." Violet yelled, jumping to her feet. "That baby died years ago. I made sure of it."

With those spiteful words, Jonah looked at his mother, got up and walked to the back of the room where his headmaster sat. Gabe watched him until he settled and gave him a nod when the boy looked at him for the first time.

"Silence." The judge roared.

"You can't treat my son like this. They are trying to cheat him. Just like he has cheated me out of money to raise my son." Her finger pointed to Gabe as spittle flew from her mouth when she spoke.

"Mrs. Thornton, sit down. Now. Or you will follow Mr. Langford from the room." Violet sat with a huff and didn't even notice Jonah had removed himself.

Turning to Ivy who was now sitting again, the judge asked a second time, "Please rise, Miss Masters-Thornton."

When Ivy stood before him, he asked, "Are you Miss Ivy Masters-Thornton, daughter of Ms Anita Masters, deceased and Mr Lamont Gabriel Thornton."

"I am, Your Honour."

"Did you agree to a paternity test? The results of which I have before me." The judge tapped the bench with a pointer finger.

"I did, Your Honour."

He asked a few more questions of Ivy and took a minute to take some notes before looking up at the small audience. "Take a seat, Miss Masters."

Ivy sat down and turned to Gabe giving him a small smile.

Fifteen minutes later, Violet Thornton was screaming blue murder as the judge accepted the petition in Ivy's favour.

"You've got it all wrong," Violet shouted.

"No madam, you are the one who's got it all wrong. The will clearly states Mr Thornton has the power to invoke this clause whenever he sees fit, and as he has invoked it to the person who is legally entitled, I see no reason to drag this out any longer." Banging down his gavel, he turned to Gabe, "I find in favour of your petition, Mr Thornton."

He gathered paperwork into a pile and pushed them aside as he selected another small pile. "Mr Chadwick, could you and your client approach the bench, please?"

Jonathon rose and stepped into the isle and waited for Jonah Thornton to join him. Together they approached the judge and waited.

"Young man," the judge began, "Do you fully understand what you are asking of the court here today?"

"Yes, Your Honour, I wish to live with my father until I am of legal age."

"I have read the documentation and interviewed your headmaster."

"He is my son, not anyone else's," Violet shouted over the judge as he spoke, "I have raised him as a single mother since he was a month old when my husband walked out on me."

"Before you continue, Mrs Thornton," the judge said, lowering his chin to look over his spectacles at her, yet again. "I have the paperwork from your first petition to the courts back when you and your husband separated." The judge shook the documents in her direction. "I have spoken with the headmaster of your son's school, who has a record of how often you have been in contact with your son over the years. And

I know very well who pays his school fees. I suggest you remain silent."

"But…!"

"Did I mention the witnesses who claim to have seen you assaulting your son occasionally, and the photos of the bruises he sustained from beatings?"

Violet's shoulders dropped, though she tried to remain in control.

The judge moved forward again and spoke quietly with Jonah and Mr Chadwick. Ten long minutes of discussion and deliberation, the judge finally sent both Jonah and Mr Chadwick back to their seats.

"Mr Jonah Thornton, please rise."

Gabe turned in his seat to watch his son. He stood with his shoulder's back and his cheeks were a dark shade of red. In that moment, Gabe recalled another person who remained strong against evil. Was it wrong for him to be so proud of his son?

"I find in favour of your petition." The judge began, "As of today, you are now the responsibility of your father, Mr. Lamont Gabriel Thornton. All monies being paid for Jonah's upkeep to Mrs. Violet Thornton will cease as of today. I wish you well, young man." Turning to Violet, who was remonstrating loudly with her counsel while rummaging around in her handbag, the judge said, "Violet Thornton, on the evidence put before me today, and by your own admission, I advise you, Mr Chadwick intends on pressing charges for receiving stolen property. Counsellor, someone will be in touch with you and your client shortly."

When the Judge dropped his gavel, declaring the end of the hearing, Jonah ran into his father's open arms.

IVY

Watching on as Gabe hugged his son, Ivy swallowed against the burn in her throat. She was going to meet her brother. A fact she was oblivious to only two months earlier. Cameron's arm was around her as they both stood watching the elation for all present.

"Thank you, Duncan," Gabe said, holding out his hand to Jonah's headmaster.

"It was my pleasure."

The two men began chatting when Jonah stepped forward and held out a hand to Ivy. "Miss Ivy Masters-Thornton, I can't tell you how wonderful it is to meet you in person. When Aunty Scarlett mentioned you for the first time, I couldn't believe my good fortune. Having a sister means more to me than anything. That you're an Aussie is right up there with claiming bragging rights."

Both Ivy and Cameron laughed, "I can't tell you how excited I was to hear you existed. Finding out I had cousins was one thing but a brother, well that's amazing." She dropped his hand and pulled him into her arms. With her brother's arms wrapped around her and Cameron's hand on her back, Ivy didn't think it could get any better.

"Excuse me, Mr Salisbury," the clerk called, "The judge is ready to see you all now."

Gabe gathered his family, and followed Mr Salisbury into the judge's chambers.

"Thank you all for coming in. Please take a seat," the judge indicated the chairs and waited for all of them to settle around the table. "I have asked you all in here so I can read out the detailed wishes of Miss Ivy Masters."

Gabe sat back with his arms settled in his lap. Ivy smiled when Cameron clasped her hand, yet again. Her father probably thought he knew the distribution of the will backwards. He was in for a treat.

The judge began, "The estate is in trust as follows. Miss Masters has bequeathed equal portions to Master Charles Thornton-Parkes, Master Lyle Thornton-Parkes, Miss Donita Thornton-Parkes, Master Jonah Thornton and Miss Ivy Masters-Thornton." Gabe broke down and cried. Ivy couldn't believe her father expected her to ignore her brother in this. Somehow Ivy sensed her mother looking down on her saying, 'well done, my girl.'

The judge waited a minute before continuing, "The estate managers are Mrs Scarlett Thornton-Parkes and Mr Lamont Gabriel Thornton, as is currently the case. My job here is done. I wish all families could be as respectful as you've been in your dealings, Miss Masters."

"Thank you, Your Honour," The words croaked from Ivy as she shared her first genuine smile since arriving this morning. She leaned into Cameron's one-armed hug and rested her head on his shoulder.

"Thank you for your presence here today and I wish you all the very best for the future." The judge held up a finger as people responded, "What I like most in my profession seeing justice done. Miss Masters, nearly twenty-five years ago I sat in a courtroom and listened to the most horrific tale of events. That story has remained with me to this day. To finally meet you and know the risk your mother took to save her unborn daughter and Mr Thornton and his sister, were not only courageous but selfless. I see many traits in you that I saw in your mother all those years ago."

Ivy swiped at her tears as they streamed down her face. "You were the judge for the trial which convicted those men of their horrendous crime to my mother?"

"I was. You did her proud today. Will you have time to stick around for a while before you head home to Australia?"

"No, Your Honour. Cameron and I both have to get back to work." When the judge laughed, everyone joined in. Ivy was now a wealthy woman, and she was rushing back to her business. Yes, she understood the irony of her actions.

A PROUD MOMENT

GABE

The lounge room at Gabe's house was bursting with conversation and good wishes. Gabe invited the whole team back to celebrate the outcome. Ivy huddled in the corner with her brother and cousins. They were all getting to know one another.

"Thanks Cameron," Gabe said, as he sidled up beside him. "Your support of Ivy is remarkable."

Cameron stood back, taking in the surrounding scene. "Ivy's the remarkable one."

"Yes, she is. So much like her mother."

The doorbell rang, and Phil led his family into the room. "Uncle Gabe," he said, greeting his uncle with a slap on the back, "We hear congratulations are in order."

"You made it," Gabe said, hugging his nephew and great niece at the same time. Portia struggled to get down and ran over to Ivy who was in Clem's arms. "V, V, V," the little girl called with her arms held high for Ivy's attention.

"Hey little lady," Ivy picked her up. Portia cuddled in and held on tight.

"Thank God that's all over."

Nancy, Audrey, and Thomas joined them with drinks in hand. "I still can't believe hiring Cameron would lead to all this," Thomas told her.

"I can't believe not only have I found my father, but now I have more family than I know what to do with." They all laughed.

"Excuse me, everyone," Gabe said to the chattering, excited group. "If I may, I'd like to propose a toast," everyone who didn't have a glass found one and they all formed a semi-circle around Gabe. "My beautiful sister and I would like to propose a toast to family."

"To family," everyone echoed.

"To every one of you here today who has helped me get to this moment. I have many regrets in life, but none include my beautiful children, nieces and nephews. Thank you for being a part of my life."

The little ones cheered and giggled.

"To Ivy Masters. What you did today has secured the family estate for generations to come, and I thank you. You not only barged your way into my life, but you made me realise for the sake of my children, I needed to act and fight back. Today, I have the most important people in my life by my side. And that's because of your commitment to dare to find your father. Thank you." Gabe opened his arms and Ivy walked into them.

"Thanks to you all for your support and love. Please enjoy lunch and our company." Gabe finished, with his arms still wrapped around Ivy.

EPILOGUE

IVY

Looking at her reflection in the mirror again, made it at least the tenth time she studied herself in less than five minutes. Sophie, Tessa, and Lindy convinced Ivy she needed a black dress, so they spent the morning shopping. Now, she stood in her bedroom above the bakery and looked at herself from every angle. Did she really look okay? Was she dressed suitably?

The dress they'd all fallen in love with was a black, full-length with a split continuing up to mid-thigh. Ivy argued it was more for a date with her man than a night out with her father. Studying the mirror again, she could see its appeal but hoped her father didn't think she was over the top.

She recalled their conversation last night when Gabe asked, "Would you do me the honour of a night of wining and dining? There may also be some dancing."

She'd laughed and declared, "I don't actually dance."

"Then it'll be my pleasure to teach you," Gabe promised.

A grimace spread across her face. Poor Cameron, they'd only just arrived back home five days ago and he'd had his head down working to make up for the week they'd been away. He was hoping for a night alone with her and it broke her heart to tell him Gabe planned a special night for just the two of them and she couldn't refuse. Not that she wanted to.

There was a knock on the door and Ivy took a last look in the mirror, picked up her keys and bag and headed down to where her father was waiting for her.

"Hi," Ivy said, wanting to add 'Dad', but it just wasn't rolling off her tongue comfortably yet. She'd practised in the shower a few times, but the word sounded awkward and weird. Well, maybe someday soon she'd be able to honour him with his correct title.

"Wow!" Gabe declared, taking in her appearance. "You look stunning, just like your mother." He caressed her face, then pulled back, shaking his head, "Sorry. No sad thoughts. Come on, young lady, let's cause some gossip," he teased.

In the car, Ivy looked over at her father, "Where are we going?"

"I want to show you Amaroo." She watched out the front window as dusk was quickly turning to night.

The drive out to Amaroo Estate was full of chatter about everything that came to mind. The trip, estate business, the bakery, Cameron, Scarlett and her family, Jonah, and Cameron again. The plans for Thornton House, and then Cameron some more.

"You realise that's the third time you've mentioned Cameron," Ivy said to her father as he turned down the long drive of the estate.

"You realise he's a good man, right?" Gabe countered.

The swirling in her stomach returned, but this time it was from delight. "Yes, I do."

As the mansion came into view, Ivy noticed lights on all over the house.

Gabe pulled up out the front and Ivy gasped, "Oh my God," she looked at her father.

Her door opened, and she took in the man in uniform who offered her his hand, "Miss Masters," he said in greeting.

"Higgins?" Ivy's mouth dropped open.

"At your service, miss." He gave her a bright smile which had the corners of his eyes crinkling.

Gabe joined them around her side of the car, "Everything ready, Higgins?" he tugged the sleeves of his tuxedo before offering her his arm.

"Certainly, sir. The table's set for two and the music is playing softly."

"Thank you, Higgins."

"What's going on here?" Ivy asked as she fell into step beside him.

"Exactly what I promised, wining, dining and dancing." Gabe walked up the steps and into the foyer of the mansion.

Inside, a man dressed in a dark grey suit offered to take her shawl. She handed it to him and took Gabe's offered arm again. He guided her down a side hallway with the most amazing decor and pictures hanging on the wall. It was the history of a bygone era. The history of Amaroo Estate.

Ivy was speechless as she took in all the decor and grandeur. Eventually she spoke, "This place is amazing!"

Her father smiled beside her. "I'm glad you like it because it's yours."

Ivy stopped, trying to process what he'd said. "Mine? What am I going to do with this?"

Gabe just smiled and led her further down the hallway. He stopped at a doorway with a sign overhead, it read, 'Waratah Tea Rooms'.

"Mum loved Waratah's," Ivy said, without thinking.

"I know. She used to tell me I could keep my English roses, she'd take a Waratah any day."

Ivy looked inside when she heard someone calling her name. She swallowed hard and fought back tears.

"Oh no, what is this?" Everyone was there, her family and friends from town. Everyone knew and loved Ivy. People she'd rub shoulders with at the local footy club were here in their best evening wear, but why?

"Go greet your guests," Gabe said as he kissed her cheek and nudged her forward. She looked at the full room, then back to her father. "Go on." He urged.

She took in the packed room. Standing room only. Ivy walked around greeting people who were congratulating her on the opening of her new restaurant. By the time she saw her father again, he was standing with Scarlett and Spencer with a drink in hand. Beside them were Clem, Portia, and Phil, along with Audrey, Thomas and even Nancy. When she caught sight of Jonah, she opened her arms wide and he ran towards her. Her baby brother, who at only fifteen was only an inch or two shorter than her. They'd existed in this world, never knowing one another until now. They held each other close, neither one willing to break the contact.

Wait staff entered the room with trays of canapés. Ivy watched as people sampled the food. It was funny to see her friends, Chester's Run locals dressed in their finest for a purpose she hadn't fully grasped. Next, champagne flutes were being handed around and after she accepted a glass from Jonah, he tugged her into the middle of the room where she stood with her English family, who were catching up with her Australian counterparts. Tessa, Harry, Lindy and Jack all looked stunning, dressed for an occasion she'd known nothing about.

"What's going on?" She hissed at Lindy as her eyes roamed the room. Lindy ignored her question, instead she surveyed the room. "This place is beautiful, isn't it? With so much history. Gabe has done a magnificent job renovating it, hasn't he?" People chatted and laughed. Ivy looked around and noticed eyes were watching her closely, as if something else was going to happen.

"I can't see Cameron," she told her brother.

"I haven't seen him all night." Jonah didn't meet her eyes as he tried to stretch up above the crowd, looking. "Hang on, I'll go see if he's outside."

Where was Cameron?

Watching her brother walk away, Ivy understood at this moment, she was looking for the only other person who really mattered. Her heart plummeted at the thought of this grand party and knowing he couldn't bring himself to be a part of it.

She cast her eyes down. Maybe this was too much for him to handle. That thought saddened her, he'd been doing so well lately. Maybe she pushed him too hard. Ivy schooled her features, looked up, and plastered on a smile when Scarlett gave her a sweet smile as she and Lindy talked.

The sound of a guitar filled the air, Ivy turned to see Sophie standing next to the musician. She didn't miss the way they looked at one another as he strummed out the first few notes of *Endless Love*. Sophie's voice caught the attention of everyone in the room, including Ivy's. Her mouth dropped open. No one mentioned Sophie could sing. The crowd silenced as the music and their beautiful voices blended into song.

CAMERON

Cameron turned to his brother and Gabe. This was his moment.

"Here's Jonah," Liam said as the young lad walked down the hallway.

"Are you ready?"

Cameron nodded. He wasn't always ready for things out of his comfort zone, but he was certainly ready for this.

"I'm ready!" he said as the men who would walk with him gathered around.

"Let's do this," Liam said to the group. For once, Cameron was grateful for his brother's self-assurance. As they began, Nate and Caleb joined him and took their places on either side of Jonah. Cameron's nerves rose, but he ignored them. He had to if he was going to get through this. Jack and little Bradley joined the throng, walking beside Gabe. Cameron needed these men with him. Their support as he took this most important step of his life, meant everything to him.

Sophie and Owen belted out the final words of the song. The guests' eyes were on Ivy as he led the group, his troop, into battle. Liam's arm around his shoulder became his strength. He tamped down the tingling in his chest and the heart palpitations, he would fight for the hand of this beautiful woman.

Cameron gave a nervous tug on the sleeve of his tux. He sought out Ivy and noticed her beautiful gown. She was stunning. He couldn't think straight. He was so grateful to their families, who assisted him and Gabe in planning this surprise.

He watched as the women closed around her, just as he had the support of his men. Ivy looked to Lindy, Scarlett, and Tessa, then back to him. A look of questioning in her eyes. He clenched the small box in his left palm and continued to stride forward, never faltering. He smiled as her Aunty Darla and Uncle Tony walked up and stood to her left. Tony gently gripped her elbow when she greeted them with wide eyes.

The penny clicked. He could tell.

Everything around them faded away as Cameron got down on one knee before her. Ivy's hand flew to her mouth as a soft melody surrounded them. Liam stepped up beside his brother and held out a microphone. Liam suggested it knowing Cameron's voice wouldn't carry.

He began, "Ivy Masters, you are the most wonderful person in the whole world. You have a heart of gold and patience that could never be rivalled." He gave a chuckle, "You'll need that if you plan on being with me."

The crowd laughed.

He saw her mouth widen into a smile and tears resting on her lashes. "I know we haven't been together long, and the time we have was spent working out I'm a jealous idiot and discovering your family. But in that time the love and dedication you showed made me fall in love with you. I love you deeply, Ivy." He paused, swallowed, and gathered his next words.

"Will you accept me as your life long partner, as we build a life and family together? Will you agree to be my wife?"

Sophie removed Ivy's glass from her shaking hand. Raising her hands to his cheeks she cupped them and nodded, "I have loved you from the day you walked into Aunty Darla's place at Christmas. The moment you smiled at me, I lost my heart. Cameron, we haven't known each other long but I believe you and I are meant to be together. Yes, I'd be honoured to be your wife."

"The ring," Liam whispered in his brother's ear.

It took a moment for Cameron to realise what he needed to do. He unclasped his hand and presented Ivy with the small burgundy velvet box. He fumbled it open and held the ring up to her.

"Oh," Ivy said in a whisper, "That's stunning." She leaned in closer and cupped his cheeks and placed her lips on his. The cheers from the guests had them pulling away from the kiss laughing. "Do I have to put it on myself?"

Liam gave him a gentle nudge and Cameron realised he had to do something, "Um, no, I can do that." Taking the ring carefully from the box, he slid it onto her long, shaking finger and held her hand admiring it. "I love you with all my heart, Ivy."

"I love you, too."

"Everyone please ready your glasses," Liam said into the microphone. He turned to Gabe, "Would you like to do this?"

"Thank you, young man, I'd be honoured."

Liam handed over the microphone and everyone waited.

"I can't explain how privileged I am to be standing here on behalf of Ivy's mother, Anita and myself. I wish you both every happiness. No matter what life throws at you, you are a team and you can face anything together." He paused and looked from Ivy to Cameron and back again. "To Ivy and Cameron." He raised his glass.

"To Ivy and Cameron," they all repeated.

The congratulations lasted long into the evening.

They were surrounded by family and friends and the delight on Ivy's face was amazing. Hardly leaving each other's side, they mingled and tasted the food shipped in for the occasion.

"So," Ivy said to her father when most of the guests had left, "Do my fiancé and I get a proper tour of this place?"

"Of course." Gabe called out to the guy playing the guitar earlier. "Owen, would you like to take these two on a tour of Amaroo?"

"By all means," Owen said with a grin. "It would be my pleasure."

Owen gave Ivy and Cameron the grand tour of the mansion. Downstairs there were four separate dining areas each with their own kitchens. Upstairs was accommodation for guests and of course Ivy and Cameron. This place was Gabe's present to his daughter and now his home away from England and Thornton House.

Once the last of the guests left, Scarlett and Gabe, as hosts, ensured the staff finished cleaning up.

Cameron walked Ivy upstairs to their unit tucked away on the far side of the building. His arm was wrapped around her and he carried her shoes in his spare hand.

"I'm not sure if I told you how stunning you looked tonight," he said as they walked down the corridor with the plush, burgundy carpet muffling their footsteps.

"Well, I must say you scrubbed up okay yourself in that tuxedo." Her face transformed. "You took my breath away."

Inside the room, Ivy looked at her ring again. "I can't believe Gabe gave you this ring to give to me," her fingers were outstretched as she studied the large diamond solitaire.

"It was the ring he'd given your mother on their engagement. She'd returned it to him with a kiss the last time they met and his hope was that it'd find its way to you someday. It was the best way I knew to have your mother present on our special day."

"Seriously, the most wonderful way possible."

"Are you happy?" He asked her.

"Happier than I ever thought possible. Cameron, tonight was the most amazing engagement party in the whole world."

He drew her in close and held her, breathing in her scent, taking in her smile, and allowing his mind to settle. This was the hardest thing he'd ever done, yet he wouldn't change a thing for the world.

"We have our entire lives together. When shall we get married?"

Ivy threw her head back and laughed. "Let's recover from the engagement party first."

"Alright. But please don't make me wait too long."

He pulled her closer and touched his lips softly to hers. His world changed so much since Ivy came into his life. He couldn't wait to see what their future had in store for them.

The End

ABOUT THE AUTHOR

Cheryl lives in a picturesque town just out of Melbourne, Australia with her husband, two adult children, two Border Collies, a small pond of gold fish, chickens, the local birdlife and one rather cantankerous cat.

When she's not at her desk writing or at work you'll find her listening to audiobooks or podcasts while walking, doing a jigsaw puzzle or two, on the ride on mower or occasionally weeding the garden. She loves getting up early and taking photos of the sunrise. Walks along the river path with the dogs is just one of the ways she nuts out a plot problem in her mind.

Cheryl is grateful for the peace and quiet the early hours of the morning bring. As well as the company of the dogs and cat as she works. Tearing herself away from the desk to get ready for work gets harder and harder as the storyline progresses to 'The End'.

www.cherylrosariowriter.com

ACKNOWLEDGEMENTS

To Nas Dean, thank you again for all your support on this journey. Your patience and support continued as I tackled Betrayed Expectations. As with the publication of my first book, you have answered all my queries and steered me forward to bring Ivy and Cameron's story to life. I look forward to doing it all again.

Once again my thanks goes to Matt Woods, for his time and patience in getting another cover out into the world. I'm so excited of our achievements. I can't thank you enough for your expertise, time and support.

To Alois, Emma and Bruce, Matthew and Daisy, Matt and Aimee, Jemima, and Tilly, thanks for your ongoing encouragement and allowing me to chatter on about the stories in my head. I love sharing these achievements with you all.

To Michelle and Katie, not only are you ladies my beta readers but you also proved a worthy sales team. It's your belief in my stories that keeps me focused. Thank you both once again for being in my corner.

To each and every one of my readers who took a risk on a new author, I thank you. The beautiful messages of encouragement after Betrayed Hearts were wonderful and so was your eagerness for the release of Betrayed Expectations. I hope you enjoyed Ivy and Cameron's story as much as I loved creating it.

Book 1 Betrayed Hearts - Released October 2020

Book 2 Betrayed Expectations - Released July 2021

Book 3 Betrayed Past - Planned released middle of 2022

COMING SOON

Betrayed Past

Concealing an old identity to survive. Falling in love with a woman behind a mask. Can they overcome the past or will the truth destroy them?

Though Reuben's love for Maggie grows, he struggles to find meaning in his work and is holding on to unanswered questions about her past.

The anonymity of living in a big city is comforting to Maggie. When Reuben accepts his dream job in Chester's Run, she wants him to be happy, but worries for her safety in a small country town. Despite her fears, she lands a great job, develops wonderful friendships and watches Reuben flourish.

Settling in and slowly discovering her old self, their connection only strengthens. They find a place of peace and a lifestyle to fight for. When her past catches up to her can she keep Reuben safe and still survive?

Sign up to my newsletter for more information about books in this series and other books I'm writing at

www.cherylrosariowriter.com

www.ingramcontent.com/pod-product-compliance
Lightning Source LLC
Chambersburg PA
CBHW050800190726
48285CB00005B/1734